Hades's Haunt

A Widdershins Magical Mystery
Book 1

Jo Buer

Dedicated to Class 6 2022

A talented group of authors, illustrators and poets.

Thank you for the non-sweary swear words.

Contents

Chapter 1

I hadn't planned any of this. Not one ounce.

I turned the envelope over in my hand again. I had fingered it so much it had become grubby. The corners were crumpled from living in my handbag for the best of three weeks. My mother had scrawled one word—a name—on the front: Mara. A great aunt I hadn't known existed until Mom passed.

For the millionth time, I considered opening it. But I didn't. I held it up to the window instead. A pointless effort. Streetlights were few, and when we passed one it offered no clue to the envelope's contents. I rested the envelope back on my lap and glimpsed my face in the window, drawn and shadowy amongst the tendrils of blonde hair that had escaped from my ponytail. I sighed. The cabby's eyes met mine in the rear-view mirror, and he arched an eyebrow. I forced a smile.

That's the way, Alice. Fake it 'til you make it. No point feeling sorry for yourself. Other people have been through worse.

Of course, I agreed with myself, feeling temporarily buoyed by my optimistic inner voice. I mean, I'd only lost my mother ... my house ... my job ...

Boy, the list *was* getting long.

I straightened my shoulders. Here I was on my way to meet Great Aunt Mara. To my knowledge, my last living relative. While Mom had never mentioned her, she had left explicit instructions in her will that I hand-deliver this letter to Great Aunt Mara. So here I was.

I'd spent a good amount of time over the last few days imagining what Great Aunt Mara might be like. She'd be kind, of course, like Mom. Maybe even spoke in feel-good sentiments like "Happiness is a choice"—one of Mom's favorites. I envisioned her as every grand-motherly cliché I had seen on TV: a warm smile and plump figure; gray, permed hair; and an apron around her waist marked with flour from where she'd wiped her hands after making cookies. And when she saw me, she'd wrap me in a big hug and invite me to live with her.

Warmth filled my chest at the thought.

The taxi pulled to a stop at an intersection and waited for a car to pass. I glanced at the taximeter, mentally calculated how much was on my card, and swallowed. We had to be getting close.

Come on, Alice. Keep it positive. Not long now and you'll be with your aunt, sipping tea, snacking on cookies, and laughing and hugging as you share memories about Mom. It was a nice thought.

I caught the cabby's eye in the mirror again and puzzled for a moment. Why did he keep staring at me like that?

I gave him another wide smile. Kill 'em with kindness, my mother always said.

Shaking his head, the cabby turned his attention back to the road and pulled into the intersection.

It was almost like he was reading my thoughts.

I shifted my focus to the view out my window. For the most part, Widdershins looked how I expected a small village to look at night. Quaint shops nestled up against each other, closed signs hanging in their windows, illuminated by the streetlights. A large sign with a black-and-white cow boasted "The Holy Cow General Store". Beside that stood various other shops: a florist, a small clothing boutique, an antiques store with an old wheelbarrow planter parked out front.

We made our way around a town square—a central park with a grove of tall trees illuminated by the occasional in-ground light. My focus traveled back to the array of shops around the town center. On one corner sat an old two-story, red-brick building with the word "Bank" scribed into the masonry. Farther around the square was a small café with a pale green-and-white striped awning over its door and windows. A sign above the door read "Miss Maisy's Tea Shoppe". I suspected the center looked rather charming during the daylight, but at night, the shadows thrown by the streetlights seemed sharp and unwelcoming.

None of that, Alice. There's no point getting cold feet now.

We turned down a side street and drove through a more residential part of town. Whimsical Victorian cottages with gingerbread trim lined both sides of the street. The farther we drove, the larger the front yards got, setting the houses further back from the road. A mixture of excitement and nervousness bubbled in my chest.

This was by far the most reckless thing I had ever done. I was pinning a lot on believing Great Aunt Mara was a charitable person.

I'd had a lot to organize after Mom passed—her funeral and sorting through her belongings. Losing my job hadn't come as a surprise. What with my mother being sick and not being able to afford care, I hadn't been the most reliable employee. And when the bank came for the house, I couldn't do anything. Any inheritance was long ago eaten away by medical bills. So I used my meager savings to put a few boxes into storage. I packed a duffel bag of my own belongings, booked a flight, flew across two states, hired a taxi, and here I was. Moments away from starting a new life.

I hoped.

The one thing I hadn't done was call ahead. Great Aunt Mara had no idea I was coming.

The executor of the will had given me Great Aunt Mara's phone number along with her address. Mom's instructions had been explicit. I was to hand-deliver the envelope. I just couldn't bring myself to call ahead first. What if Great Aunt Mara told me she didn't want to see me? That she had no interest in a great niece? No, it was better I just showed up. Once she saw me, of course, she'd want to help me, I reasoned. We were family. And ... I had zero back-up plan.

The cabby flicked me yet another look in the mirror. Was he judging me?

I knew it wasn't possible he was reading my mind, but just in case, I sent him the thought: *How long until we're there?*

The car swerved over to the side of the road and pulled up alongside a cobblestone wall overgrown with ivy.

Oh.

I took a moment to still the sudden hitch in my chest. We were here. Coincidence, that was all.

He was still watching me in the mirror, and his eyes seemed to smile. Then he winked at me.

What the guacamole?!

Refocusing on his meter, the cabby pressed a few buttons on the dash. It spurred me to unbelt and gather my belongings. I hadn't brought much, just my jacket, purse, and duffel. The envelope still lay on my lap. I reached into my purse and withdrew my bank card after a moment of searching. My heart momentarily stopped when I saw the cost. As I handed my card to the driver through the gap in the seats, I said a quick prayer to whoever was listening.

Once he returned my card, I stuffed it back in my purse along with the envelope. I slid across the seat, dragging my belongings with me.

"Thanks," I said, exiting the car. The night air was too warm for a jacket, so I tied it around my waist, then swung my purse strap over my shoulder. The cabby said nothing. I'd barely closed the door when he pulled away from the curb and took off down the street. With mixed emotions, I stood there on the pavement, watching the lights retreat. Here I was, at night, alone in a strange place about to meet a long-lost relative who didn't know I was coming.

Who will be thrilled to meet you, my thoughts tried to console me.

Yes, she will, I thought back in reply.

I turned to survey my whereabouts. A few yards back, a gap showed in the stone wall. Hoisting up my duffel bag in both hands before me, I shuffled my way toward it. Stonework arched over a tall wrought-iron gate. Engraved in the stone above the gate, and barely visible from the light of the nearest streetlamp, were the words "Hollyhock Cottage".

Cute, I thought.

I maneuvered my duffel to my left hand and jiggled the gate with my right. It stayed closed. Squinting, I traced my hand along its bars, searching for a latch. Sure enough, I found one. I lifted it, and precariously balancing on one leg, I pushed the gate open with my foot. Its screech set my teeth on edge. A cobbled footpath wound its way through an overgrown garden. A few garden lamps illuminated the path enough for me to see where I was going. I tried to ignore the ominous shadows untouched by their glow.

The path veered to the right, and I hobbled along it, scuffing my feet across the stones under the weight of my duffel. My pulse sped up. I was almost there. I grinned, then quickly smoothed my expression.

Play it cool, Alice.

Not that anyone was watching me.

Although ...

A sudden unease settled over me. Maybe I *was* being watched. Yes. I was almost sure of it. A heaviness, like eyes were observing my every move.

Just my imagination, I consoled myself. *An overactive imagination.*

I rounded the corner, and the feeling intensified. Security cameras, maybe?

A rustle in the undergrowth to my left made my heart leap into my throat. Paralyzed, I scanned my surroundings. *Just a bird or a mouse,* I reasoned, before continuing down the path, the weight of my duffel dragging at my pace.

A yellow moon peeked out from behind the branches of a tree, still not offering enough light to see into the shadows. A wave of relief washed over me as the cottage grew clearer. It was nothing like I had expected. Its style predated the Victorian era, and instead of wood cladding and gingerbread trim, the cottage was a hodgepodge of cob-blestones. A steeply pitched roof of slate-colored shingles allowed for tall gables, giving the cottage a witch's hat appearance. Small rectangle windows with wooden trim and lead crosshatching were illuminated from within. Someone was home. I exhaled sharply.

I could still feel eyes on me, making my skin prickle. I did one last scan of my surroundings before taking the last few steps to the door. And there they were, two amber eyes blinking slowly at me. A cat. A black cat perched on a stone pillar at the end of the garden. A nervous giggle escaped.

"Hey, puss-puss," I cooed at it. I had never been a cat person, but if it belonged to Great Aunt Mara, then it made sense to be nice.

The cat stared, unmoving. For a second, I wondered if maybe, in the dim light, I'd mistaken a statue for the real thing. A cat statue was no weirder than the gnomes or flamingos I'd seen in gardens before. The statue blinked, and a flicker of its tail corrected me. It was very much alive. After slowly tracking its eyes up and down my body, it haughtily put its nose in the air and turned away.

"Well, nice to meet you too," I said.

With a tail swish, the thing lackadaisically stretched and jumped down from its pedestal. Obviously unfazed by my being there, it saun-tered past me toward the front door of the cottage.

Juggling my duffel in one hand again, I repositioned the strap of my purse on my shoulder. Time to meet my destiny. I sucked in a deep breath, planted a wide smile on my face, and set off after the cat.

Chapter 2

A lantern hanging in the corner illuminated the front entrance. The door appeared to be made of solid slabs of wood, railroad crossties maybe, with a large iron ring hanging in the center as a knocker. I followed the cat up the few steps and placed my duffel on the ground, readying myself to knock. The cat barely even paused before placing its right paw on the door close to the doorjamb and, to my surprise, pushing it open, just enough for the strange feline to squeeze through. A ray of amber light from inside stretched across the portico to meet my sneakers.

A flicker of unease passed through me. Why would an elderly woman leave a door unlocked at night? And not just unlocked, but not properly closed either? How else would the cat have been able to open it? I gave my head a quick shake, trying to dispel an onslaught of bad thoughts.

Grasping the cold iron doorknocker in one hand, I rapped three times and listened with pricked ears for a sign of life within. Nothing.

My heart beat a little faster. Maybe I should have called? I still could. I pulled at my purse and rummaged for my phone. *It would be a bit awkward, wouldn't it? Calling while I was literally on the doorstep. No less awkward than just showing up*, I argued back.

I scrolled through my contacts until I found Great Aunt Mara. My finger was poised to tap the call button when a noise sounded in front of me. I jumped, and the phone flew from my hand. I made a fumbled grab for it, but I was too slow, and it hit the stone pavement at my feet. I scrambled to pick it up, relieved to notice its screen remained uncracked. When I stood up again, a woman faced me in the doorway. My eyes widened, heat rising in my chest.

She was slightly shorter than me, her countenance stern. With short, spiky, salt-and-pepper hair, she appeared to be in her fifties. Her lips were painted a matching shade to her knee-length, red-sequined dress. She crossed her arms across an ample chest and arched one thin eyebrow in calm amusement.

I couldn't say a thing. Words failed me.

"Well, close your mouth, child, or you'll be catching flies," the woman said, dropping her arms to her sides and smoothing the fabric over her wide hips.

My mouth snapped closed, jarring me to my senses, and I mumbled an apology. Any confidence I might have had combusted into flames, making my cheeks feel like they were on fire.

"You certainly took your time," the woman said, tapping one emerald pump impatiently on the stone floor. "But you're here now. In you come."

She turned her back on me and started down the hallway.

It took me a second to realize what was going on. *Oh, Alice, you've got the wrong address*, I chided myself. For one, this woman was much younger than Great Aunt Mara would be, and two, there was no way Great Aunt Mara was expecting me.

"Come on, no time for dilly-dallying," she said over her shoulder as she moved farther away from me.

Too stunned to argue, I grabbed my duffel to follow her. Maybe she knew Great Aunt Mara or could point me to the right address.

As I entered the house, a tall sideboard stood to my left, holding an ornamental bowl of colored rocks. A large painting of what might have been the cottage and its gardens hung above it. The hallway had a slate floor and ended with stairs going up to another level. Candle-like sconces cast a yellowish glow on the walls. There was little time to take it all in. I was already losing sight of the woman as she turned into a room near the end of the hall on the right. I quickly closed the door behind me and hurried after her.

The cat was perched on one of the newel posts at the bottom of the staircase. It watched me, unblinking, before flicking its tail and narrowing its eyes.

So it's going to be like that, is it?

"Leave your bag at the foot of the stairs. You can take it up after," a distant voice called out.

I wasn't going to argue. I was done with lugging it around. I'd collect it on my way out again. After plonking my bag at the foot of the first step, I left my jacket on top, all the time staying out of paw's reach of the cat in case it took a swipe. With the way it was eyeing me, it seemed like something it might do.

I entered the room on my right. Before I could take in my surroundings, a disembodied voice called out from an adjoining room.

"Chamomile or peppermint?"

Chamomile or peppermint what?

I was standing in what looked to be a family room. The room was cozy. A couple of wingback chairs flanked a heavily cushioned three-seater couch, between which two small side tables held stained-glass lamps with dragonfly motifs. A coffee table sat in the middle, atop an oval oriental rug. The focal point of the room was an open fireplace with an ornately carved wooden surround and a solid mantel full of photo frames and candles. It took me a moment to recognize that the carvings on each side of the fireplace were phoenixes rising from the ashes. On the left of the hearth sat a cast-iron pot akin to a cauldron.

"Well?" the voice called back. "Chamomile or peppermint? I have no plans on giving you anything stronger or you won't sleep."

Holy cheese. Was this woman expecting me to stay?

Come on, Alice, make your apologies, explain you're not whoever she thinks you are, and be on your way!

Where? I argued back. Where would I go?

"Chamomile, please," my voice squeaked, cringing at my cowardice.

Unsure of what to do with myself, I moved closer to the fireplace mantel to inspect the photos. I caught my reflection in the glass of one and saw I was chewing my lip. I stopped and tried to focus on the pictures before me. One photo caught my attention.

The photo was black and white of two women with broad smiles in old-fashioned swimsuits and floppy wide-brimmed hats. Between them was a girl of maybe eight or nine years of age swinging on their arms. The girl's head was tilted back in laughter, her blonde hair flying out behind her. Small waves hit the shore in the background and a seagull flew overhead.

It was the quintessential picture of a perfect beach outing, and yet my stomach flip-flopped as I took in all the details. The young girl seemed so familiar. Frighteningly familiar. She looked like me. Only I had never been to the beach. Not as a child. The first time I felt sand under my toes was on my sixteenth birthday, when Mom and I went on a road trip to celebrate.

"You look like her."

I jumped.

The cat had reappeared and was winding between the woman's legs as she walked into the room holding a tray with two steaming teacups. How did she not trip in those heels?

"Still catching flies, I see." She gave a sigh, placing the tray on the coffee table.

I snapped my jaw shut, heat returning to my face.

The woman gestured for me to take a seat on the couch while she took the wingback. She crossed her legs and showed way more thigh than I'd hoped to see on someone of her age.

Now's the time, Alice. Tell her who you are and that you're at the wrong address. Then go do what you set out to do. Find your Great Aunt Mara.

"You've found her," the woman said. She lifted a cup from the tray and gently brought it to her lips.

Had she read my mind? What did she mean I had found her? I glanced around the room, trying to get my thoughts in order.

The cat jumped up onto the arm of the couch, settled onto its belly, and crossed its front paws, watching me as if I were its entertainment for the night.

"Really, Alice. Sit down before you faint away. Perhaps you can tell me why it took you so long to get here?"

Holy cheese. Was the room swaying? How did she know my name?

On wobbly legs, I took the few steps to the couch, plonking myself down before my legs gave out. I swear the cat shook its head at me before closing its eyes to sleep.

"How do you know my name?" I croaked.

"Because, *Alice*." The woman sighed as if it really was quite logical. "We're family. Your mother must have finally accepted that too. It's hard to argue with facts when you're dying."

I swallowed back a lump in my throat.

"Now, now, no point crying about it. We all have to die someday. Drink your tea. It'll make you feel better."

The woman picked up her cup, leaned back in her chair, and took another sip. She nodded, encouraging me to do the same.

My head spun with a million questions. Was this woman Great Aunt Mara? Had the executor of the will called ahead to say I was coming? Not knowing what else to do, I picked up the remaining cup of tea. I focused all my attention on steadying my hands so as not to spill the hot beverage.

The cup was warm in my hands, and I paused. This woman said we were family, yet how was I to know she was telling the truth?

The warming scent of chamomile filled my nostrils as I lifted the drink to my lips. The liquid ambrosia slid down my throat, melting away my tension, and I sank further into the couch cushions. I'd had chamomile tea before, but nothing like this.

"It's a special blend," the woman said, her eyes sparkling. "Now, I suppose you have some questions for me. However, let's start at the beginning, shall we?"

I nodded dumbly, more relaxed than I'd felt in a long time. Had I been drugged?

The woman rolled her eyes. After another sip of her tea, she pointed at the photo I'd been studying on the mantle.

"You look like her," she said, "because that precocious little cherub was your mother. The woman on the left is Isabella, your grandmother, and if you haven't put it together yet"—she arched an eyebrow, and I shifted a little in my seat—"the other woman is me. Mara."

She took another sip of her drink, allowing time for the bomb she'd dropped to settle.

"*Great Aunt* Mara?" I questioned.

She tsk-tsked. "I hardly think I need such an aging title. No matter how great I might be, Mara is fine. Thank you very much."

My cheeks flared again.

"Now it's your turn. Hades and I"—she nodded in the cat's direction—"were expecting you weeks ago."

"How?" I asked.

"Because," Aunt Mara said, drawing out the word as if she were trying to teach a very complicated math problem, "when one's mother dies, one generally seeks family. Oh, don't look at me like that."

I bit my lip to ensure my mouth hadn't fallen open again.

"I knew your mother wasn't going to keep you in the dark forever. I assumed she'd make some mention of me in her will at least."

If it hadn't been for the envelope I'd been entrusted with delivering, I would still be in the dark. Saying nothing, I tried to take it all in. Great Aunt Mara was nothing like I expected—though I hadn't had long to expect anything. Not even on her deathbed had Mom mentioned living relatives. Were there others? Was my grandmother alive too?

The cat opened one eye and watched me. Judging me, I bet.

"Your grandmother died before you were born," Great Aunt Mara said matter-of-factly. "You and I are the last of the Lovell lineage."

I swallowed hard. I hadn't asked anything aloud.

"And if we're to get along, Alice, you need to call me Mara. Or Aunt Mara, if you must. But no more of this Great Aunt malarky."

It was like the woman was in my head. "How?" I half whispered, my brain cartwheeling, and my tongue suddenly feeling thick and sluggish.

Aunt Mara started swinging one foot, her frustration evidently building. "She really told you nothing?"

Hades closed his beady little eye again, as if unsurprised by my ignorance.

"Oh, never mind. There's time enough. But any more insinuations that I'm old"—she paused for dramatic effect, gesturing her teacup at me—"and you'll come to realize I'm not always Glinda the Good Witch."

My thoughts crashed together in a jumble. I scanned the room, taking in details I hadn't registered before: the crystals and incense holder on the sideboard, the deck of tarot cards on one of the side tables, the broomstick standing in the corner of the room. Suddenly the cast iron, cauldron-like pot sitting on the hearth and the moody black cat beside me implied something a whole lot different.

Aunt Mara let out a laugh, not exactly a cackle, closer to a chuckle, her eyes twinkling. Maybe she really could read my mind. I no longer cared if my jaw was hitting my knees. It was completely ridiculous. Impossible. Unfathomable. And yet ...

Hades stood up, arching his back in a stretch before repositioning himself on the couch arm and crossing his front paws. And then, I swear it, he winked at me.

What exactly was in my tea?

Chapter 3

My mother was an optimist. Her repertoire of cliché self-help slogans knew no bounds. Right up until she got sick, Sunday mornings were for hot chocolates and warm blueberry scones at Barnaby's Coffee House. While we people watched, we played a game, choosing a maxim for each person.

"Happiness is a choice," Mom whispered across the table as a grumpy old man grumbled at the cashier because there were no newspapers to read with his morning coffee.

I'd smush my face with my hands to stop from laughing out loud.

"Always bring your own sunshine," seven-year-old me whispered back when a pretty twenty-something danced through the door in a sunflower yellow T-shirt and tie-dyed skirt.

When I was in my teens, I'd watched a couple in a corner booth. They were arguing in harsh undertones. The woman's face was flushed with anger, and the man looked like he would have sold his soul to be anywhere else. Leaning forward, the woman pulled a ring from her finger and slammed it on the table in front of the man, grabbed her purse, and stormed out. The man sank down in his seat, giving a glance around the room. I was too slow to turn away, and when his eyes locked on mine, a tidal wave of pain washed over me. I focused on my tabletop, my cheeks flaming and eyes prickling with tears.

Mom reached across the table and placed her hand over mine. "Better to have loved and lost than never to have loved at all," she whispered to me. Something in her tone made me believe she meant it. I wasn't so sure I did.

She gave my hand a quick squeeze.

"Everything happens for a reason."

When Mom died, I held on to these adages, as ridiculous as they were. Not because I believed them but because I *wanted* to believe them. Even up to her last dying breath, Mom had seemed happy. I wanted that.

Happiness is a choice, I reminded myself, opening one sleep-blurry eye to survey my surroundings.

The chamomile tea had nearly knocked me out last night, so when Aunt Mara had shown me to my room, I hadn't argued. I had hoped a good night's sleep would offer some clarity. I wasn't sure it had. However, today was a new day, and it would do me no harm to face it with the optimism of my mother—

"For the love of Hercules!" I squealed as my eye locked on Hades sitting on my bedside table, contorted in a weird yoga pose, licking his nether regions.

Ew! Cats were gross. And was he sitting on my phone?

Keep it positive, I reminded myself.

Hades paused mid-lick and glared at me like I was the one out of line. He bent down, keeping his eyes glued on me, took one more long slow-motion lick down under, then stood up, stretched, and gracefully jumped to the ground and sauntered out the door.

He had an attitude, no doubt about it. *Cattitude!* I snorted.

Sitting up, I surveyed the room. It was cute. Cozy even. Big, with a vaulted ceiling. The sun shone through the leadlight windows, where I guess I'd forgotten to pull the drapes the night before. A crystal prism hanging from a window made rainbows dance on the wall.

The bed was comfy, with a colorful quilt and several different-sized pillows. On the wall opposite the bed was a small open fireplace with a reading chair. A wrought iron clothing rack in lieu of a closet stood in the corner, beside which stood a dresser. An old-fashioned secretary desk and bookcase stood near the windows. A couple of faded oriental rugs sprawled across the knotted wooden floorboards.

This is more like it, I thought, my mood shifting as I admired my surroundings.

Without thinking, I reached for my phone to check the time. I caught myself in the act. Though cat butts were probably cleaner than most, there was no harm in finding a disinfectant wipe or something to clean it with first. I found some cleaning wipes under the sink in the bathroom and gave my phone a quick go over. I wasn't sure what weird and icky diseases a person could pick up from a cat butt, but neither was I willing to find out.

I had a growing list of questions for Aunt Mara, and my stomach was aching with hunger. I'd barely eaten since lunch the day before. After a quick shower, spritz of dry shampoo, and a dash of mascara, I headed downstairs to the kitchen I'd seen in passing the night before.

The house was eerily quiet, and the kitchen was empty. The clock on the wall read nine. I'd slept in. A surge of disappointment made my tummy growl. Along with fantasizing that *Aunt* Mara (I wasn't making the mistake of calling her "Great" again) was a cookie-baking, grandmotherly-type figure, I guess a part of me thought I'd wake to a lavish breakfast to celebrate our unusual family reunion. Considering my first introduction to Aunt Mara, I probably should have known better. She'd appeared more like a cabaret singer than the caregiver type. Also, she sort of scared me. Still, family was family, and I was happy to take what I could get.

I paused in the middle of the floor. Silence. I was sure she wasn't in her room. I'd walked past before heading downstairs, and her door was ajar and her bed made. Maybe she went out for the day? Maybe she had a job? *Or maybe,* I thought, crossing my fingers, *she'd gone out to pick up breakfast?*

Seriously, Alice! There are more important things than food.

I could scold myself all I wanted, but I wasn't sure I believed it. Food was, I remembered, a core foundation of Maslow's Pyramid.

"Aunt Mara?" I called out, knowing the half-whisper volume wouldn't yield results. Straightening my back, I feigned a little more confidence. "Aunt Mara?"

Nothing. I took stock of my surroundings. A shopping list with some items crossed off hung on the fridge. The kitchen island held a fruit bowl with a few apples and brown, speckled bananas. My stomach gurgled, and I gave in. I snapped a banana off from the bunch, peeled back the skin and took a bite. My stomach sighed in gratitude.

Half expecting to find a note, I continued a quick search but came across nothing.

A chime rang through the house, and I squeaked in surprise. So there was a doorbell; I just hadn't seen it.

It rang again. Whoever it was seemed impatient. It took me a moment to realize that with Aunt Mara gone, I'd have to answer it. Banana in hand, I headed to the door. Whoever was on the other side had now resorted to knocking. After taking a last bite of banana, I panicked and searched for a place to stash the skin, settling for behind the bowl of rocks on the sideboard.

I hid the peel as best as I could, wiped my hands on my jeans, took a deep breath, plastered a smile on my face, and opened the door.

"Oh. You're not Mara."

"No. I'm not," I said, smiling.

He was maybe my age. Early-twenties. Slightly taller than me. I had obviously caught him off guard because a myriad of expressions flashed across his face before settling into a pink flush. His hands played with the strap of his messenger bag hanging across his body.

"I'm Alice," I said, holding out my hand before quickly dropping it to my side.

Since when did you shake hands? Awkward, Alice.

"I'm Mara's ..." I struggled for words. What was I? Long-lost great niece? It seemed a lot to hit a stranger with.

"Mara's niece," the guy answered. "She said you were on your way."

My eyebrows shot up. She'd told others about me?

"I'm Jaystar," he said. "My parents were hippies." He raised and dropped a shoulder by way of explanation and threw me a crooked grin.

He didn't look like a hippy. He wore dark skinny jeans and a crisp navy shirt with white flecks. A Celtic-styled tattoo on the inside of one forearm peeked out from under a rolled-up sleeve. His dark hair looked like he'd not only forgotten to comb it that morning, but he was also prone to running a hand through it.

I instantly liked him.

"I've got some things for Mara." He fussed with the buckle straps on his bag, inserted his hand, and tugged at something inside. With a jerk, he pulled free a bundle wrapped in brown paper and tied with a string. A second bundle, I recognized as an artist's roll, came flying out with it. It landed on the cobblestones and unraveled, spilling some of its contents.

I bent down to rescue the ink pen and nibs as they rolled into the crevices between the stones. He made a scramble too, tossing the other package beside him.

When I reached for a small prismatic vial of blue-black liquid, he swatted my hand out of the way.

"I've got it!" he said.

Stunned, I sat back on my haunches and held out the few items I'd collected for him to take. One by one he went about delicately placing each item in its rightful place. Saving what I assumed was the ink vial for last.

"It ... it was a gift," he said, heat rushing his cheeks again.

"You're an artist?" I asked.

"Mm ... hmm," he mumbled.

"And a good one too," a voice cut through.

Both of us looked up from where we were crouching on the ground.

Aunt Mara towered over us. She'd chosen something a little less cabaret and more beach-casual to wear today: peep-toe wedge shoes with a glimpse of turquoise toenail polish, three-quarter jeans with rolled cuffs, a snug white t-shirt, and a turquoise kaftan. A thick assortment of bangles and bracelets adorned her wrists. She held Hades in her arms. His expression was less than impressed.

"Roowl!" The beast flashed his fangs, and Aunt Mara bent down, placing him on the ground. Hades took a couple of steps toward Jaystar, making him lose his balance and land on his butt. Hades turned heel, tossed his head in the air and, with tail high, strode off toward the front door. He had ignored me completely.

Jaystar sneezed. "Allergies," he said.

"I'm assuming that's my package there." Aunt Mara pointed to the brown paper parcel lying on the stones.

Jaystar scrambled to his feet. "Yeah, Mom asked if I could drop it off on my way to school." He picked up the bundle and passed it to Aunt Mara with shaky hands.

"Do you plan on getting up off the ground anytime soon?" Aunt Mara asked, turning her attention to me.

It was my turn for my face to burn. I stood up, wiped my palms on my jeans, and pretended I was more composed than I felt.

"School?" I asked. "On a Sunday?"

"Yeah—" His answer was interrupted by another sneeze, and he allowed Aunt Mara to take over the conversation.

"Jaystar studies at Crescent Community College. His painting is the one hanging in the entranceway."

I bit my lip as the image of the banana peel I'd stashed under it on the sideboard came to mind.

"It's good," I said. Despite having dabbled in a few art classes myself, I still knew nothing about art. But it had looked good to me. I caught Aunt Mara's steady gaze and glanced away.

Jaystar was back to playing with the straps on his messenger bag.

"You should go along and check it out," Aunt Mara said.

The painting? Did she think I had lied about seeing it?

Aunt Mara sighed. "The *college*," she said. "You should check out the college. If you plan on sticking around for a while, it might be good to focus your energies somewhere."

Sticking around for a while? My brain struggled to keep up. It had been less than twenty-four hours since I'd turned up on Aunt Mara's doorstep. My skin prickled with excitement.

"You're staying?" Jaystar asked, a wide smile creeping across his face.

My mouth opened, but no words came out. Could it really be so easy? Aunt Mara wanted me to stay?

Aunt Mara rolled her eyes, gave a small shake of her head, and wandered off inside, her wedges making a clip-clopping sound on the cobbles as she went.

"I ... I guess I am?" I said.

"Cool." Jaystar ran a hand through his hair. "You could check it out with me now?" He started bouncing on his toes, then quickly stopped. "Well ... of course ... unless you've got other plans?"

Before I could answer, he sneezed again.

"You really are allergic to cats?" I asked.

"Yeah, although none as bad as Hades. That cat can have me sneezing just by looking at me."

While I didn't know much about allergies, I didn't think that was how it worked. Then again ... something was off about that cat.

I'd made up my mind. Aunt Mara thought I was staying, and with no other plans, job, or place to stay, checking out the local college didn't seem like such a bad idea. And I liked Jaystar. He was as real and awkward as me. What's more, we shared a similar opinion of Hades. So what if he didn't like his art tools being touched? I'm sure he had his reasons.

"Let me just grab my things," I said.

I got to the door and turned around. Jaystar was bouncing on his toes again. I grinned.

Within a few steps into the hall, a disembodied voice called out.

"Banana peel?"

I cringed. How in Hercules did she know EVERYTHING?

Because she's a witch, the voice in my head reminded me.

Nonsense.

I grabbed my hidden banana peel and headed to the kitchen to discard of it.

There was no such thing as witches, right?

Chapter 4

The sun was already beginning to warm my arms and the back of my neck. I sucked in a deep breath, basking in the sweet scent of jasmine and lavender and a bouquet of fragrances I couldn't name. My knowledge of plants was limited beyond the most common. I recognized only a handful among the artist's palette of colors on either side of the cobbled path. Ivy climbed the stone walls. Hollyhocks in a rainbow of hues stood tall and proud. Cheerful marigolds beamed from a surrounding bed of green, where white and lilac-blue blooms also fought for attention. Other than the gentle padding of our sneakers on stone, birdsong, and the gentle hum of honeybees, all was quiet.

Jaystar was the first to break the spell.

"So what do you think?" he asked.

I wasn't sure if he wanted my thoughts on our surroundings, my somewhat eccentric and intimidating Aunt Mara, or college courses.

I must have stayed quiet a beat too long because he answered my silent question.

"About enrolling at the college?"

"Well, I haven't seen it yet," I reminded him. "To be honest, it hadn't really crossed my mind to go back to school."

"You'll like it," he said. "For a small campus, they offer a lot. Lots of weekend and night classes, too." His eyes lit up as he talked.

"What kind of art do you study?" I asked, genuinely interested.

"Graphic design. Painting. A little bit of everything, I guess." He grinned, one hand resting on the strap of his messenger bag. His foot kicked against a loose stone on the ground, and it bounced down the path.

"I do the brochures and marketing materials for Mara's Apothecary. Or will, when everything's officially signed off. At the moment, I mainly help with the packaging, labels and stuff, for the teas she sells at Christo's and from the cottage." He gave a one-shoulder shrug.

"Apothecary?" I asked. I tried to remember what an apothecary was. Wasn't it a place that sold medicines or the like? Aunt Mara didn't seem the type to run a pharmacy.

Jaystar's brow furrowed. "Well, yeah. You know, herbs, ointments, teas ..." his voice trailed off. "How long have you known Mara?" he asked.

Heat crept back to my cheeks.

"Mara?!" a shrill voice from the other side of the wall cut Jaystar off. "Mara! If that's you, I have a bone to pick!" A yappy dog started barking as if to punctuate the point. "Mara!?"

"It's me, Mrs. Whittle. Jaystar Stevens."

"Jaystar?" the voice called back, hitching in tone. "Does your grandmother know you're here?!"

Jaystar grimaced, shutting his eyes tightly. On opening them, he gave me a helpless look then cupped a hand to his mouth and yelled back toward the fence. "I'm just running an errand, Mrs. Whittle. For Mom."

I could swear someone muttered among the yapping on the other side of the fence.

"Sorry, Mrs. Whittle, I've got to run." He nodded at me and picked up his pace.

I scurried along beside him.

"Who's with you?" Mrs. Whittle demanded.

Was she really following us along the fence line?

I opened my mouth to reply, but Jaystar grabbed my arm. His eyes grew wide, and he put a finger to his lips. I indicated I understood, and he dropped my arm.

We arrived at the tall wrought iron gate I remembered from the night before. Ivy grew over the stone archway. An apple tree in the corner spread its branches overhead, shutting out some of the sun and sending a shiver through my body. Even in daylight, the tall gate and high stone walls looked ominous, and an uncharitable thought floated through my mind: Was Aunt Mara trying to keep something out or keep something in?

What's with the sudden weirdness, Alice? Don't ruin a good thing.

I shook my head, trying to dispel any creeping negativity. I owed it to my mom to keep things positive.

Jaystar stepped ahead of me and opened the gate. It squealed in protest, a clichéd tribute to every horror movie made.

Positivity starting now! I told myself, wincing.

"We're going to have to run," he whispered, gesturing down the footpath past where I assumed yappy dog and Mrs. Whittle lived. It didn't take a genius to guess he wanted to avoid talking to her at all costs.

I stepped through the gate, and Jaystar closed it behind me. He crept along the sidewalk, staying as close to the stone wall as possible. I followed suit.

The wall ended where I guessed Mrs. Whittle's property began. A pale pink picketed fence continued along the sidewalk, interrupted by a small white wrought iron gate in the center, and ending at a tall hedge on the boundary of the next property.

Jaystar paused between the property lines. He eyed me and mouthed the word, "Ready?"

I gave him a puzzled look.

Was Mrs. Whittle really so bad? I wasn't sure how I felt about running away from a neighbor on my first day in Widdershins. Wasn't it a bit unkind? Immature, even?

He held up three fingers, silently counting down: Three ... two ... one!

Jaystar sprang forward, and without thinking, I launched myself after him, tripping over my feet in the process and windmilling my arms wildly, trying to regain balance. Jaystar glanced back at me and, seeing me struggle, ran back and grabbed my hand just as the concrete came up to meet me. He then dragged me down the footpath, with me stumbling beside him, engulfed in laughter.

A shrill yapping followed us down the fence line. In my periphery, I glimpsed a small white dog throwing itself at the picketed fence, growling and barking, teeth snapping.

"Brucey! Brucey, come to Mommy, darling!" Another piercing shriek joined the commotion.

"Brucey?" I gasped between breaths. Bruce was not the name I'd give a bichon frisé. I was laughing so hard at the absurdity of things, tears gathered in my eyes. I couldn't see Jaystar's face to know what he was thinking.

We had almost reached the neighboring hedge. I stole a glance over my shoulder, trying to keep from stumbling as I did so. A doughy woman, hair in curlers, dressed in a fluffy pink dressing gown, waddled across the lawn, calling for her beloved Brucey.

It was all too much.

Jaystar slowed down and came to a stop. We were far enough down the street that Mrs. Whittle couldn't see us. He let go of my hand and bent over, hands on his knees and head down. His body shook, and I wondered for a moment if it was possible he was more unfit than me. It took a second for me to realize he was laughing as hard as I was, which sent me into another fit of giggles.

"Do you always run away from old ladies and their dogs?" I asked between breaths.

Jaystar stood up and attempted to compose himself. He wiped his eyes with the palm of his hand, then shook his head.

"It's just that ... well ... Mrs. Whittle ..." He ran his hand through his hair, and we continued at a more leisurely pace down the street.

"She's a little ..."

"Noisy? Nosy? Pink?" I offered.

Jaystar snorted.

"All of those things, I guess. She's a little intense," he added. "Her husband used to be the mayor. He died a few years back. Now she thinks she runs the town. Her and Brucey." The corner of his lips quirked upward.

I pressed my fist to my mouth to stifle another wave of giggles. Something about the name Bruce or Brucey reminded me of old balding men, not cutesy pedigree pooches.

Jaystar readjusted his bag's shoulder strap across his shoulder.

"I've been on the receiving end of one of Mrs. Whittle's tirades one too many times. I wasn't about to invite another one. If you think Bruce is yappy—" He snorted again.

"I'm guessing she doesn't like Aunt Mara much? She said she had a bone to pick with her."

Jaystar grimaced. "They've been feuding for years."

He hadn't taken long to reach the village square. The red-brick bank I remembered seeing the night before rose beside us. Across the road was the central park, lush with maple, oak, and willow trees. Paths led from the park's perimeter to a pavilion at the center. We turned a corner, and I marveled at the few store fronts we passed, equally quaint in the daytime.

"Why have they been fighting?" I asked.

"I've heard a whole list of reasons. Mrs. Whittle complains about weird sounds, lights, and even smells coming from the cottage. She held a town meeting once to accuse Mara of being a witch."

Oh lordy!

Jaystar sniggered. "Only a handful took it seriously, of course. Most people love your aunt or at least know enough not to make trouble."

The smell of freshly brewed coffee wafted toward me, and I salivated. The banana had not been enough to start the day.

"I think the thing that most has her panties in a twist is Hades," he continued.

"Hades? He's just a cat." A cat with an attitude, but a cat all the same.

"He poops in Mrs. Whittle's flowerbed, if she's to be believed." Jaystar grinned, and I found myself doing the same. "Hearing it from Mrs. Whittle, the cat's got it in for her—and for Brucey. My mother's a bit of a green thumb, so Mrs. Whittle sought her advice on plants to deter cats. You know, lavender, geranium, marigolds. Nothing worked."

I could believe it.

"He winds up Brucey too."

My focus drifted. We were approaching a café with a green-and-white striped awning. My stomach gave an audible groan, the scent of coffee and pastries making my mouth water. A sandwich board on the sidewalk read "Miss Maisy's Tea Shoppe".

"Do we have time to go in?" I asked, stopping to eye the display of goodies through the window.

A crease formed between Jaystar's eyebrows, and he shifted his weight.

"There's a café on campus. We should go there," he said.

"Jaystar Stevens!" A voice admonished him from behind. "You can't seriously be considering stealing business from your grandmother!"

Jaystar's face fell, and he lowered his gaze.

"Hello, Mrs. Frieda," he said, chastened.

"Grandmother?" I asked.

"Jay-star!" Mrs. Freida said, emphasizing each syllable.

Older women were a force to be reckoned with in Widdershins, I realized.

Mrs. Frieda, in her plaid church dress and hat, looped an arm through mine. "Come on, my dear. You must try Maisy's famous blueberry scones."

My heart leaped.

Mrs. Frieda tilted her nose in the air and led me through the door into a cozy tearoom, leaving Jaystar to shuffle along after us.

The tea shop was cute. White tiles with little black diamond inserts covered the floor. Small, round tables with crisp white tablecloths were spaced throughout the room. A floral design in blues and greens embroidered the tablecloths' edges. The room itself was painted a pale green with beautiful paintings of flowers arranged with ornate teacups and tea pots hanging on the walls. I wondered if they were Jaystar's. A tall shelving unit held jars of tea and china teacups. A young mother with a little girl sat at a corner table nearby and a pang of nostalgia and grief hit me all at once. I tore my gaze away.

An old-fashioned cash register sat on a counter beside a fresh bouquet of flowers, beneath which was a cabinet filled with pastries, muffins, quiches, and tea sandwiches.

The harsh sound of steel hitting tile behind me made me jump. I spun around to see a woman my age with a name badge on her shirt, a look of horror on her face, and a jug of milk lying at her feet.

As she seemed frozen, I grabbed a handful of napkins from the counter and bent down to soak up the milk.

"Are you okay?" I asked. The milk was already settling into the grout lines between the tiles. The soggy clump of paper in my hand had barely made a difference. Jaystar kneeled beside me with a dishtowel in hand. The woman broke away from her trance and slipped her phone into her apron pocket.

"Are you okay?" I asked again. All color had drained from her face. I guessed dropping the milk had really startled her.

"I ... I'm fine ..." she mumbled.

"What's all this, then?" A short woman with warm cheeks and a grandmotherly aesthetic joined us. Her gray hair was pulled into a bun at her nape, and she had an apron wrapped around her middle. In all ways, she resembled the image I'd conjured of Aunt Mara before I'd met her. She rested her hand on the young woman's shoulder.

"It's just milk, my dear. Go get another from the fridge."

I met the young woman's eyes before she hurried off behind the counter. I could have sworn I saw fear in them.

"Jaystar! This wasn't your doing, was it? Getting Lucy all flustered?" The old woman had a hand on her hip and a teasing smile on her lips. I guessed at once that this was Miss Maisy, proprietor of the tea shop and the grandmother my new friend had tried to avoid. Jaystar stood up, soggy dishtowel in hand. He went to speak, but Mrs. Frieda beat him to it.

"Your delinquent grandson was trying to stop his friend here from patronizing your shop!" Mrs. Frieda's tone was sharp as she glared coldly at Jaystar.

No love lost there, I thought.

I shifted on my feet, quite conscious how all the eyes in the tea shop were fixed on us.

Miss Maisy considered her grandson for a moment, then shook her head in disappointment. The twinkle in her eye gave her away. And just like with Jaystar, I felt an instant fondness for her.

Mrs. Frieda harrumphed. "Well, when you're ready, I'll be at my table, expecting the usual, please, Miss Maisy. And although she doesn't know it yet, this young lady would like the same." Mrs. Frieda pointed at me before moving to sit at a table beneath a painting of pink peonies.

Miss Maisy's attention turned to me. Her eyes crinkled as she eyed me up and down. She then grasped my hands in her own. I tried not to wince as the paper napkins turned to mush in my palm.

"A friend of Jaystar's?" she asked, as if this were something unusual.

Nodding, I stole a glance at Jaystar. He was studying his feet, avoiding my eyes. Why was he so uncomfortable being here?

"I'm Miss Maisy. Welcome to my tea shop. Come, come." She let go of my hand and steered me toward a table beneath a painting of purple pansies and a china teapot. "Mrs. Frieda likes to dine alone."

"I'm Alice," I said, aware that I still had to ditch the napkin and wash my hands. Miss Maisy ushered me to a chair, and Jaystar came to the rescue, offering to take the napkins in his own soggy dishtowel. I was at a loss with what to do with my hands. I knew what I wanted to do—wash them with soap and water—but Miss Maisy had pulled out a chair opposite me and plonked herself down. I made do with wringing them awkwardly.

Miss Maisy's expression had changed a little. She was studying me now with narrowed eyes, as if she were trying to place if she'd seen me before. She leaned forward, elbows on the table, as if to see better.

"Now, I've lived in Widdershins most of my life," she began. "My children grew up here, and now my grandchildren are growing up here, and I pride myself in being able to say that I know well the goings on here. However, I don't think I've seen you here before ..."

I squirmed in my seat, unsure where she was headed.

"Yet you look awfully familiar." She tilted her head to the side.

Thankfully, Jaystar appeared beside me, offering me a warm moist dishtowel smelling of lavender.

"For your hands," he said.

With relief, I took it from him and wiped my hands before setting it aside.

Jaystar's eyes locked on his grandmother. I could almost feel him pulse with nervous energy beside me.

"Alice is new here," he said. "She wanted to try one of your famous blueberry scones."

Miss Maisy continued studying me.

"To go," he added hastily. "We ... ah ... I'm showing her around the campus."

He didn't give either me or his grandmother a moment to speak. Instead, he looped his arm under Miss Maisy's and tried to lift her from her chair. Something was going on though I couldn't pinpoint what. He was acting rude. And yet, the way Miss Maisy was scrutinizing me was a tad unsettling.

I'd instantly liked both Jaystar and Miss Maisy, and I'd always believed myself a good judge of character. Mom had teased me about it.

"Oh, Alice," she would say. "Believing everyone is good doesn't *make* them good."

Miss Maisy finally stood up, gave me a warm smile, shot a look of annoyance at her grandson, and headed back to the counter. Jaystar took his grandmother's place and slumped forward, elbows on the table and his face in his hands. He let out a low groan.

I glanced around the room again. The few patrons who were there had returned to their own food and conversations. Lucy seemed to have recovered from dropping the milk jug and was now carrying a tray with a teapot, teacup, possibly milk and sugar, and a plate with a tasty-looking scone over to Mrs. Frieda. For a moment, Lucy's eyes locked on mine, then she turned away. My stomach rumbled, and I instinctively put a hand over it as if I could silence it. It had felt like hours since I'd bolted down the banana.

Jaystar met my eye. His hair was standing on end from running his hands through it.

"I'm so sorry," he said. "I shouldn't have brought you here."

His pained expression didn't line up with my experience so far.

I did another quick sweep of the tea shop. It hardly seemed like a place he shouldn't have brought me.

No drunk gang members passed out on the floor.

Check.

No dead bodies slumped across a table.

Check.

But by the anguish on his face, it was as if we were seeing two completely different things.

"It's lovely," I said. "I'm happy to be here. And your grandmother seems really nice."

"She can't know," he half whispered, leaning forward across the table.

"She can't know what?" I asked.

Lucy was now watching us. I could see her out of the corner of my eye. She was standing by the counter, rag in hand, ignoring Mrs. Frieda waving for her attention.

Maybe she was crushing on Jaystar, I thought.

Miss Maisy appeared out of nowhere.

"What did you say your last name was, dear?" She placed a cute green-and-white polka-dotted cardboard box in front of me, which I guessed held my scone. She also set down two to-go cups. By the smell, and where we found ourselves, I assumed they contained freshly brewed tea. Jaystar leaped to his feet, knocking the table. The paper cups wobbled, then stilled.

"Sorry, Grams," Jaystar said, grappling with the buckles on his messenger bag. "Alice isn't from around here. I'm sure you won't know." He'd yanked out his wallet and was rummaging through it for change.

"We really have to run. I have an assignment due." He shot me a look of urgency.

I was slower to rise. It didn't make sense. If Miss Maisy had lived here most of her life, she was sure to know Aunt Mara. And no one would believe Jaystar had an assignment due on a Sunday.

"Thank you for the tea," I said, "but I hadn't ordered ..."

"It's on the house," Miss Maisy replied.

Jaystar vibrated with impatience.

"You do look very familiar, though, Alice. Are you sure you don't have relatives in Widdershins?"

Jaystar stood behind his grandmother, shaking his head vehemently and mouthing the word "no" at me. But really, what harm could there be? If I was going to be staying a while, like Aunt Mara had encouraged, then it was only a matter of time before Miss Maisy found out.

"Lovell," I said. "I'm Alice Lovell."

Jaystar's jaw dropped.

Time stood still as an explosion of emotions crossed Miss Maisy's face.

"Lovell?" she growled, her eyes blazing.

"Mara Lovell's great niece," I said, grimacing at the "great" part.

Miss Maisy inhaled sharply.

"By all things sugar and sherbet," she whispered, shaking her head as if she couldn't quite believe it. "I knew it!" she suddenly raged. "She sent you here, didn't she?"

I recoiled. What was happening?

Miss Maisy swooped up the paper cups of tea and the cutesy carryout box and dumped them back on the tray.

My stomach dropped.

"And don't think you're getting your hands on any of my special blends! You can tell Mara it'll be over my dead body before she'll ever steal from me again!"

My brain was struggling to keep up. Jaystar's grandmother was accusing Aunt Mara of being a thief?

Maisy spun on her feet to face her grandson, who seemed to have shrunk to half of his height.

"And you!" She poked him in the chest with a finger, making him stumble backward. "You thought it okay to bring *her* here?!"

I pulled on Jaystar's arm. My chest felt tight, and tears prickled my eyes. I focused on the doorway.

"Alice isn't our enemy, Grams. She's new here. We just came in for a bite to eat."

It was no use. Miss Maisy wasn't listening.

I tugged on Jaystar's arm again. Though grateful he was standing up for me, I was desperate to leave.

"The Lovell's are bad news, Jaystar, and you know it! And you've just brought one into my shop. They will ruin us, and this will be all on your head, my boy! I expected more from you." Her lip curled with disgust, and she jabbed him in the chest again with her finger.

I inched Jaystar back toward the door. Miss Maisy continued her tirade, but the roaring of confusion in my head drowned out most of it.

Think, Alice. What would Mom say? I sifted through as many maxims as I could remember.

See no evil, speak no evil, hear no evil.

Everything happens for a reason.

Always look on the bright side.

Everyone wants happiness. No one wants pain. But you can't have a rainbow without a little rain.

None fit the situation.

As soon as my fingers found the door handle, I hauled myself and Jaystar out onto the pavement where I gasped for air. The wind had been knocked out of me.

"And don't think you're welcome back here until you grow a little more sense!" Miss Maisy spat her final farewell at her grandson before slamming the door and turning the opening sign to closed.

The few customers within the tea shop gawked at us through the window before, one by one, turning away. Wide-eyed Lucy was the last.

41

Chapter 5

"I'm getting the impression Aunt Mara's not well liked," I said, my heart heavy.

We'd been walking in silence for a block. At first, it had been at a rapid pace, both of us eager to put as much distance between ourselves and Maisy's Tea Shoppe as we could. As we slowed, I wondered if I'd made a huge mistake in coming to Widdershins. I had been so excited to find out I still had a living family member, it hadn't mattered that Mom had kept her secret from me. Family meant a new start. A chance at happiness. Finding out my one living family member was a pariah wasn't the new beginning I'd hoped for.

"Nah," Jaystar said, kicking at a loose stone and readjusting his shoulder strap again. "It's just Grams." He remained focused on his feet.

And Mrs. Whittle, I thought.

"I shouldn't have let you go in there."

I bit my lip. He *had* tried to stop me. I hadn't listened.

"They used to be best friends, you know?"

"Who?" I asked, mulling over my current situation.

Well done, Alice. Your first day in Widdershins and you're exiled from a tea shop.

"Grams and Mara. They even went into business together for a while. Something happened though, and now they just snipe at each other. Grams can hold a grudge like no other." He let out a low whistle.

I knew so little about Aunt Mara, I realized.

"I'm sorry for getting you in trouble." I bit my lip. I'd always hated getting in trouble. I could still feel tears prickling beneath the surface.

"I'm family," he said, shrugging a shoulder. "It's different. Plus, she needs my help at the shop. She'll be grouchy for the next week or so, but it's nothing I can't handle."

Jaystar seemed to perk up, and as we turned a corner, I saw why. A sign on the grass curb read "Crescent Community College."

From the footpath it was pretty unassuming, somewhat like a two-story office block. Square. Beige brick facade, with only a few trees to soften its aesthetic. It seemed out of place compared to the quaint township we'd just walked through.

"Is it closed?" The reflective glass on the windows gave no sign of whether lights were on or if anyone was inside.

"It is," Jaystar said. "It's Sunday. Day classes only happen on Tuesdays and Thursdays, most of the classes happen at night, and then on Saturday there's a range of hobby classes. It's a small school in a small town," he said, by justification.

So what were we doing here? "Is there a café?" I asked without really thinking.

Jaystar raised an eyebrow.

"I'm hungry," I said in return. Being yelled at had in no way curbed my appetite.

He grinned.

We headed to the front entrance. Glass doors looked into a nondescript entryway with a narrow hall on the right and stairs leading off to the left. I admit it surprised me when, after more rummaging in his bag, he pulled out keys on a lanyard. He selected one, slid it into the lock, and opened the door.

Things still weren't making sense. What school gave out keys to their students?

"I also kinda work here," Jaystar said. He held the door open for me to enter.

So that made three jobs: graphic design for Aunt Mara, helping his Grams at the Tea Shoppe, and working here.

"Right," I said, not sure how to reply.

"I'm an assistant in the arts department," he continued, ushering me down the hall. "I look after supplies, help the lecturers with their class prep, and do a bit of tutoring on the side. It helps to keep the cost down and also means I can come in and use the studio whenever I want."

Cost? Sugar-sticks, Alice. You hadn't thought of that! My heart sank. Even if I found a course I liked, I doubted I could afford it.

"Oh ..." he said as an afterthought. "And yes, there *is* a café here. It's open seven days. You'll love it."

As long as it had food and no one yelling at me, I was sure I would.

"I just need to stop at the office. I have an essay to drop off, a lesson plan to pick up, and I thought we could grab you some brochures so you can get an idea of study options ...” His voice trailed off, and his expression turned sheepish. “Unless ... you know what you want to study?”

So that was it. Somehow Aunt Mara must have known I had a track record of flibbertigibbetiness, as my mother called it, and had told Jaystar. Just like she’d told Jaystar I’d be visiting. It was becoming clearer that Mom had been in contact with Aunt Mara before she died. Why had she kept it from me?

As for the flibbertigibbetiness, Mom hadn’t been wrong. I lacked stick-to-itiveness. In the search for “my thing”—something I was good at and something I enjoyed—I had tried nearly everything: photography, coding, creative writing, baking, dog walking, interior design, and painting. I’d even tried belly-dancing, flower-arrangement, and nannying. Suffice to say, none of these were “my thing.”

“Keep curious, Alice, and you’ll find it. One day.”

I hope so, Mom, I really do.

We arrived at a small reception area with a counter loaded with brochures and a window looking into an office. Jaystar flicked on a light, unlocked a door to the office, and slipped behind the counter. As he made his way to a wall with cubbies and went about switching his essay for his lesson plans, I browsed the array of study options in glossy leaflets. Since I was here, I saw no harm in grabbing a few. For a small campus, they offered a wide breadth of activities. I took a handful of pamphlets, wrapped them in a school prospectus, and stuffed them into my back pocket. They stuck out, but it was the best I could do, considering I hadn’t brought my bag with me.

“All done?” he asked, flicking off the office switch.

"Yup," I answered, slapping my butt cheek in response. I had meant it to show the brochures I had stuffed into my pocket, realizing too late how weird it could look.

Wow, Alice. Let's add social adeptness to the list of things that aren't your "thing".

Jaystar hadn't seemed to notice.

"This way," he said, moving past me and indicating for me to follow him down the hall.

When we reached the other end of the building, we were greeted with another set of glass doors. Jaystar pushed a button on the wall, and they opened onto a forecourt. An open expanse of lawn with a couple of shade-bearing trees was the focal point. A few picnic tables and benches sat around the perimeter. What really grabbed my attention, however, was the flashy coffee house with the big sign reading, "Christo's Café". My stomach flip-flopped with anticipation. Finally. Food.

Jaystar must have seen my face light up on seeing it because his own face broke out into a massive grin.

"Come on," he said, gesturing toward the coffee shop with a nod. "I want you to meet someone."

Christo's Café was a different beast altogether from Maisy's Tea Shoppe. It had an artsy, metro, high-vibe aesthetic, and possibly half of the population of Widdershins. Glass windows and doors stretched from floor to ceiling. The floor was polished concrete, the walls were natural slate, and a giant feature wall was created from red subway tiles. Coffeehouse music and the strong aroma of roasted coffee beans lured me in. People sat in booths whispering over their steaming mugs. Young families indulged in mouth-watering breakfasts. A group of cyclists congregated on their bikes outside, and a few solitary customers tapped away on their laptops or scrolled their phones while sipping drinks and nibbling on bagels.

The place was buzzing with creative energy.

A tall, gangly figure strode toward us, arms wide.

"Jaystar!" he cried out in some sort of European accent before drawing him into an embrace. "So good to see you!" He turned his attention to me. "And aren't you just darling?" His eyes sparkled, accentuated by the smile lines crinkling at the corners. He scanned me up and down, placing one hand on his hip with a flourish and mm-hmm-ing me with approval.

"I'm Christo." He held out his hand in greeting. "The proprietor of this grand establishment." With a wave of his arm, he urged me to take it all in.

When he took my hand in his and gave it a shake, I found his energy so cheerful and buoyant, the rest of the day's stresses slipped away.

"I'm Alice," I said.

"Mara's niece," Jaystar quickly interjected.

Inside, I cringed, waiting to see what Christo's reaction would be.

Wide-eyed shock flashed across his face before settling into curiosity.

"Well, well. Tickle my whiskers," Christo said, massaging the stubble on his chin for a moment while he looked me up and down for a second time.

"I can see it," he said. "Yup, you've definitely got her joie de vivre." He winked at me.

I wasn't sure I agreed, but it was certainly refreshing to meet someone who liked Aunt Mara.

"Come, come," he said, resting a hand on my lower back and guiding me toward a booth. "Let's get you seated and find a menu. I can tell you're starving."

Was I ever.

I slid onto my bench, and Jaystar parked himself opposite me. Christo signaled a server by the counter and surprised me by sliding in beside Jaystar.

"So how do you know Aunt Mara?" I asked, curious.

He gave Jaystar a questioning glance. "Well, *everyone* knows Mara," he said. "She's larger than life around these parts."

From what I had seen so far, that seemed to be a fitting statement.

"She's the reason this place is booming," he said in a conspiratorial whisper.

Business *did* seem good. Although not packed to capacity, there were more customers than I had expected, being as hidden away as it was. What Aunt Mara had to do with it, I couldn't even guess.

A server in tight black jeans, white shirt, and gray apron brought menus over to the table. When I glanced up to thank him, my eyes fell on his name badge.

"Bruce?" I said in surprise, shocked to have come across the name twice in a day. What was with small towns and archaic first names?

Says the girl named Alice?

"Yeah?" the server said in surprise. "Do I know you?"

Christo considered me quizzically. A quick glance at Jaystar told me he knew what I was thinking.

"Oh ... oh, sorry," I stammered. "I thought you were someone else."

Who? Dog-Bruce?

Jaystar's face twitched.

Man-Bruce squinted at me, finished handing out the menus, and mumbled something about being back with water.

Christo watched him leave, annoyance showing on his face, then catching himself, quickly beamed in my direction. I was dying to know what the café had to do with Aunt Mara, but Christo bet me to it with a question of his own.

"Well, Little Alice, I need to know *everything*! What took you so long and how long are you staying? Mara has been talking about you solidly for the last six months." His words flooded forth, and he leaned forward over the table as he spoke.

My head swam. Another person who knew about me from Mara before I had any idea she existed.

When I took too long to respond, he continued talking.

"When Mara started talking about you coming to stay, well, don't tell your aunt, but we were taking bets in the kitchen whether or not you were real." He chuckled.

Man-Bruce came back, balancing a tray in one hand with a carafe of water and three glasses. He placed a glass in front of each of us before filling them and placing the carafe on the table between us.

"Have you decided what you'd like to order?" he asked in a bored tone. He placed the tray under his arm and pulled a small pad and a pencil from his apron pocket. Not once did he make eye contact with us. I made the automatic judgement that the success of Christo's Café was not due to this charismatic server.

Be kind, Alice, I quickly admonished myself. Maybe Man-Bruce had been having a bad day.

"I'm ready," Jaystar said, snapping me back into my body. I hadn't even checked out the menu yet. Scrambling to open it, I knocked my glass, making the water lap at its sides.

"I can come back if you need more time," Man-Bruce said in a slow, robotic tone, ignoring Jaystar's readiness to order.

Christo gave Man-Bruce a stony look. "Bruce. Jaystar is ready to order, and we don't keep our customers waiting, do we?"

Man-Bruce held Christo's eye a moment too long, then peered down at his notepad, shrugged his shoulders, and sighed loudly, pencil poised to take his order.

While Jaystar ordered, I scanned my eyes down the length of the menu. It contained a full range of breakfasts, including different muffins and pastries and other delights. No blueberry scone, so I settled on a blueberry muffin instead. On the last page of the menu were the beverages. I trailed my eyes over all the usuals—coffees, teas, sodas, even smoothies. Down at the bottom was another list titled "Better You Beverages."

Man-Bruce moved on to taking Christo's order. I guess he was joining us for brunch.

I glanced over the selection of Better You Beverages. They were unusual, given they had a name and a price but no hint of what was in them. Rainbows and moonbeams, I guessed, going by their names.

Curiouser and curiouser, I thought, in tribute to my namesake.

Soul Healing. Attitude of Abundance. True to You. True Love. Bad Be-Gone. Stick-to-itiveness, (I made a mental note of that one). Cosmic Clearing. And so on, and so on.

Man-Bruce tapped his pencil impatiently on his pad. It was my turn. "Just a blueberry muffin to eat, thanks, and ..." A drink. I needed to order a drink. "The Better You Beverages ... are they tea?" That was my best guess.

Christo saved Man-Bruce from answering.

"Those"—he raised an eyebrow and grinned—"are how Mara and I met. I can't believe she hasn't told you."

I could. It went without saying she hadn't told me much.

Man-Bruce looked up from his pad, a strange expression on his face.

"What would you recommend?" I asked.

"Ahh," Christo said, massaging his chin and winking at Jaystar. "What do you think, Jay Man?"

Jaystar tilted his head as if thinking.

"I know!" Christo said, in an eureka moment. "It's perfect!" He traced his finger down the list. "Ahh, here we are. Welcome to Wonderland."

He chuckled to himself. Jaystar snorted, and I smiled. It wasn't the first time someone had made such a reference to my name. It was all in fun, and besides, I found Christo's lightheartedness infectious.

Man-Bruce rolled his eyes with bored disdain. "Really?" he asked, drawing out the word.

"Yes, really," I said. *Kill him with kindness, Alice.* "One Welcome to Wonderland, please." I beamed an exaggerated smile his way.

Man-Bruce let out a harrumph before turning his back to us and heading for the kitchen.

A cloud of darkness crossed Christo's face. Just as suddenly, it disappeared.

Spurred on by a few questions from Christo, I filled in both Jaystar and Christo on how I came to be in Widdershins. Both were shocked to learn that until a few weeks ago, I hadn't known Aunt Mara existed.

They were just as surprised to hear I wasn't sure I'd be staying. Though I was hopeful, everything—of course—depended on Aunt Mara. As Jaystar and Christo had understood it, she'd been planning for months for me to move in with her. It was a perplexing position to be in. Aunt Mara and I had a lot to talk about. Not least, I still had to give her the envelope that brought me here.

"Tell me about Aunt Mara," I said, just as Man-Bruce brought over our food and drinks. He placed our orders in front of us with a grunt and left without saying anything further.

Christo shook his head. "Thank you, Bruce!" he called in sing-song sarcasm.

"Don't get too used to him," he said with a chortle. "I get the feeling he won't be around much longer. In fact, this works out perfectly. If you decide to stick around, then I'd have a vacancy." Christo gave me a wink, and Jaystar perked up in his seat beside him.

Oh lordy! Poor Man-Bruce. At the same time, a ripple of excitement buzzed through me. Day one, and I'd landed myself a job!

"Sounds great!" I enthused.

Sorry, Man-Bruce.

"Perfect," he said, turning from me to Jaystar and back. "Give me until the end of day to finalize things here…" He jerked his head toward Man-Bruce, who was bent over the counter on his phone, ignoring the woman in line waiting to be served. "I'll plan to have you set up by the end of next week."

The blueberry muffin was delicious. It was larger than I expected too. The Welcome to Wonderland turned out to be tea. An iced tea. I had never tasted anything like it in my life. It contained kiwifruit, strawberries, and mint, but also other tastes and aromas I couldn't place. It made my skin tingle pleasantly, and it somehow made colors seem sharper and my mind clearer. Maybe it *had* been made with rainbows and moonbeams.

"You mentioned Aunt Mara had something to do with this tea?" I asked Christo.

The two men across from me were devouring their eggs on sourdough, bacon, and sausages. Their meals were three times the size of my muffin, but had eating been a race, they were lapping me.

"Well, you could say so," Christo said between mouthfuls.

Jaystar choked a little and coughed into his elbow until he gained control.

"The Better You Beverages are a joint effort between Mara and me. You see ... Mara has a bit of a *reputation* around these parts."

I had suspected I had seen a bit of her reputation, and I steeled myself with what was to come next.

"A talent. With herbs and teas and such. We have customers who swear by them. A cup of Attitude of Abundance and they find twenty dollars on the road. A mouthful of True Love and they walk out the door smack bang into Mr. or Ms. Right."

Maybe I had chosen the wrong tea.

I eyed Jaystar skeptically.

He one-shoulder shrugged me again and went back to chewing. After a moment, he swallowed. "It's true," he said. "People either love her or hate her because they think she's a witch."

A crumb of blueberry muffin sidled down the wrong pipe, and it was my turn to splutter. Christo passed me a napkin. I wiped at my eyes and sipped my Welcome to Wonderland until I'd semi-regained my composure.

"But there's no such thing as witches, right?" My cheeks flushed as I realized how ridiculous I sounded.

Oh, come on, Alice. Put your big girl pants on. You're not in a fairy tale. Of course there are no such things as witches!

A thought struck me, and I addressed Jaystar. "Is that why your grandmother hates her? Because she thinks Aunt Mara's a ..." Nope. I couldn't even bring myself to say the word.

"Not exactly," he said, shifting in his seat and dropping his gaze to his plate.

"You've meet Miss Maisy, have you?" Christo asked. "Oh, dear. I bet finding out who you were went down like a lead balloon."

I frowned. It certainly wasn't the "Welcome to Wonderland" I'd been expecting.

"Mara's the competition," Jaystar said, pushing the last bite of his toast around his plate.

"Oh," I said, trying to piece it together. Who knew such a small town would have so much conflict over teas?

"It's more that they share the same supplier, if you ask me," Christo said.

"Supplier?" I asked. What was this? The hidden world of herbal drug dealing?

"My mother." Jaystar gave a groan.

Christo filled in the gaps. Aunt Mara and Miss Maisy had gone into business together roughly twenty years ago. They had studied herbology together and along the way became best friends. Miss Maisy had always wanted her own tea shop and so together they created a range of teas, using what they'd learned, and went about selling them from Miss Maisy's shop to the locals. The thing was, some teas did better than others. It turned out Aunt Mara had a gift— as if her teas were imbued with magic. People came from all over for these special teas while Miss Maisy's teas sat on the shelves, gathering dust.

With business booming, and less time to grow the herbs themselves, the women enlisted Miss Maisy's daughter-in-law, Jaystar's mom, as a plant supplier. She was an expert horticulturist, so it was a win-win. Except for the bubbling discontentment between Aunt Mara and Miss Maisy. Aunt Mara was tight-lipped about what made her teas special. She never shared the full recipes, not even with her best friend. Without Aunt Mara or her recipe book, they couldn't be replicated.

Only, Aunt Mara hadn't enjoyed being at Miss Maisy's beck and call when an order came in, especially if Aunt Mara had other plans. Aunt Mara, I learned, had an enviable social life. Miss Maisy disliked having the success of her shop dependent on Aunt Mara and hated that she had no access to her tea recipes. Their business partnership, and soon their friendship, unraveled, with each going their separate ways.

Business slowed for Miss Maisy no matter how hard she tried to revive it. Though her teas were good, they didn't have the x-factor Aunt Mara's contained.

Aunt Mara took a laid-back approach to the whole thing. Sometimes she'd sell teas from her cottage and sometimes from local eateries. She never shared the recipes, only advised of potential allergies.

And she continued using Jaystar's mom for supplying herbs when she needed it. Jaystar's mom had never really gotten along with her mother-in-law, and when Jaystar's dad died, money was scarce. Miss Maisy wanted her to stop doing business with Aunt Mara, but Aunt

Mara paid better, and so, when there was a choice to make and a mouth to feed, she'd sometimes supply Aunt Mara first.

Yikes. I understood now why Miss Maisy had been so inhospitable.

Hurt people, hurt people, Alice.

Yes, they did. But to lose a friend over some tea recipes?

The way Christo told it, Aunt Mara hadn't stolen from Miss Maisy— not deliberately anyway. If customers followed Aunt Mara, that had been their choice.

I had well and truly finished my Welcome to Wonderland drink by the end of the story. Jaystar had sat quietly through most of it, despite the retelling of his family history. He seemed pretty nonchalant about the whole thing, like he'd accepted it all a long time ago. My insides tightened at the thought of what might happen if Miss Maisy were to find out about Jaystar helping Aunt Mara.

When I'd asked about the Better You Beverages, Christo told me it had been a successful one-year business trial between himself and Aunt Mara. Christo offered themes for the drinks based on the needs of his customers, and Aunt Mara created the teas. She earned a commission on tea sales and also on increased traffic based on these sales.

"So what's next?" I asked.

"Well ... I've been trying to convince your aunt to expand the business further. There's a massive untapped market out there, overseas even. I have everything lined up, *if* she's willing to be a little less"—he chewed his lip for a moment—"um ... private with her recipes, we could hire more people. Make a killing." He beamed a wide smile at me. "She's stubborn, as you know, but she'll come around."

I *didn't* know. I knew nothing other than what he and Jaystar had told me about her.

Something wasn't adding up. What made Christo think Aunt Mara would give in and share her tea recipes with him when she never did with Miss Maisy? And if Aunt Mara was so against expanding her sales, like Christo had implied, why had Jaystar mentioned he was making marketing materials for her?

Well, Alice. If you want an answer, ask.

"Well, she must be more into the idea than you suspect if she's looking at marketing materials and signing off on shop space," I said.

A sharp pain coursed through my shin, and I jumped in my seat, taking a moment to register Jaystar had kicked me. His wide eyes pleaded with me to shut up.

Oops. Had Aunt Mara been keeping her plans a secret? I wondered.

"What do you mean, shop space?" Christo asked, his eyebrows drawing together.

Jaystar interrupted me before I could say anything.

"I think Alice misunderstood," he said, avoiding eye contact with me while I fought the urge to rub my leg. "I'd said I was helping Mara with some labels ... for the stuff she sells from the cottage. I have to get her to sign a contract—you know ... intellectual property rights and such as a creative freelancer."

Christo looked at me for confirmation. That hadn't been what Jaystar said, but I read the room and nodded.

"Sorry," I said. "My bad." I shrugged and tried to shake off a blanket of unease.

The conversation and the food had run its course. Man-Bruce hadn't returned to check in on our meal or clear our table. Christo stood up and told us our meals were free. We thanked him and said our goodbyes. Though he had smiled and said all the right things, as he walked off with our dishes in hand, I couldn't help thinking something had changed in his demeanor.

"What was that about?" I whispered, leaning forward across the table when Christo was out of earshot.

Jaystar winced. "I'm sorry," he said. "When I mentioned Mara's Apothecary, I figured you knew ... being family and all. I didn't know this was all new to you. Mara had asked I keep it quiet. It looked like Christo was in the dark about it too, so I guess Mara's gonna kill me." He squirmed in his seat.

"Or turn you into a frog," I said, trying to make light of the situation.

"What are your plans for the rest of the day?" Jaystar asked, changing the subject.

"Actually, I should head home," I said. *Home?* "To Hollyhock Cottage," I corrected.

Jaystar looked crestfallen.

"Mara and I have a lot to talk about. I am glad we got to spend this time together though." I smiled. It had been an eventful morning, but I really had enjoyed Jaystar's company. I also had an uncomfortable amount of study possibilities crammed into my back pocket and a potential job offer. Overall, the morning had been a good one.

Sorry, Man-Bruce, I thought again, feeling a little guilty that in a few days I could be his replacement.

"Of course," Jaystar said. "I can walk you back to the cottage if you like." He scooted across the bench and stood up.

I sighed with relief. I wasn't confident I'd be able to find my way back on my own. Navigation and a good sense of direction were other skills I lacked. Also, I wasn't too thrilled with the idea of walking past

Miss Maisy's or Mrs. Whittle's without backup. Thinking of Mrs. Whittle, I wondered what the chances were that I'd come across two Bruce's in one day. Both with bad attitudes.

It probably wasn't worth thinking about.

We made it back in good time without mishap. No angry grandmotherly figure waited to ambush us as we snuck—yes, snuck—past Miss Maisy's Tea Shoppe. We also avoided crossing paths with Mrs. Whittle and Dog-Bruce, as I was now intent on calling him. Not that I expected there to be a time when Dog-Bruce and Man-Bruce should be confused.

At the cottage gate, we said our goodbyes. I thanked Jaystar again for showing me around, protecting me from his grandmother, and for introducing me to Christo. I smiled to myself as he bounced away on the balls of his feet while clutching the strap of his messenger bag. He was cute, I decided, in a nerdy-arty way.

I followed the cobblestones back toward the cottage, basking in a renewed sense of hope that maybe things were looking up. A black-capped chickadee flittered down the path ahead of me, as if to affirm the thought. The cottage came into view, reminding me of something out of a fairy-tale. I sent a quick thank you to Mom. Whatever strings she was pulling from the beyond, an adventure lay before me. I still couldn't understand why she'd kept all this hidden. Time would tell, I guessed. Maybe Aunt Mara could shed some light on the matter.

The front porch came into view, and my blood ran cold. My eyes locked on the graffiti scrawled in red paint across the front door.

One word. One I was becoming all too familiar with.

Witch.

Welcome to Wonderland, Alice, I thought.

Chapter 6

"Now, don't go getting your knickers in a twist. It's not the first time, and I dare say it won't be the last." Aunt Mara pushed her glasses up the bridge of her nose and turned back to the pot she had boiling on the stove. Glass jars filled with various herbs and spices littered the bench beside her. She gave the contents of the pot a stir, then leaned over a notebook she had opened beside the array of ingredients. She let go of the wooden spoon she had been stirring with and traced her finger along the words in her notebook, her mouth moving as she read. The handle of the wooden spoon continued moving around the circumference of the pot as if she were still stirring.

I scrunched my eyes tight, then opened them again, relieved to see I must have imagined it.

Aunt Mara picked up a jar of what looked like small pink candies or crystalized dried fruit, unscrewed the lid, took a pinch between her thumb and forefinger, and dropped it into the steaming pot.

I was sitting on one of the tall stools at the kitchen island. In front of me lay the pile of folded and creased pamphlets I'd taken from the college. I'd go through them later. Right now, I wanted to know why someone had graffitied Aunt Mara's front door and why I wasn't allowed to call the cops.

"Alice," she said, turning to face me again, clearly exasperated, "I have no intention of bothering the sheriff over something as benign as this."

"Benign?"

"Yes. If I were to bother the sheriff's department every time someone broke into the house or painted my door, the local law enforcement would never get time off!"

Holy cheese!

Had someone broken into the cottage? Because if they had, it seemed to me, that sort of thing was exactly what law enforcement should be bothered with!

"Now, never you mind about any of it. It's being taken care of." She turned back to whatever she was cooking on the stove. It didn't smell like anything I'd eaten before.

I wasn't going to get anywhere further with Aunt Mara. Christo had called her stubborn. Now I understood why.

I sighed. My good mood was fading. I had so many questions I wanted to ask Aunt Mara, but the graffiti on the door had gotten under my skin. Who would do such a thing?

From that morning alone, I could think of two people: Mrs. Whittle and Miss Maisy. Although I couldn't really imagine either of them as the graffitiing type. Who else could Aunt Mara have possibly upset?

Hades leaped up on the island beside me and went about licking his paw and cleaning his face. I didn't think it particularly hygienic for the cat to sit on a food-prep surface.

He stopped mid-lick and glared at me. The tip of his pink tongue poked out between his teeth. I shuffled back in my chair.

"Hades. Leave Alice alone," Aunt Mara admonished without turning around. How *did* she do that?

Hades squinted at me and I instinctively gave him the stink-eye back.

Two can play at this game, cat!

He glared at me and gave his paw another long lick. I poked my tongue at him. It seemed fitting.

"You two really must learn to get along," Aunt Mara said, spinning around to face us, one hand on her hip and a wooden spoon in the other.

Hades's eyes widened in innocence. He stretched backward onto his hind legs, butt in the air, then shifted his weight forward to standing, and casually jumped down from the island. He left the room with head high and tail in the air.

"Right!" Aunt Mara said, watching Hades leave. "I have some time while this simmers, so you might as well ask me some of those questions crashing around in that brain of yours."

She placed the spoon on the bench by the stove, pulled up a stool opposite me, and then took her glasses off, placing them beside my pile of leaflets.

I swallowed. Now the time had come, I didn't know where to start.

"Well, why don't we just start at the beginning?" Aunt Mara said, inferring my thoughts. "Your mother never approved of my way of life and, stubborn child that she was, thought it better for you to be as far removed from it as possible."

Sugar-sticks. Aunt Mara certainly didn't beat around the bush.

"No, I don't," Aunt Mara said.

My jaw dropped and I bit my lip to hide it. Was I really that easy to read?

"Yes," Aunt Mara said, clasping her hands on the counter between us.

I swayed a little on my chair. What kind of witchcraft was this?

"The kind that your mother forfeited her heritage for, apparently."

Good grief. I was starting to see stars. A migraine. That would explain it.

All is good in my world, I tried to affirm to myself. *All is well.*

"You really do need to get better at hiding your thoughts, Alice."

I grabbed onto the edge of the island to steady myself. What was going on?

Aunt Mara blew out an exasperated breath.

"I told your mother she was doing you a disadvantage by not telling you. You come from a family of witches, Alice. I'm a witch. Your dearly departed, and ridiculously stubborn mother, was a witch. And you, my dear ..."

Don't say it. Don't say it!

"... are a witch."

Not only were stars dancing in my vision, but the room was spinning, too.

"And Hades?" I squeaked. Now I really was losing my mind. Lock me up and throw away the key.

"Oh, for crying out loud," Aunt Mara admonished me. "Hades is a cat!"

Right. Hades was a cat, and I was apparently a witch. Except, I'd never shown any hint of magical abilities. I had enough difficulty doing normal everyday adult stuff, like remembering to do my laundry and holding down a job. Aunt Mara was obviously insane.

"Really, Alice. You're being dramatic. You have a letter for me from your mother, I believe. Go fetch it, and you can hear it in her words." She stood up and returned to stirring the pot on the stove.

Breathe, Alice, I reminded myself. I hadn't told her about the letter, though it was possible Mom had told her about it before she died. If they'd been in touch, it would explain why so many people knew about me and were expecting me in Widdershins.

I went upstairs and retrieved it from my duffel. I had fingered it so many times, trying to intuit what it said. Now, I was going to find out.

When I returned to the kitchen, I was surprised to see Aunt Mara had put away the jars of herbs and spices, put a lid on the pot and taken it off the stove to cool, and was now back sitting at the island, glasses balanced on her nose, flicking through the brochures I'd brought home. I'd only been a minute. She certainly moved fast.

On seeing me, she shuffled the brochures and restacked them in a pile.

I handed Aunt Mara the envelope with a shaky hand and took a seat opposite her.

She handed it back to me.

"You open it," she said.

Despite my confusion, I knew better than to argue.

I slipped my fingernail under the seal and gently tore it open.

A black ball of fur launched itself onto the island and positioned itself in front of Aunt Mara, watching me intently. As she ran her hand down Hades's back, he purred. I had an audience, it seemed.

I pulled out the leaves of paper inside, swallowing hard on seeing my mother's cursive handwriting on the yellow legal paper on top. My eyes found Aunt Mara's, and she gave me a nod.

Alice,

If you're reading this, it means time has been cruel, and the Reaper has come for me earlier than I would have liked. It also means you've followed my instructions and are in Widdershins with your aunt.

My eyes welled. She'd written this for me.

From nowhere, Aunt Mara passed me a tissue box. I took one and dabbed at the corners of my eyes like that would somehow calm the threatening flood.

I suspect she's already told you what I so selfishly kept secret. It's true. We are witches. All I wanted for you, my daughter, was a normal life. Safe from magic and all its mayhem. I did the best I could to give that to you. And I think I succeeded. We had a wonderful life, just the two of us, full of love and joy; and I want you to remember me for the normal life we had.

The tears were streaming now. We did have a wonderful life.

But the expense was high. I kept you from your family, and I kept you from your heritage. When I saw you struggling with your place in life, unsure of your abilities, bouncing from one thing to the next and losing confidence in yourself, I knew I'd made a mistake. I may have given up magic and renounced being a witch, but it was unfair of me to not give you the choice.

I glanced up at Aunt Mara and sniffed. I'd been reading it all quietly to myself, yet somehow I felt she was hearing every word. Aunt Mara nodded for me to continue.

I reached out to Mara several months ago, and I know I can move on in peace now, knowing we've made our amends. She has been much more forgiving than I deserve. I never thought through how much it would pain her to not have you in her life.

So here, Alice, is my dying wish:

Spend a year with your aunt at Hollyhock Cottage, and let her show you your heritage. She'll teach you spell-craft and the herbal arts, div-ination, and the laws we must abide by. You'll have full access to the family Book of Shadows. And maybe, during this year, you'll find the part of yourself you thought was missing.

Being a witch, and especially a Lovell witch, is both a blessing and a curse. At the end of the year, you'll be equipped to decide for yourself what life you want: the magical or non-magical. It is your rightful choice to make.

If, in a year's time, you choose to continue to walk the Wiccan Way, Hollyhock Cottage will be yours, but as lovely as the cottage is, do not let that influence your decision.

My mind raced. What did Mom mean, Hollyhock Cottage would be mine? It belonged to Aunt Mara. Whatever my decision, I couldn't take it from her.

"Hollyhock Cottage does *not* belong to me," Aunt Mara answered.

I no longer doubted she could read my mind.

"Hollyhock Cottage has been in our family for hundreds of years. It was built over ley lines; it's a conduit for magic, and it is always passed down to the first born female Lovell. When Isabella, your grandmother, passed, your mother inherited it. When she gave up her magic, it should have gone to you, but you were kept away from Widdershins, ignorant of your inheritance, so it went to Hades."

"Hades?" I asked, incredulous. "Shouldn't it have gone to you?"

"That's not how it works," Aunt Mara said.

"Wait, wouldn't that make Hades twenty-something years old?" He looked like a kitten.

"Lovell cats don't age like other cats," Aunt Mara answered simply.

I eyed the furball across from me. He looked good for a twenty-something feline. A twenty-something feline who owned a house.

"And if after a year I decide to go back to my old life ...?"

What old life, Alice? Your old life was with your mother, and there's no going back to that.

I sniffed.

"We'll cross that bridge if we come to it. Finish the letter."

I love you, my beautiful daughter. I know whatever happens, you're destined for a wonderful life. You're destined for something big. I'm sorry I'm not there to share it with you.

Remember, my darling, happiness is a choice.

Much love,

Mom.

I wiped at my face with the palm of my hand. I had so many conflicting emotions. Mostly, I missed Mom.

Nothing in the letter explained why she had kept me in the dark all this time and had turned her back on magic. She said she'd wanted a normal life for me, but what was normal? Normal was different for everyone.

Behind Mom's letter was paperwork for the cottage. I wasn't sure what lawyer would sign off on a cat owning a house, but there it was in legal-speak, with everything needed to transfer ownership to me in a year's time if it was what I wanted.

"There you have it," Aunt Mara said. "You're a witch."

It was a lot to take in.

"So I have powers?" My voice cracked as I spoke.

"They'll make themselves known when you're ready for them. You've been away from magic most of your life, so you can expect to be a late bloomer."

I wasn't sure if I was happy about this or disappointed. Trying to digest it all, I bit my lip. I still had so many questions. "You'll teach me though?"

"Everything I can, but later. You need to settle in first." She pushed the pile of brochures from the community college closer to me. She'd put one on herbalism at the top of the pile. I didn't remember grabbing that one. "There are some things you need to know now, though, Alice." Her tone was more somber than usual, and my skin prickled.

"You're not to tell *anyone*. Non-Magicals, that is. It's imperative Non-Magicals stay in the dark. You can get in a lot of trouble if you break this rule."

I nodded dumbly. Aunt Mara's tone was serious, and frankly, the idea of getting in any sort of trouble scared me.

My mind was reeling, and was spent. I put my mom's letter and the paperwork on the cottage back in the envelope. It was only four in the afternoon and I felt like I needed a nap.

"Aunt Mara?" I asked, remembering something Mom had written in her letter. "What is a Book of Shadows? Mom said I would have full access to it."

A line formed between Aunt Mara's brows, and she took a moment to answer.

"A Book of Shadows is a grimoire. It gets passed down the Lovell line with every Lovell contributing spells, recipes, and magical knowledge they obtain throughout their lifetime."

Perfect reading material before a nap, I thought.

"Right now it's out of commission," she said.

My face dropped.

"You'll have access to it soon enough, but right now I have my suspicions you're not the only one wanting to get their hands on it."

I shivered. That sounded ominous.

Aunt Mara stood up, with Hades following suit. It was weird to think that he was now my landlord.

Hades considered me before jumping down off the island and leaving the room. Maybe Aunt Mara was right—maybe I *should* make more of an effort to get along with Hades.

Aunt Mara looked like she was readying herself to leave. I suspected question-time was over. She paused, her forehead crinkling again.

"Alice, I really am pleased you're here," she said. I saw in her eyes that she meant it. She seemed to want to say more, but a buzzing sound interrupted the moment. Aunt Mara reached into her pocket and pulled out her phone.

"Hello, Marion," she said. Aunt Mara offered little more than some hemming and hawing in response to the person on the other end of the line. She shot me a glance, making me wonder if I had come into the conversation somehow. Her jaw tightened, and she turned her back to me. Seconds later, she hung up.

"I'm going out for a while," she said, her tone softer. "I don't expect to be too long, but there's plenty of food in the fridge and pantry if you get hungry. And Hades is here if you need anything."

I wasn't sure how to respond. Aunt Mara had said herself he was just a cat, even if he was a Lovell cat, whatever that meant.

She stuffed her phone back into her pocket and moved across the room, before turning back to me.

"And, child ..." she said. "I agree with your mother; I also think you're destined for something big." Her lips curved upward as she walked out the door.

Holy cheese. I might just be in Wonderland, after all.

Chapter 7

How I really felt about everything, to be honest, was a little panicked.

In just twenty-four hours, I had met my last living relative and had found out witches were real. And I, in fact, was one—or at least, my mother and aunt thought I was. The jury was still out on that. Plus, in a year's time, I might inherit Hollyhock Cottage. That alone was more adulting than I thought myself capable of.

My head spun. I was torn between taking a nap or busying myself to quiet the turmoil.

In the end, I decided on tackling the graffiti on the front door. It would feel good to have it cleaned up before Aunt Mara got home.

I made my way over to the kitchen sink to look for cleaning supplies. The cupboard below the sink stored little more than dishwashing liquid and dishwasher tablets, a pack of sponges, and a pair of pink rubber gloves. I took the gloves and a sponge, but I'd still need to find a bucket and some cleaner.

Laundry, I thought. Surely, I'd find more cleaning products there. Which meant I would have to go exploring.

It turned out the laundry room was easy to find, although not where I expected it to be. A door under the stairs opened into a room that looked like a much newer addition to the cottage. It was equipped with a modern washer and drier, a deep sink, and a long bench for ironing and folding. Two doors led off from it. The floor had slate tiles, and the backsplash was a pale turquoise color. In the corner, a yellow bucket sat beside a broom and mop. A cordless stick vacuum cleaner perched on the wall, charging. I guess even a witch couldn't wave a magic wand and expect the house to tidy itself. I was a little disappointed.

A bottle of household cleaner sat under the bench. It would do the trick. But first, since I was already snooping, I thought I'd check out where the other doors led. I was living here now, so I wasn't really doing anything wrong, I reassured myself.

It was a garage. A standard, empty garage. Strangely, it never crossed my mind that Aunt Mara had a car. The driveway, I guessed, must exit the back of the property. I made a mental note to take time to explore the grounds of the cottage tomorrow.

I closed the door and walked across the laundry room to the other door. Just as I reached out for the doorhandle, a chime rang out, making me jump. It wasn't until the second refrain I recognized it as the front doorbell.

Oh, sugar-sticks. Whoever was at the door was going to see the word "witch" scrawled in red paint. I hurried into the hallway, wondering how to explain the graffiti on the door. Anxiety crawled across my skin.

Come on, Alice. If Aunt Mara wasn't worried about it, why are you?

Maybe because if Mom's letter was to be believed, it hit a little close to home.

I reached the door on the third ring and pulled it open.

Nothing could have prepared me.

Man-Bruce stood there, mouth agape, obviously as surprised as I was.

"It's you?" we chorused in shock.

"You're not Mara," he said, stating the obvious in a flat voice.

"No, I'm not," I said. I attempted my sunniest smile.

Kill him with kindness, I reminded myself. Something about the guy set my teeth on edge.

Man-Bruce let out an exaggerated sigh, like my being there inconvenienced him.

"Were you needing something?" I prodded.

"I'm here for a pickup."

We stood staring at each other for a moment. His fingers twitched at his sides.

"A pickup?" I asked.

"You know. The stuff." A harshness edged his voice though he kept the volume low. His gaze darted around like he expected someone to be watching.

"I'm sorry?"

"The stuff!"

His eyes took on a wildness, emphasizing the shadows beneath them, which I hadn't noticed at Christo's. I took a small step backward with one hand on the door, an uneasiness settling in my belly.

Was this some sort of drug sale? Was Aunt Mara in the business of more than just herbal teas? It was a sobering thought.

Man-Bruce drew in a deep breath. "Mara said she'd have it ready for me. It was all organized. The tea. You know? The *special* tea."

My stomach flip-flopped.

Okay, Alice. Jaystar said Aunt Mara sometimes sells teas from the cottage. Maybe she did have an arrangement with Man-Bruce.

"Look," I said, feigning a confidence I didn't feel. "Mara's not here at the moment, but if you let me know your last name, maybe I can find it for you."

I had no idea where to even start, but with the look Man-Bruce was giving me, I suspected he wasn't going anywhere until he got his tea. Aunt Mara seemed like an organized person, so maybe I'd get lucky and find it with no trouble.

"Maximilian," he mumbled

"Sorry?" I asked.

"Maximilian." Now that he was getting what he wanted, his voice had returned to its usual apathetic drone. "It's my name."

Of course it was. Bruce Maximilian. The antithesis, in my mind, to the weedy guy standing in front of me.

"I'll be back in a minute," I said, closing the door behind me. I grimaced, knowing the word "witch" would now be staring him in the face.

Hades was watching me from the staircase newel as I headed down the hall.

"Meeyowl!"

I caught a glimpse of his canines.

"My, what sharp teeth you have."

"All the better to eat you with!" the wolf said.

I eyed him suspiciously, and then remembered my promise to be kinder to him and more positive in general.

I flashed him what I hoped was a warm smile.

"Okay, Hades. Where would Aunt Mara keep her magical potions, or herbs, or whatever? Where would they be, puss-puss?" I cooed.

He rolled his eyes, unimpressed at my attempt, stretched his back into an arch, and jumped down onto the floor.

He turned his back to me and headed toward the door under the stair, checking over his shoulder once as if he wanted me to follow. It was possible I was reading too much into Hades's mannerisms, but without any better ideas of where to start my search, I figured I might as well follow him. I hadn't explored at least one room in that part of the house.

He stopped at the door under the stairs, and just like I had seen him do with the front door, he pressed a paw lightly to the door, and it opened. Something to ponder later, I told myself.

Hades led me into the laundry and did the same with the door I'd been called away from opening.

The door opened to a staircase trailing downward.

Brilliant. He was taking me to the basement. I could only imagine what horrors a basement harbored in a witch's cottage.

Remember Alice, positive thoughts attract positive things. Another of my mother's mantras.

I sucked in a deep breath and reached my hand into the gaping darkness, hunting for a light-switch.

I found it almost immediately. The narrow stairwell lit up. It twisted to the right near the bottom so I couldn't see where it ended. Hades was wasting no time trotting down the stairs. I followed behind at a more fearful pace and Hades was out of sight within seconds. It was with relief when I turned the bend and found myself in a well-lit, cozy workspace-*cum*-library.

A workbench with a sink and various chopping boards, bowls, mortars and pestles, and knives spread across one wall. Wooden floor-to-ceiling shelving units held jars of dried herbs and the like, on another. Calligraphic labels read *Mugwort, Rosemary, Dandelion Root, Chamomile, Sage, Rosehips*, and a multitude of names, some I'd heard of and many I hadn't. A couch with embroidered cushions and a quilted throw sat in front of a tall bookcase overflowing with books on all things magical and what I had believed was mythical until today. More books were stacked in piles on the floor and on a coffee table. Everywhere I looked lay crystals and rocks, decks of oracle cards, and other New Age trinkets. Bundles of herbs hung from a string suspended across the room. Others were laid out on racks to dry. They perfumed the room with a heady bouquet. No doubt this was Aunt Mara's workspace.

Hades waited for me on the other side of the room. He held up one paw and was very focused on cleaning it, as if he were saying, *Now you're here, my job is done.*

"Alright, cat. Where's Man-Bruce's what-cha-call-it?"

Hades stopped grooming and narrowed his eyes at me, as if I were stupid. And maybe I was. It took me a moment to realize he was standing in front of shelves lined with paper bags. Hades stepped aside so I could have a closer look. Each bag had stiff edges and not an out-of-place crease. A bordered sticky label with a calligraphic name held it closed. As I flicked through, I noticed they had been arranged in alphabetical order. Moving down a few shelves, I found the M's, and sure enough, one label read: "Maximilian, Bruce."

Hades sauntered off, his job done. I pulled out the bag and looked it over. The label had come unstuck, torn slightly at the corner, and the bag was slightly crumpled, at odds with the others. While tempted to peek inside, I thought better of it. It was none of my business, and the sooner I got back upstairs, the sooner I could get rid of Man-Bruce. I took the stairs two at a time, switched off the light at the top landing, and re-entered the laundry. The bucket and cleaner reminded me of my original plan, prior to Man-Bruce showing up on the doorstep. I huffed. One thing at a time.

Man-Bruce was furiously texting away on his phone when I opened the door. He barely glanced up.

"You've got it?" he grunted.

"Yeah," I said, handing it out for him to take.

Relief flashed in his eyes as he grabbed hold of it.

I held it for a moment longer. It felt weird to ask, but I didn't want to lose Aunt Mara business.

"Have you paid?" I asked.

His eyes locked on mine. "It's all been taken care of," he said, yanking it from my grasp.

I had no idea if it was true, but I couldn't do much about it.

He pocketed his phone and turned his back on me. Without another word, he headed down the path toward the road.

"Come again," I called out, and instantly kicked myself for doing so.

Really, Alice!

Clearly, I was made for customer service. I snorted.

I turned around to go back inside, then remembered the door.

How in Hercules ...?

It was clean. No spray paint marred its surface. No "Witch" scrawled in imitation blood. A quick glance at the ground showed no sign of paint drips either. I touched the door with my fingers. Dry.

Had Man-Bruce somehow cleaned it? Not possible. It was amazing he could squeeze his phone into his pocket. He had no room in his skinny jeans for cleaning products. Plus, from what I'd seen so far, the man had zero interest in helping others.

Then who?

I thought back to when I last saw the graffiti. I'd been trying so hard to avoid drawing attention to it, I realized that the last time I saw it was actually the first time I saw it.

Could Aunt Mara had cleaned it before she left?

I didn't think so. The garage was empty. If she'd taken her car, then she wouldn't have come out the front door, and there was too little time between her leaving and my searching for cleaning products. We would have crossed paths.

It made no sense.

Had I imagined it?

Really, Alice? You're gaslighting yourself?

No. I saw what I saw. Which meant either I was going mad or something weird was going on at Hollyhock Cottage.

Chapter 8

By seven o'clock, I was starving again. After a hunt through the fridge and cupboards, I settled on making myself a sandwich. I had never been much of a cook though I'd taken classes one summer while I was on a hunt to find my "thing". Yet a pastrami and lettuce sandwich was still about as gourmet as I got. Hades was eyeing up my dinner from where he sat perched on the counter. Every so often, his tongue flicked out of his mouth when I took a bite. It took me a moment to realize he was probably hungry. I wasn't sure what his feeding schedule was or if he even had one, but I wasn't going to begrudge him food, especially as he helped me to find Man-Bruce's stuff and send him on his way.

His bowl was on the ground in the corner. Feeding him had never crossed my mind. In my defense, I had thought Aunt Mara would have been home hours ago. At the bottom of the pantry, I found a plastic container of cat food. I carried it over to his food bowl and crouched down to take off the lid. Hades wove himself around my legs, purring and head-butting me. I guess the way to a cat's heart was kitty kibble.

A measuring cup sat on top of the kibble. I used it to scoop up a quantity and drop it into his bowl. I figured he wouldn't care if I had given him too much.

Hades devoured his food by the time I'd returned to my seat to take another bite of my sandwich. It was possible he enjoyed his food as much as I did mine. I felt a little guilty I'd made him wait.

I finished my sandwich as Hades rigorously groomed himself. That cat sure liked to be clean. Just as I swallowed my last mouthful, he stiffened, mid-lick. His ears pricked and twitched as if he were hearing things I couldn't. I froze, my own senses on high alert.

When the doorbell rang, I again nearly jumped out of my skin. Was the cottage always this busy?

"Coming," I called out. I dropped my plate into the sink, making a mental note to deal with it later, and headed down the hall to the front door. I hoped it wasn't Man-Bruce again.

"Mara Lovell?" a man's voice boomed. "Open up, this is the WBI."

So, not Man-Bruce. And what was the WBI?

I was only a few paces away from the door when the visitor started banging with the knocker. Did nobody have patience in this town?

I guess Hades had warmed up to me since I fed him. He kept close beside me, nestling up to my leg when I reached the door.

"Mara! Open up!"

Whoever it was, was in a mood. I wasn't sure I wanted to open the door.

"Mara's not here," I called back, biting my lip. Hades head-butted my leg.

"Well, if she's not here, where is she?"

How was I supposed to know?

Hades head-butted me harder before walking over to the door and scratching at it.

Really? Now he wanted to go outside? Didn't he have some sort of magical power where he could open the door himself?

"Hades? Hades, if that's you, let me in, puss."

Hades turned and gave me a weird look, then pressed his paw to the door. And just like that, it opened.

I was gobsmacked. Hades was a traitor. How was I supposed to keep out intruders if the cat went about opening the door for people?

The door swung open, and a dark figure filled the frame. Hades launched himself at him, and to my shock, nestled into his arms and starting purring.

"You're not, Mara," the man said.

This was beginning to feel like déjà vu.

Two shorter figures stepped out from behind him and flashed badges at me. I paid no attention to them; I was too focused on the man in front of me.

He was a good deal taller than me and maybe a handful of years older. He wore a collared shirt tucked into belted slacks and a long charcoal-gray overcoat better suited to colder weather. He had dark wavy hair, long enough to tuck behind his ears, and dark stubble on a chiseled jaw. And he had the bluest eyes I had ever seen. He could have stepped out of some glossy high-end fashion magazine. Any other time, I might have been weak-kneed in his presence. Instead I was hit with an intense wave of resentment.

Hades had turned to mush in his arms. The cat was purring loudly and dribbling like a baby. His paws puddling the air as he lay belly up against the man's chest. No doubt about it; Hades was smitten, and I was kind of jealous. Hadn't I just fed the brute? Wasn't he supposed to be a Lovell cat?

"Miss? Miss? Can you tell us your name, miss?" One of the shorter guys was trying to get my attention. I hadn't been listening.

"I'm Alice," I said, "Alice Lovell. Mara's great niece." I cringed at the word *great* again and hoped Aunt Mara never found out I had said it.

A whisper of shock flitted across the tall man's face, quickly disappearing behind a stern countenance. His eyes scanned my face, and I fought against turning away. Instead, I made myself stand up straighter, and I pulled my shoulders back. He lowered Hades to the ground. Hades let out a perturbed mew and threw daggers at me with his eyes.

Traitor, I thought, glaring back at him.

The man on the right stepped forward this time. "Miss Lovell?" he questioned. "We need to talk with your aunt. Do you know where she is?"

"I've already told you. Aunt Mara's not here. If you have a message for her, I'll pass it on when she gets back." I attempted a smile to soften the edge in my tone.

"When do you think she'll be back?" Boss-Man asked.

"I'm sorry," I said, ignoring his question. "I never got your name."

The man on the right opened his mouth to answer. Boss-Man held up a hand to silence him. He then tilted his head slightly, as if to work out if I was serious or not. Obviously, he thought he was somebody.

"I'm Eli," he said, his eyes glued to my face. The two men flanking him gave each other a nervous glance.

"Eli ...?" I asked, waiting for a last name.

"Just Eli," he said.

Right. Got it. My hackles went up.

He looked at me like he found something funny.

"This is Crowley"—he pointed to the stocky, balding man on his left—"and Nix"—he indicated the lanky bird-like man on his right. Crowley and Nix nodded at me, simultaneously crossing their arms in front of their bodies, as if they were bodyguards.

"As we mentioned, we are from the WBI. It's really important we speak with your aunt." His eyes refused to leave mine.

"Well, as *I* have mentioned, Just Eli, my aunt is not here right now." My jaw clenched. I was losing my patience. I considered closing the door on them but figured Hades could just as easily open it again.

"Right. Well, we'll just wait inside until she returns," Eli said. He jerked his head at Crowley, indicating for him to enter. Instinctively, I put up my hand to stop them.

"I don't think so," I said. Beads of sweat formed on the back of my neck and my pulse sped up. One woman, home alone, versus three men and a cat, because it was obvious whose side Hades was on. It was an unfair fight.

The three men glanced at each other.

"You know what WBI stands for, don't you?" Eli said the words slowly, studying me while he did so.

I had no clue. It must have shown on my face.

"The Wiccan Bureau of Investigation, ma'am," Nix quickly supplied.

"There's been a murder," Crowley stated.

Eli kept his eyes focused on my face.

"I'm sorry, what?" I asked, a chill settling on my skin. Wasn't Wiccan synonymous with witchcraft? And what did he mean, murder?

"We're from the Wiccan Bureau of Investigation, ma'am."

"There's been a murder."

Nix and Crowley repeated themselves.

Oh lordy! I wasn't sure if I was more shocked by the fact they had mentioned a murder, or that Tweedledee, Tweedledum, and Boss-Man knew about witches.

"I don't know what you mean," I said, playing dumb. Aunt Mara had told me to keep our magical lineage under wraps.

"You said you were Mara's niece, right?"

I nodded.

"Well then, you know we're the governing body for investigations into the misuse of magic, particularly as it pertains to the harm or homicide of an innocent?"

Little flashes of light danced before my eyes. I took a step back and rested a hand on the sideboard in the hope the room might stop spinning. No luck.

"Ah, Boss?" one of the Tweedles said as my legs crumpled beneath me and the lights went out.

When I came to, a heavy weight sat on my chest, and I had the unnerving feeling I was being watched. I opened one eye at a time before blinking and focusing on the face pressed up to mine.

Hades was sitting on me, his wide eyes unblinking. Behind him, two faces crowded in. Crowley and Nix awkwardly studied me and then eyed each other.

"Boss. She's awake," one of them called out.

I nudged Hades off me. He jumped onto the neighboring chair, and I maneuvered myself into a seated position.

I was on the couch in the living room with my legs stretched out before me. Nix and Crowley backed away and wandered around the room, avoiding looking at me.

Well done, Alice. Witchy law enforcement mention murder, and you faint.

I was mortified and my insides had turned to liquid.

Eli entered from the kitchen and handed me a glass of water. "Here," he said.

I tried to stop my hand from shaking as I took it from him.

"Are you okay?" he asked while Tweedledee and Tweedledum wandered off into another room.

"How long have you known Mara?" Eli asked, cutting right to the chase.

Pulling the glass away from my lips, I answered. "Twenty-four hours, give or take."

Eli's eyes narrowed, and he massaged the bridge of his nose as if he were getting a migraine. "And ... how long have you known you were a witch?"

Boy, oh, boy. I deliberated whether to answer. I wasn't supposed to talk magical things with Non-Magicals, but as far as I could tell, someone who was investigating the misuse of magic didn't fall into this category.

"Aunt Mara told me a few hours ago," I said.

His mouth fell open, and he quickly clamped it shut.

A crash from the kitchen drew our attention. A shame-faced Crowley stuck his head around the doorway.

"Sorry, Boss. Just knocked over a vase."

Eli shot him a look that made my heart jump.

I wouldn't want to be on his bad side, I thought.

He turned his gaze back to me and narrowed his eyes.

"You said there had been a murder?" I gulped as I said it. "What does that have to do with Aunt Mara?" Horrible thoughts raced through my mind. What if Aunt Mara was hurt? Sweat beaded on the back of my neck again. I took another sip of water.

Eli let out a sigh. He picked up Hades, plonked himself onto the chair, and repositioned Hades on his knee. Hades settled in and closed his eyes. I swung my legs around so I was sitting properly on the couch, facing Eli.

"You're Maggie's daughter? Am I correct?"

I nodded dumbly.

"Right. Mara's mentioned you. She also said she and your mother were estranged, so she didn't get to see much of you."

I nodded again. Although, to my knowledge, she'd seen nothing of me.

"I'm assuming you're here because Maggie's passed?"

Tears prickled behind my eyelids, and I blinked them back.

"Right. I'm very sorry for your loss," he said, dropping his eyes.

"Why are you looking for Aunt Mara?" I asked again.

"Your aunt is a suspect in a murder investigation. I wanted to get to her before Widdershins's Law Enforcement did. They'll complicate things. I've known your aunt a long time. I don't normally take on these types of cases, but I owe her."

"What kind of murder?" I asked. My voice was higher than normal. Hades opened one eye and stared at me.

"When did you last see Mara?" Eli asked, avoiding my question.

I bristled. I just wanted him to answer my questions.

"A few hours ago," I said. "Around four, I think. She got a phone call and left. She said she'd only be gone a short while."

"Boss!" came a voice from down the hall. "We think we've found something."

"Hold up," Eli called back, then turned back to me. "And you've been home the whole time? Since she left?"

"Yeah," I said, unsure what he was getting at.

The line between his eyebrows deepened.

Eli picked up Hades and plopped him onto the ground. I got short-lived satisfaction watching the cat glare at him before sauntering off. In a few quick strides, Eli was at the doorway to the hallway.

I followed, nervous as to what Tweedledee and Tweedledum had found.

"Under the stairs," a voice called out. I followed closely behind Eli. He was tall and broad, and I felt rather dwarfed in his presence.

My heart jumped into my throat as I realized they'd probably found Aunt Mara's basement workspace. I wasn't sure she'd be thrilled with people rummaging around there.

The door to the basement was wide open, and the light on, illuminating the stairs curling down to Aunt Mara's workspace. Eli filled most of the narrow space as he made his way down the stairs. I followed at a slower pace, not convinced I wanted to know what they'd found.

Chapter 9

"Monkshood," one of the Tweedles called out. I couldn't see which one. Eli still blocked my view.

I pushed past him to see what the fuss was about. Crowley held a jar in his hand. A neatly calligraphed label was visible. Nix was on the other side of the room, rummaging through a filing cabinet I'd overlooked the first time I'd visited.

"You can't do that!" I protested. It seemed wrong, them going through Aunt Mara's things without her being there.

Nix ignored me.

Turning to Eli, I tried again. "He can't just be going through her things." I pointed at Nix, who was pulling out files and flicking through papers.

"Actually, he can," Eli said, unsmiling. "It's why we're here." He turned to Crowley. "Bag it."

"We found this too, Boss," Crowley said, moving toward the workbench where a giant book sat. I followed Eli over to the bench.

My skin tingled. It seemed familiar, yet I couldn't remember having seen it before. It was huge, with a leather cover engraved with patterns and sigils I didn't understand. It looked old, and for some reason I felt incredibly protective of it.

"Get away from it," I said, my skin heating up.

Both Crowley and Eli ignored me.

"Where was it?" Eli asked.

"Hidden behind a bunch of books on the bookcase."

I spun around to the bookcase. Books sprawled haphazardly every which way. Gaps showed on the shelves, and more piles than I remembered lay on the floor. Crowley had pulled it apart in his search and not bothered to put anything back properly.

A fire unfurled inside me.

"Don't you need a search warrant or something to do this?" I snapped.

They continued to ignore me.

"Here's the strange thing," Crowley said, as he and Eli leaned over the book.

It was all strange if you asked me.

I managed to squeeze in between them. Crowley opened the book and started turning pages. They were all blank. No words. No pictures. Nothing.

"What is this?" I asked, fighting the urge to slap Crowley's hand away from touching it.

"It's your Book of Shadows," Eli said, finally answering me.

A light went off in my head. This was my family's grimoire.

"Why are the pages blank?"

"Good question," Eli answered. "We'll take it with us." He gestured to Crowley to pack it up.

"You can't," I argued. "It belongs to my family."

"She's right, Boss. I've already checked. It's been spelled. We can't take it from the room. In fact, the entire room's been spelled. Magic won't work down here. I mean, maybe Mara's does, and Miss Lovell's too, being family and all, but otherwise it's been bound up well and good. There's some serious magic at play here."

My brain raced ahead, trying to understand what Crowley was saying. Eli turned to me, his eyes exploring my face.

"I don't suppose, in the few hours you've known you're a witch, you've learned any magic?"

I was numb. Too many conflicting emotions were muddying my mind. I shook my head.

"Figures," he said, pinching the bridge of his nose. "Right. Put it back where you found it, Crowley. We'll get the High Council involved only *if* and *when* needed. In the meantime, we know it's here." He walked away and then, eyes scanning the bookcase, he turned around again. "And tidy up your mess!"

"Yes, Boss," Crowley said, gathering the Book of Shadows up in his arms.

"Tell me again, Miss Lovell, when did you last see Mara?" His voice was calmer now, but no less threatening.

"Four, four-thirty," I said, trying to make sense of what was going on. All my emotions were heightened. I wasn't sure if I was going to burst into flames with anger, dissolve into a sobbing mess, or faint again.

"And have you even been down here, in this room?"

"Well, yeah," I said. "One of Aunt Mara's customers came by to pick up some tea or something from Mara."

The room fell silent, and Crowley and Nix stopped what they were doing. Eli arched an eyebrow at me.

"And ...?" Eli prompted.

"So I came down to see if I could find it ..."

An even more pinched expression appeared on Eli's face. Crowley and Nix exchanged a glance.

The blood drained from my face. It didn't take a genius to sense I'd said the wrong thing.

Before I could say anything else, the doorbell rang. Again. I wanted to scream at whoever it was to go away. This evening was turning into a nightmare. I didn't think I could deal with facing any more visitors. What I needed to do was get rid of the ones I already had.

I held my breath, unsure what to do. The others were quiet. All of us frozen.

The doorbell chimed again, which seemed to spur Eli into action.

"Okay, this is what we're going to do. Nix, you're going to go upstairs and do a cloaking spell around this room. Under no circumstances do you drop it unless you hear from me."

"But, Boss ..."

"I know. It bucks protocol, but we'll deal with the consequences later. Crowley, you put the room back how you found it. No one can know we were here."

"Mara will know."

"Of course she will! That's not who I'm worried about. Miss Lovell, you're going to go upstairs. You're going to tell the sheriff you're Mara's great niece and Mara is away. She'll be back tomorrow. Buy us some time, hopefully. You can tell her you'll let Mara know to contact her when she's back. Do NOT mention this room, the monkshood, being a witch, or having had any visitors today, got it?"

"The sheriff?" I asked.

His expression told me enough. I wasn't to argue. Maybe it was a witchy sense that told him who was at the door, if that was even a thing.

The doorbell chimed again.

"Look," he grabbed my shoulders and made me face him. "I know you're new to this, but right now, you're a suspect in a murder investigation. A serious one."

Was there any other kind? I wondered. Then his words hit. *I* was a murder suspect?!

"Up there"—he pointed up the stairs—"is the sheriff. I don't know how much she knows, but if she gets any whiff that something is out of place and you're involved, she'll be dragging you down to the station, which is really going to complicate things. Do you understand?"

As scary as he was, concern showed itself too. It was coming off him in waves.

I nodded.

"Go!" Eli ordered, letting go of my shoulders.

For the second time that day, I took the stairs two at a time. Nix stood in the laundry, back to the door, mumbling under his breath. I slowed my pace only on reaching the hall, trying to calm my racing heart.

You've got this, Alice. Stay calm. Act innocent.

I *am* innocent! I wanted to argue with myself. I didn't even know who the victim was. I paused at the door and took a deep breath.

Remember, Alice. The most frightening monsters are the ones that live in our minds. Positive thoughts attract positive things.

My pulse slowed.

"Mara Lovell. We know you're in there. Open up," a woman's voice demanded.

"Coming," I called back.

Okay, Alice, it's showtime. Act normal. Just say Aunt Mara's gone out and will be back tomorrow. Oh, sugar-sticks! I hope she's back earlier than that. Where is she?

Focus, Alice! A man's voice interrupted my thoughts.

How in Hercules had Eli got into my head? I gave my head a good shake, as if I could dispel him.

Get out of my head! I thought back hard.

Well, focus. Open the door before she breaks it down, will you?!

The sheriff had taken to pounding on the door so hard it vibrated.

Oh, we were going to have a serious talk after I'd gotten rid of our unwanted guest. I didn't care who Eli thought he was. This was a total invasion of privacy, and I wasn't having it!

I put my hand on the doorknob and turned it. The sheriff must have been waiting for that because she pushed it open hard, making me jump back in surprise.

"Where's Mara?" she asked. No niceties.

"Hi, I'm Alice," I said, holding out my hand to shake hers.

She ignored it and pushed past into the hallway. A tall, gangly man in uniform followed suit, ducking through the doorway. He looked younger than me; his face undecided about what was stubble and what were pimples. His hand was on his holster at his side.

Glimpsing it, the sheriff turned on him. "Stand down, Jonas."

With a blush, Jonas took his hand off his holster.

What was it with people barging in? Weren't there laws against that? In fact, shouldn't they have a warrant or something?

"Can I help you?" I asked.

The sheriff glanced around. About my height, she had long auburn hair slicked back into a ponytail. If I had to guess, she was probably in her thirties.

"Where's Mara?" she asked.

Well, this was going wonderfully.

Stick to the script. Eli's voice interrupted my own thoughts.

"Get out!" I hissed at him.

"Excuse me?" The sheriff scowled.

I glanced around, trying to find an excuse. Hades brushed up against my leg. I bent down and picked him up.

"The cat," I explained. "He needs to go out." I pushed past Officer Jonas and dropped Hades on the front doorstep. He turned around, hissed, and swiped at me, making me jump back with a squeal. Then he took off in a mad sprint down the pathway.

"I guess he really needed to go," Jonas said.

The sheriff shot daggers at him, and he flinched.

Good save, Eli said.

I gritted my teeth.

"Who are you?" the sheriff asked, finally setting her eyes on me.

"I'm Alice Lovell," I said, thankful to be back on script. "Mara's great niece." I made a show of eyeing her uniform. "And you must be the sheriff?" I held out my hand again.

The sheriff just looked at it. "Markson," she grunted at me, jerking her head in a nod. She moved down the hall, opening doors and peering inside.

Speed it up! Eli ordered.

Gandhi said, To lose patience is to lose the battle, I reminded myself, ignoring Eli.

What are you? An encyclopedia of New Age proverbs? Eli growled.

"Mara's not here. She's out for the night, but I can get her to contact you when she's back?" I said to Sheriff Markson's back.

She pivoted to face me again. Her eyes narrowed, and I struggled not to fidget under her stare.

"Where is she?" the sheriff asked.

Oh, sugar-sticks, I had no idea. Did I tell the sheriff that or would that make her ask more questions?

Tell her you don't know, Eli said.

"She didn't say. She only said she'd be back tomorrow sometime." I shrugged, hoping it made me look relaxed about the whole thing. "As I've said, I can get her to call you when she gets back."

"Ms. Lovell is needed to answer some questions about a murder." Officer Jonas puffed out his chest and slipped his hand back on his holster.

"I told you to stand down, Jonas!" the sheriff growled. "Go wait outside!"

Officer Jonas slumped and bowed his head as he slunk out the door.

"Murder?" I asked, acting shocked. Maybe the sheriff would be more forthcoming with answers.

You're going off script, Wonderland!

Wonderland? Well, that was a new one.

My name is Alice*!* I thought back to him.

The sheriff and Eli growled in unison.

"We're in the preliminary stages of our investigation. However"—the sheriff paused, her eyes scanning me up and down—"it seems your aunt's herbals might be connected. You wouldn't know anything about that, would you?"

Heat rose up the back of my neck. I couldn't remember. Did I know, or did I not know? Holy cheese, things were getting confusing.

She was studying me closely.

"And what time did you say you last saw your aunt?" The sheriff raised an eyebrow and her tone had become sickly syrupy.

Careful, Eli warned. *You know nothing about the herbals, and you can't remember what time she left. If you give too much away, you incriminate yourself.*

Oh lordy. The seriousness of the situation hit home. I really was a suspect in all of this.

"Well?" the sheriff asked.

"Oh, umm, I can't really remember. It's been a long day." I tried an innocent smile, but it fell flat.

The sheriff narrowed her eyes at me, then continued down the hall. She was almost at the staircase.

"I'm sorry," I said, "but it really has been a long day. I was hoping to get to bed early. I'll get Aunt Mara to call you as soon as she returns." My heart pounded in my chest. What if Nix's cloaking spell didn't work? It might be hard to explain the man in the laundry and the two men in the basement. And if *they'd* found incriminating evidence, it wouldn't be a stretch that the sheriff might, too.

Come on, Wonderland. Wrap it up. Smile that wide-eyed innocence thing you've got going on, and get her out of here.

I'm trying! I thought back at him.

Try harder!

I knew what I would do. I'd kill her with kindness, and maybe that would get her on side, make her see we could never have been involved with a *murder*.

"Would you and Officer Jonas like to join me for a cup of tea before I turn in?" I asked.

What in damnations are you doing, Wonderland?! Eli roared.

I flinched.

"What are you playing at, Lovell?" the sheriff asked, her voice dry.

"Nothing," I stammered. What was I doing wrong?

"Seems unusual you want me to sit down and have a cup of tea with you, considering that might just be the last thing our victim did."

My mouth went dry.

Eli, what's going on? Panic rose in my chest. A white noise filled my head, making it hard to think.

Eli?

The sheriff reached into her back pocket and pulled out a piece of paper.

"Miss Lovell, do you recognize this man?" She thrust the folded piece of paper at me.

I took the paper and slowly unfolded it. From the corner of my eye, I saw the sheriff's hand move to her holster.

Whoever it is, don't react, I told myself.

Do not react! Eli's voice repeated.

I let my gaze fall onto the paper in my hand.

My stomach dropped.

Not only did I know the guy, but I might also have been the one who killed him.

Chapter 10

"**W**ell?"

The sheriff's eyes burned into my skin. I kept my gaze focused on the paper while willing my legs to not give out under me. A lump had formed in my throat, and I didn't trust myself to speak.

How was this possible? Any of it? No one deserved to die by murder.

There was no mistaking the man in the photo. It was Man-Bruce. The dead man was Man-Bruce.

Both Eli and the sheriff had alluded to poisoning. I guessed it was why Crowley bagged a jar of Aunt Mara's herbs.

"Do you recognize this man, Miss Lovell?" The sheriff's voice was pinched with impatience.

If I have to intervene and put the WBI at risk, Wonderland, you can bet things are going to get a whole lot more complicated for you, Eli growled.

"Do. You. Know. This. Man?"

I let my eyes rise to meet hers.

"The way I see it," she said, her eyes flashing, "is you talk now, or we take you down to the station and keep you there until you're willing to talk. Ball's in your court."

Could she even do that? I wasn't sure. Nor did I want to find out. I had to give her something. The truth. I needed to tell her the truth. What else was there?

Eli's frustration and anger became a throbbing pain at my temple. With it, something shifted in me. None of this was right. I hadn't knowingly killed anyone. I conceded the sheriff had a job to do, but I didn't deserve to be threatened by her—or Eli, for that matter. And as far as I was concerned, Eli had zero right making himself at home in my head!

An unusual, prickly sort of heat grew inside me. It crawled up my back, over my shoulders, and up my neck. Anger. It wasn't often I got angry, but right now, I was livid.

I held the picture out for the sheriff to take back.

"Yes," I said, keeping my voice as steady as possible while holding her gaze. I felt the fire in my eyes. "I have seen this man."

The sheriff tightened her grip on the handle of her revolver.

Don't even start! I warned Eli.

"Jonas, get in here," the sheriff called out to her sidekick.

I felt rather than saw Officer Jonas move into the entrance behind me. The sheriff took the picture from my hand, stuffing it back into her pocket.

"I saw him this morning at Christo's Café," I said. "He was our server. I was there with Christo and Jaystar—" I searched my brain for Jaystar's last name before remembering Mrs. Frieda scolding him. "Jaystar Stevens."

The sheriff studied my face. I kept my eyes on her. I would not be bullied. I had told her the truth, and I'd just given her two witnesses who could corroborate my story. The sheriff's fingers relaxed on her gun.

The voice in my head stayed silent.

"And do you know of any relationship Mara might have had with this man?" she asked, her face still stony.

"Ask her," I said, matching her tone. "Tomorrow. When she's back."

I turned my back to her and moved toward the door. Officer Jonas shuffled out of my way.

"You need to leave," I said, holding the door open. I was struggling to keep my anger contained. It was bristling under my skin. I couldn't remember having ever felt this way before. Maybe it was feeding off of Eli's emotions. But wherever it had come from, it was doing the trick.

The sheriff's jaw clenched, and she gestured Officer Jonas out the door. She paused when she got to me.

"You can expect to be hearing from us in the morning," the sheriff sneered.

I held her gaze until she turned and left. I kept my shoulders squared as they walked down to the path. From nowhere, a rocket of black fur raced up the garden path. It zipped between the sheriff's legs mid-stride, making her lose her balance and swear loudly. Officer Jonas grabbed one of her flailing arms to steady her, and she cussed him out before stomping off ahead of him.

Hades shot through the door like a bullet, bringing an icy-cold breeze with him that made my skin crackle. He skidded at the end of the hall. His pupils dilated, like he was chasing prey, and then flew up the stairs. He thundered around in the bedrooms and up and down the hall.

"Dumb cat," I muttered before slamming the door.

The intensity of my anger was fading, replaced instead with grief. Death was horrible. Any sort of death. And murder was the worst. And tonight, someone had been killed. Someone I knew, albeit not well. A heaviness settled in my limbs, and I could feel tears building. The floodgates were weakening. But first, I had other people I needed to oust from the house.

"Eli!" I called. "It's your turn."

Crowley and Nix came out from under the stairs carrying bags of evidence, I assumed, somehow linking Aunt Mara or myself to Man-Bruce's murder.

Eli followed close behind.

"You need to leave," I said to all three of them, keeping my voice as steady as possible.

Crowley and Nix exchanged a glance before standing aside, parting the way for Eli.

"You need to leave," I said again, focusing in on Eli. A rush of fire burned in my eyes. "It's late. Unless you have an arrest warrant, I want you out of this house. I'll get Aunt Mara to contact you when she's back."

Crowley and Nix faced Eli. Eli jerked his head toward the door. They left, saying nothing. Eli stayed where he was.

"Look, you're not going to get anything more from me tonight. It's been a long day. As I told the sheriff, yes, I know the victim." I choked on the last word and had to swallow hard to stay the emotion. "But I didn't kill him."

I willed back the threatening tears. There would be time enough for that when I'd gotten him out of the house.

"I'm sorry. I was rough on you back there," he said, scanning my face.

Part of me wanted to believe he was sorry, but I was still so angry with him. "Don't—Don't you *ever* do that again! Stay out of my head!" I snapped.

Though he flinched, he masked it quickly with a stern countenance.

He stayed there, watching me, until I finally had to turn away. The day's events had gotten the better of me, and sobs were building. I refused to let him see.

"Alright, Wonderland," he said. "We'll talk again tomorrow, and maybe by then Mara will be back."

I said nothing.

He took a step toward the door, then paused. His back stiffened, and he slowly turned around, glancing back down the hallway. From the corner of my eye, I saw his jaw tighten as he scanned the ceiling.

"Wonderland ..." he said, his voice lowered. "Do you have someone else here with you?"

"No ..." I said, suddenly anxious. At least I didn't think so.

I followed his gaze upward, my senses on edge. Muffled movement came from a bedroom above. I exhaled with relief. "That'll be the cat," I said.

"Right. Of course. Hades." His face relaxed slightly. He headed back out the door toward where Crowley and Nix waited down the path. Part way there, he turned around one more time.

"Oh, and Wonderland ..." he called out. "Don't leave town, okay?"

My jaw went slack.

Where in Hercules was Aunt Mara?

Chapter 11

As soon as I shut the door, my legs almost gave out. I stumbled my way down the hall, leaning on the wall as I went, until I reached the living room. I threw myself at the sofa.

Oh, this was bad.

I turned onto my side, wrapped my arms around a cushion, and tucked my legs up under me. A tsunami of tears burst forth. Man-Bruce was dead. And I might have been one of the last to see him alive. Not only that, but I may very well have been the one to have poisoned him.

The thought winded me. Me? A murderer, accidental as it was? The sheriff had inferred poisoning through tea. Which, at my best guess, was exactly what I had given Man-Bruce. I had trusted that whatever Aunt Mara had packaged up for Man-Bruce wasn't something meant to off a person. Only, how well did I know Aunt Mara? Not well at all.

Sniffing, I sat up on the sofa, feet still tucked to my side and wiped my face with my hand.

This had been the strangest twenty-four hours of my life. Not only had I gained a great aunt who had subsequently disappeared, but we were now both murder suspects.

Aunt! *Aunt*! I reminded myself, catching my mistake. No *great* about it. I didn't understand how Aunt Mara and Eli could so easily read my thoughts, but I certainly didn't want Aunt Mara hearing me call her great.

I assumed mind-reading was a witchy thing. I didn't like it. Weren't there rules around privacy? And if I really was a witch, where were *my* cool powers? Flying on brooms? Wriggling my nose and changing my hair color? Winning the lottery?

Nope. I guess I was the witch who gave the poisoned apple, or in this case tea, to the innocent—albeit somewhat rude—stranger looking for help.

I hugged the cushion to my chest. All this going around in circles was giving me a headache.

A thundering of paws racing down the stairs, through the hall, and into the kitchen, ended with a crash. My heart leaped into my throat. Though I knew it was the cat, the way Eli—Mr. Tall-Dark-and-Serious—had asked if I was alone, had unsettled me, so I called out anyway.

"Hello? Is someone there?" No reply, as I imagined there wouldn't be.

Come on, Alice. Remember, the most frightening monsters are the ones that exist in our minds— another of my mom's mantras.

Taking a deep breath, I gave my eyes another wipe.

No more tears, I chided myself. *Remember what Einstein said: "Life is like a bicycle. To keep your balance, you must keep moving."* Well, Al, this is me moving.

I pushed aside the cushion, unwound my legs from under me, and lifted myself from the sofa. More sounds of movement came from the other room.

"Hades?" I called. "What are you up to?" Pushing my shoulders back, I summoned my last reserves of confidence and marched into the kitchen. A cylindrical kitchen utensil holder had fallen over on the bench, and a steel ladle had rolled onto the ground. I picked it up and place it in the sink.

"Hades?" I called again, sure I was hearing noises coming from the hallway by the stairs. Moving through the doorway into the hall, I spied Hades right away. He stood with his back to the door under the stairs and was going about cleaning his paw as calmly as if I hadn't just heard him zooming around the house moments before.

"Well, cat," I said. "Any idea where Aunt Mara might be?" My voice quavered a bit. She had said she wouldn't be long. "Because if you know something, it would really help me out if she were here." It was ridiculous trying to appeal to a cat, but what choice did I have?

Hades eyeballed me. I stared back and his golden eyes narrowed to slits. I held his gaze. *What do you know, Hades?*

It had been worth a shot.

No way I was going to win a staring competition with a feline.

"Fine. I'm off to bed."

I fell asleep the moment my head hit the pillow. The shock had taken its toll. I woke to birdsong and sun streaming through the windows, where I had forgotten to pull the drapes again. Everything seemed so normal, so cheerful, so at odds with the memories that rushed back from the day before. I let out a groan and moved to bury my face in my pillow. A heavy weight on my bed stopped me from doing so.

Hades!

I was spooning with Hades. He was curled into a tight croissant, eyes closed, his tail curled around his body. I studied him and felt a wave of warmth, accompanied by a surge of affection. He looked so sweet and innocent. Of all the things that had happened over the last couple of days, this might have been one of the most bewildering.

He made a soft snoring sound as he slept. I couldn't resist gently stroking the fur on his forehead. I'd been a bit tough on him. He was just a cat, after all. It wouldn't do me any harm to be nicer to him, like Aunt Mara had asked.

Thinking of Aunt Mara, I strained my ears for any hint of movement downstairs. I was hopeful she might have come home during the night and she'd be able to put to rest the accusations against us.

Both the sheriff and Eli had promised they would be back, and I wasn't looking forward to seeing either of them. Not really. I was going to ignore the slight flutter in my chest when I thought of Mr. Tall-Dark-and-Serious. So what if he was handsome? He also wanted to arrest me for a murder I didn't commit and had no qualms about making himself at home in my brain. And he had taken to calling me Wonderland, which was irksome at best.

I needed a plan. I needed to find Aunt Mara. Maybe Christo would know where she was? They were business partners, so it seemed worth a shot. Also, I could offer my condolences. Even though Christo had been meaning to let Man-Bruce go from his job, it didn't mean he wouldn't be cut up by his death.

It was a weak plan. Sure, I now knew where Christo's Café was, but not whether it would be open or even if he would be there. A tragedy had just taken place. Plus, I didn't know how well-known Man-Bruce's death was. Regardless, discovering some answers was certainly more appealing than staying at the cottage waiting to be arrested.

Despite trying my best to extract myself from Hades without waking him, it was no good. He opened his eyes and yawned, showing his fangs. After a slow stretch, he glared at me and let out a sharp mew, jumped off the bed, and padded down the hall. I assumed he wanted feeding.

I picked up my phone from the nightstand and checked the screen. It was just after seven. No missed calls or texts. No messages from Aunt Mara telling me she was on her way home. Nothing.

Once I hauled myself out of bed, I had a quick shower and applied a dash of makeup. When I made it downstairs, I found Hades waiting by his food bowl, so I fed him while contemplating how best to satiate my own hunger.

A quick scan of the contents of the pantry and some mental calculations of how much money was on my card, helped me settle on another hot drink and muffin from Christo's Café. If they were open. If they weren't, I'd rethink things. The sooner I left the cottage, the less chance I had of bumping into law enforcement.

Outside, I was relieved to find the path empty. Before I could move, a flash of black fur dashed through my legs and down the cobblestones ahead of me.

Please don't go near Mrs. Whittle's flowerbed, I pleaded in my mind. I made a mental note to proceed carefully past Mrs. Whittle's just in case.

When I arrived at Christo's Café without incident, I found the café buzzing with customers, which both relieved me and made me nervous.

A group of middle-aged cyclists in blue-and-black spandex clustered around their bikes near the door. They parted to let me through. Soft rock music and a gentle hum of conversations surrounded me as I entered, and I sighed at the reminder of what *normal* felt like. I scoured the room for Christo, sure that if he was here, his tall stature and loud energy would stand out like a beacon amongst his customers. Students huddled in booths with backpacks on the seats beside them, looking like they were getting ready to leave. Anxious, foot-tapping, phone-scrolling customers, likely on their way to work, waited in line or crowded the counter where drinks were made. One man sat at a table alone, clicking away on his laptop with earphones on. I saw no sign of Christo. Nor was there a sign of mourning. I don't know what I expected. I wasn't even sure Man-Bruce's death was public yet.

I shook away an unexpected chill. It seemed wrong for everyone to be going about their normal day-to-day when someone was dead.

I lined up behind a woman waiting for the counter. She was two heads taller than me and of the build and with the attire that suggested she'd just come from the gym. While the line made slow progress in moving, I thought over my options for the day. If Christo wasn't hiding out the back or didn't know where Aunt Mara was, I needed a back-up plan. I'd already left Aunt Mara several messages to no avail, and I didn't know any of her other friends. I supposed I could reach out to Jaystar since his mom was a supplier of herbs for Aunt Mara. But what if she had been involved in setting Aunt Mara up? She'd need a motive, I had to remind myself, and I couldn't think of one. Christo had said Aunt Mara paid her well.

As far as suspects went, I was at a loss. Was the intention to kill Man-Bruce or frame Aunt Mara? Or was someone trying to do both? And that was the problem.

Lost in my daydream, it took me a moment to realize I'd reached the counter. The woman who had been in front of me had now stepped aside to wait for her drink.

"What can I do you for?" the guy at the counter asked.

Hmm. Did I order coffee or risk another Better You Beverage?

"One large mocha and a blueberry muffin to go, please." If Aunt Mara had added anything magical to her Better You Beverages, then I was going to stay away from them. Welcome to Wonderland had been a heck of an awakening.

I cringed when the barista rang up the price. Not only did Christo's appear swanky, but it also charged swanky prices. The uncharitable thought hit me that now Man-Bruce was dead, I might be in line for his job sooner than I had expected. Could that be used as a motive against me?

I swallowed hard.

When the barista returned my card, I went to step aside to wait for my order but caught myself.

"Excuse me," I said to the barista. "Will Christo be in today?"

The barista was already opening the food cabinet. He picked up a pair of tongs and went about retrieving my blueberry muffin without looking at me.

"Nah, he said he's got some stuff to tend to. I'm running the show today."

"Oh," the word fell out. "I know this is weird, but do you know where I could find him?" I bit my lip, hoping he knew.

The barista straightened and lifted his eyes to meet mine.

"Are you a friend of Christo's?" he asked. "I haven't seen you before."

"Well, yes …" I said, before correcting myself. It was too soon to call him a friend. "No. He's a friend of my aunt's."

"Honestly … I don't know."

I noticed his name badge with "Andrew" printed on it as he handed me my muffin in a brown paper bag.

"He called me last night to say he wouldn't be in, asked if I could hold down the fort. He's usually in on a Monday." His face pinched for a moment, and I held my breath in case he wanted to tell me something else.

"We get our stock on Monday. Most of it, anyway. Maybe something went sideways with our order and Christo was getting it sorted. It's possible he could be in later …"

Andrew didn't look confident that would happen. It made me uneasy.

"Ahem," a voice behind me drew our attention. A middle-aged woman in a plush cream pantsuit tapped a foot and bristled.

Andrew shot her a smile, and I stepped aside to let her order.

"Large mocha?" another barista called out, and I made my way to the far end of the counter to collect it.

The paper cup was emblazoned with Christo's Café on its side. A thin wisp of steam rose from the sippy hole in its lid. I held the mocha high to catch Andrew's eye and mouthed my thanks, then stepped away to think about what my next move was going to be. No Christo left me with no plan.

Remember, Alice, I reminded myself, *think positively and positive things will happen.*

Maybe Aunt Mara was right now sitting at home, I solaced myself. And maybe the sheriff and Eli had discovered overnight Man-Bruce's supposed murder was actually a self-inflicted accident. And maybe, I thought, I could use my witchy powers to teleport myself to a tropical island somewhere and wait until the whole sorry saga was over. Positive thinking, right?

Suddenly, I eyed a familiar face. It took me a moment to place where I had seen her before, sitting as she was, half of her face turned away from me. It was the young woman from Miss Maisy's—Lucy, the server. My skin prickled. Why was she at Christo's when she could just as easily get a hot drink from Miss Maisy's—and probably with a staff discount, too? Maybe she was here to meet someone. Or avoid someone, the thought flashed through my mind.

She nestled into the farthest corner of a booth, hunched forward over a drink, both hands clasping it as if she were warming them. Her blonde shoulder-length hair hung limp, pushed behind her ear. She was unmoving, deep in thought. Sadness clung to her like a dark cloud. I couldn't help myself. Despite my humiliating exit from Miss Maisy's the day before, I was drawn to her.

Lucy remained entranced by her drink as I approached. I cleared my throat so as not to startle her.

"Hi," I said.

After a pause, her head jerked up, and she blinked furiously before turning to face me. I raised my mocha slightly in greeting.

"I think I remember you from Miss Maisy's," I said. "Can I join you?"

The poor woman's eyes were red and puffy. She'd been crying, I realized with a start. Maybe she knew Man-Bruce. An ache grew in my chest. I slid onto the seat opposite her and placed my mocha and muffin on the table in front of me.

"I'm Alice," I said.

The woman opposite me shuffled farther back in her chair. I tried to keep a gentle smile in place, hoping it hid how awkward I felt.

"I just moved here. Two days ago, in fact."

No response. Her hands still gripped her drink in front of her, and her eyes looked through me rather than at me.

"What are you drinking?" I asked, desperate to get her talking, or else I might never have the courage to strike up a conversation with a stranger again.

Confusion washed across her face before her eyes fell on her drink. Almost in slow motion, she unclasped her hands from around the paper cup. I could make out part of a scrawl in marker across its side. Something *tea*. The something was still out of sight.

"Can I see?" I asked, nodding toward her drink.

Lucy pulled her hands back as if granting me permission. I turned the cup around to face me. It read, Bad Luck Be Gone. I remembered it as being a Better You Beverage. Probably one I should have thought of ordering.

I had nothing to go on but my intuition, so I took a deep breath before asking, "Did you know him?" My voice was barely a whisper. It was also possible I was totally off track.

Lucy lifted her eyes to me again. Her bottom lip tremored, and fresh tears rolled down her cheeks.

Jackpot, I thought, the ache inside me growing.

"I'm so sorry," I said.

She sniffed and wiped her nose with the back of her hand, then gave me a little nod.

"I'm Lucy," she said, in a small voice.

"Was he family?" I asked.

She nodded, eyes welling again. "We ... We ..." She choked on the words.

I reached my hand across the table and placed it over hers, giving it a small squeeze.

Instantly, a tingly surge of energy coursed through my hand, up my arm, and spread like wildfire through my body. The room around me vanished, and I was weightless, looking down on two people, their arms wrapped around one another. I recognized Lucy right away. She stood on the pavement, her arms draped around the neck of a man whose back was to me. Over his shoulder, I saw Lucy's face. She was smiling, her eyes bright and cheeks flushed. The man nuzzled his face into the curve of her neck, and Lucy threw her head back and laughed. She was in love. It beamed out of her, and I couldn't help feeling a warmth unfurl inside me. The man lifted her so her feet were just above the ground and turned, allowing me to see his face.

My stomach dropped. Deep down I'd known who I would see, but it still sent a bolt of shock ricocheting through me. Man-Bruce's eyes were animated in a way that reflected Lucy's. A far call from the man who had turned up at the cottage insisting on his herbal pickup.

Just as suddenly, I was back in my body again, sitting in a booth at Christo's Café. I reeled back in my seat, tearing my hand from Lucy's and feeling as if I'd been sucker-punched.

Holy cheese! Either I'd just had a weird out-of-body experience or the stress from the last couple of days had me losing my mind.

I gave my hand a small shake, trying to dispel remnants of pins and needles in my fingertips.

Lucy's eyes were wide as she stared at me.

Before I could say anything, a shriek cut through the white-noised bustle of the café. I twisted in my seat and gaped as a streak of black darted across the room, whizzing through people's legs and under tables, leaving a trail of squeals and curses in its wake.

A willowy cyclist club man lunged for the thing but missed and hit the polished concrete floor hard. Another club member helped him up. One woman stood on a chair, pointing and screaming like the whirlwind of fur was the devil itself. Andrew the barista ran around with a broom in hand, chasing the frenzied feline. My stomach somersaulted, and a cold sweat broke out across the back of my neck.

Think happy thoughts, Alice. Think happy thoughts. There's no way ...

A couple more customers joined the chase. Tables were pushed aside, cutlery crashed to the floor, and chairs were knocked over in the chaos. The cat parkoured its way around the space, clearly oblivious to all else but its prey —a large man in cycling attire.

Please don't be Hades. Please don't be Hades.

While my heart threatened to break free from my chest, my limbs wouldn't move. I tore my attention away to glance at Lucy; her face drawn in fear. Her mouth had formed a silent scream and her eyes were wide disks following the cat as he flew around the room.

What I didn't understand was why no one was helping the man being chased!

His cycling companions, many of whom had now entered the café to join the pandemonium all ignored his cries and sobs as he clambered over tables and chairs, waving his fleshy arms and trying to escape the beast chasing him. Sweat dripped down his forehead, his cheeks puffed, jowls wobbled, mouth gasped for breath.

Everyone was so focused on the cat, no one had thought to shield the man. His face turned a carmine color, and I worried if someone didn't do something fast, he might suffer a heart attack.

Please don't be Hades. Please don't be Hades, I repeated.

The man was slowing down; I had to do something. The cat was enjoying this too much. Its eyes were black saucers and something about its features made me think it was ... smirking?

Oh lordy.

I hoisted myself up so I was standing on my seat, cupped my hands around my mouth and hollered as best as I could across the uproar: "Hades!" The cat ignored me. Christo's patrons did not.

Faces turned to stare and alternatively, glare at me. Andrew, broom still held high, took a few steps toward me, a V etched between his brows. "Is he yours?!"

The accusing tone hit hard. More steely eyes turned on me, and my cheeks flared. If hefty spandex guy wasn't heading for a heart attack, I sure was.

"No ... well ... not exactly ..." Other than coffee house music still playing in the background, and staggered sobs coming from Spandex-Man, Christo's Café was quiet. More eyes pierced me like knives. I wanted to explain I'd only just met Hades; he was my aunt's cat, not mine, but from behind the crowd, a scream cut me short. Over the heads of my audience, I watched as Hades launched himself through the air. Claws spread, he threw himself at his prey, hitting the man in the chest. Spandex-Man's arms flew up in fright and he staggered backward. The ball of fur was still latched to Spandex-Man's chest as he fell, slamming into the ground. My hands flew to my mouth in horror. Had Hades killed him?

A chill ran through me. Everyone's attention was still on me. Behind them, a man lay supine on the concrete floor. Unmoving.

"If he's your cat, you need to take him and leave!" Andrew's tone was cutting. Murmurs went up from the crowd.

"Why would you even bring a cat here?" someone else called out.

Behind them, Spandex-Man was coming to. Tears streamed down his face. My legs felt weak. There was no explanation for what I saw. It was impossible.

Hades had snagged one of the man's socks in his mouth, and he was dragging the three-hundred-plus pound man across the floor of the café toward the door.

It defied physics.

A whimper came from behind me. I'd almost forgotten about Lucy, but I couldn't tear my eyes away from the scene behind the crowd. The crowd, no longer interested in the cat, turned all its fury on me. They continued to hurl questions and accusations my way.

Behind them, Spandex-Man struggled against the vise-like grip of a twelve-pound cat. He flailed his arms and pounded his fists on the ground like a toddler. But Hades had a hold of the man like he weighed nothing.

Maybe he didn't.

My legs sagged beneath me. Spandex-Man's flailing limbs seemed to slip through solid objects like they were water.

How in Hercules…

My legs buckled fully, and I slumped back onto my seat, ignoring the surrounding voices.

My eyes met Lucy's. She had grown even paler than before. Like she'd seen a ghost.

Holy cheese. Maybe she had.

Chapter 12

"You can see him?" I asked, ignoring the surrounding uproar.

Lucy's eyes widened. She scrabbled out from behind the table, knocking her drink over as she did so. The lid flew off her cup, splattering me with Bad Luck Be Gone.

Oh, if it were only that simple.

She pushed her way through the mob closing in around our booth. I lost sight of her as Andrew filled my space.

"What's wrong with you? Of course she can see him!" His voice exploded as he slammed a fist on the tabletop, trying to get my attention.

"Lucy!" I called out, scrambling to get out of the booth and follow her.

"Who brings a cat to a café? You owe me a drink." One of the cyclist crew blocked my exit from the booth. He was a wiry man, still wearing his bike helmet, with the remains of a drink splashed across his front, much like me.

Kindness. Kill them with kindness, I reminded myself, cringing at my automatic choice of words.

"I'm so sorry," I said. "I don't know how he got here." And I honestly didn't. It was a bit of a distance from the cottage to Christo's Café. He must have followed me.

"You need to leave," Andrew said, his voice tight.

"She should be barred!" spilled-drink cyclist guy growled. When a few people voiced their agreement, he turned to Andrew. "We're here having a drink for our friend Gerry, and *she*"–he pointed a finger at me, and I shuffled uncomfortably, still unable to get out of my seat—"*she* brings her cat. Into a café! Gerry hated cats! Is this what it's all about? Some cruel joke?"

"Yeah!" one of his spandex-attired friends called out.

"I'm so sorry," I said again, trying to lift myself out from behind the table. I threw my best pleading doe-eyed look at Andrew, hoping he might let me leave. It seemed to work.

He drew his lips into a thin line of disapproval before taking a step back, allowing me room to stand. A quick jerk of his head in the door's direction and a grunt was all I needed to high-tail it out of there. A cacophony of protests followed me.

I didn't stop until I was out of sight of Christo's Café. What was happening? Two days and I'd been kicked out of two cafés. Any chance of part-time employment was looking slim.

Bad Luck Be Gone had left an unattractive splatter across the front of my shirt. It was hardly an advertisement for good luck, if that's what Aunt Mara's special elixir was supposed to conjure. I'd neglected to grab my mocha in my haste to leave, but fortunately, my paper-bagged muffin had made it out intact. My stomach gave a low growl in appreciation. Even the local pariah had to eat, I guess.

I continued down the street. With no other idea where to search for Aunt Mara, I'd resigned myself to heading back to the cottage and whatever—and whomever—awaited me there. My mind was still a jumble of questions, not the least about what had just happened back in the café. I saw no sign of Lucy or Hades or Hades's spectral hostage.

Was I going mad? I opened up the paper bag. The muffin had become slightly smushed in the chaos, but if food couldn't quell a descent into madness, I didn't know what could. Smushed or not, the muffin was good. It didn't help my mood though.

Upon finishing, I licked my fingers of the last few crumbs of muffin and threw the paper bag in the nearest trash bin. Turning the corner, my stomach flipped. Farther down the street, a crowd was gathering. A police car and ambulance were parked in front of Miss Maisy's Tea Shoppe. I could just make out Officer Jonas's gangly figure trying to hold back the rubberneckers intent on blocking the doorway to the shop.

Please don't be Hades again. I sent a prayer up to whoever was listening. One public humiliation was enough for one day. Also, the longer I could avoid crossing paths with the sheriff and her protégé, the better.

A bike whizzed past me on the footpath, making me jump, and I pushed myself up against the wall of the building. Using it to my advantage, I took a few steps back so I could peep out from around the corner of the building without being seen.

Miss Maisy's form came into view in the doorway of the tea shop. Though her back was to me, I glimpsed enough from around the form of Officer Jonas to see that she was dressed in a bright apricot-pink dress, waving her arms and shouting words that were drowned out by the surrounding commotion. Another figure came out to join her. Even if the uniform hadn't given her away, her stiff posture and fiery red hair would have. The sheriff looked to be trying to calm her while simultaneously scolding Officer Jonas for not keeping the crowd back. It was amazing what one could tell from arm movements alone.

A figure broke off from the crowd, skirting Officer Jonas, and making a beeline for Miss Maisy. I recognized Jaystar immediately and felt a strange sense of relief. Whatever drama was unfolding, at least Miss Maisy had her grandson with her. Jaystar wrapped an arm around her, and I was thankful to see Miss Maisy didn't push him away based on her last harsh words. Jaystar guided her out of the way of the door, which, held open by the sheriff, was now occupied by someone else in uniform.

The crowd finally made space, and I watched with a sinking feeling as two paramedics, a gurney between them, made their way to the ambulance. I clung to the corner of the building, willing my legs to keep me upright.

As the paramedics lifted the stretcher into the ambulance, I glimpsed the covered form of a body, with nothing but an arm hanging limp from under the white sheet, visible to us onlookers.

This was bad. This was really bad. No amount of Mom's feel-good, think-positive adages were going to dull the shock of seeing a dead body. Because that's what I was seeing. There was no doubt in my mind. Whoever was on that stretcher was dead.

Nausea swirled in the pit of my stomach, and I wondered how long it would be before I lost my breakfast. The doors of the ambulance closed. Lights flashed and sirens blared for a moment and then fell dead. The vehicle then pulled out onto the road, before speeding off in what I supposed was the direction of the local hospital. Or morgue. I didn't know how these things worked. Other than having my mother pass away, my life had been blissfully free of the nuances of death.

Now that the ambulance had gone, people started to leave. I'd lost sight of Miss Maisy and Jaystar when the gurney was being loaded into the ambulance. Leaving Officer Jonas to manage the few stragglers still trying to get a glimpse into the Tea Shoppe, the sheriff moved inside.

Now was my chance. I needed to get past the Tea Shoppe without being spotted by either Miss Maisy or the sheriff. I suspected it wouldn't do me any good being caught at a potential crime scene after my last run in with the sheriff. I knew of no other way to get back to Hollyhock Cottage, which seemed like the best place to regroup, even if Eli might be there waiting for me.

Taking a deep breath, I let go of the wall beside me and tried out my legs. A little jelly-ish, but they'd be fine once I started walking, I told myself. I only had to get to the end of the block; then turning the corner I'd be out of sight, and I could sprint back to Hollyhock Cottage. Who knew? Mara could be waiting for me there. The idea cheered me a little. She seemed like a take-charge person. I bet she would sort things with the sheriff and Eli. If my mom were here, she would have fixed things ...

A cloud of grief was on my periphery, so I pushed it away. There would be time for that later.

I stepped out from behind the side of the building. Head down, I put all my focus on the few steps ahead of me, with the child-like belief that "if you can't see them, they can't see you." *Them* was pretty much everyone at this point.

From the corner of my eye, I could see I was drawing level with the Tea Shoppe. My heart sped up, but I tried to keep my pace steady so I didn't draw any attention. I stole a glance ahead, making sure the way was clear. At the end of the block, a flash of black fur disappearing around the corner made my stomach lurch. Was it Hades? Again? What was he up to? Had he been at Miss Maisy's too?

I willed my feet to slow down when all I wanted to do was chase after the darn cat and find out what was going on. I tried mentally screaming at him to slow down. If Eli could get inside my head, maybe I could do the same with Hades.

It took me a second to notice the sound of shoes on asphalt, pounding across the road toward me. I willed myself to act natural, to keep going.

Please don't be the sheriff, I pleaded to whoever was listening.

My stomach churned. Whoever it was, they were getting closer.

"Alice?" a voice called out, making my legs nearly buckle under me. "Alice. Hold up!"

It was with relief I recognized his voice—Jaystar, thankfully with no one else with him. I gave a small wave but continued walking. Until I was out of view of the Tea Shoppe, I was not inclined to stop. Plus, Hades was getting away.

The corner was so close; I picked up my pace despite my best efforts.

"Alice, wait up!"

I was almost there.

Just as I reached the end of the block, his hand grasped my shoulder. I squealed automatically and then ducked out of sight of the Tea

Shoppe. My breath was heavy and labored, and I bent over, hands on my knees, trying to calm my racing heart and regulate my breathing.

"Alice? Are you okay?"

I stood up and brushed a strand of loose hair from my face. "Of course," I said, a smile plastered on my face. "How are you?"

I wasn't fooling anyone. Worry and confusion were stamped all over his features. "Didn't you hear me? I was calling you."

"Oh," I said, not really sure of what else to say. I had never been good at lying. "I'm sorry. I just ..." I hesitated, ultimately choosing to stay as close to the truth as possible. "I thought I saw Hades."

"Mara's cat?"

"Yeah," I said, wiping my sweaty palms on my jeans. I really wanted to get back to the cottage, but Jaystar deserved more than me fobbing him off.

He shifted his messenger bag on his shoulder while he studied my face, then dropped his gaze to the stain on my shirt. His eyes narrowed.

I crossed my fingers behind my back that he wasn't someone else who could read my mind.

"Is everything okay at the Tea Shoppe?" I asked, not sure the subject was going to calm my nerves any. "Is your grandmother okay?"

He shrugged, his eyes flicking away for a moment. "I guess," he said.

I raised an eyebrow.

"Well ... I mean, *Grams* is okay. But right now, she's giving an earful to poor Sheriff Markson."

Poor Sheriff Markson? I would have liked to have seen Grams lay into *poor* Sheriff Markson.

Be kind whenever possible, and it is always possible, I reminded my-self. Thanks Dalai Lama.

I stole a glance down the road, wondering where Hades was now. Had he headed back to the cottage? And what had he done with Spandex-Man?

"Mom sent me around to drop off some teas and herbs. I'd told her what happened yesterday—getting kicked out of the Tea Shoppe—and she thought it might help get back on Grams good side," he said with a half-smile.

He fell into step beside me as I started back in the cottage's direction.

"Why was the sheriff there?" I asked, knowing it had something to do with the body in the ambulance.

His expression fell again.

"One of grandma's customers, Marion Marigold. I guess she had a heart attack or something. I was out the back when it happened."

"Oh," I said. Something about the name Marion rang a bell, but I couldn't place it. "That's awful. I'm so sorry. Don't you need to be there for your grandmother or for questioning or something?"

He looked at me quizzically again. "Grams is fine. Mrs. Frieda is there, so Grams sent me on my way. And it was a heart attack, not murder. If the sheriff needs any more information from me, she knows where I live. Widdershins is a small town. Almost everyone knows everyone."

My shoulders relaxed a little. If it wasn't murder, there was one less felony I could be accused of.

"Did you know Marion?" I asked. The niggling feeling I'd heard the name before was bothering me.

"Yeah. Not well. But like I said, everyone kinda knows everyone." He kicked at a small rock, and it went rolling down the sidewalk into the gutter.

"She was Widdershin's resident billionaire," he said. "A good sort, a little eccentric, but a good sort all the same. She liked to give back to the community and invest in lots of local start-ups and things." His tone was somber.

I couldn't help wondering what she thought of Aunt Mara. She was at Miss Maisy's when she passed, so had she been team Miss Maisy?

In a rush, I remembered where I had heard the name before. Aunt Mara had been talking to a Marion on her phone right before she left the house on Sunday.

"Were Aunt Mara and Marion friends?" I asked.

Jaystar gave a one-shoulder shrug. "Yeah. I mean, Marion got along with everyone. She had no interest in community dramas. She didn't care about the feud between Mara and Grams. In fact, the only tea she drank was one of Mara's, but the only place she'd drink it was at the Tea Shoppe. She liked the atmosphere of the place. Only Marion would get that kind of allowance from Grams." He shook his head and let out a low whistle of admiration.

She certainly sounded like someone special. After my own interaction with Miss Maisy and hearing the history between her and Aunt Mara, I found it hard to believe she would let anyone drink Aunt Mara's tea on her premises.

We were approaching Mrs. Whittle's house. I hoped she was inside and wouldn't notice us. I'd had enough drama for one day. It also meant that we were nearly at Hollyhock Cottage. I wasn't sure if Jaystar was planning to follow me all the way to the cottage. While

I enjoyed his company, who knew what was waiting for me there. A friend might not be such a bad thing right now—or it could get awkward quickly.

"Remember Man-Bruce?" I asked?

Jaystar regarded me, obviously puzzled. After a moment, recognition flashed in his eyes. "The guy from Christo's? Man-Bruce? As opposed to the dog named Bruce?" He grinned.

I nodded.

Alright, Alice. Spit it out. Worst case, he runs for the hills and thinks you're a murderer. Best case, he'll know where Aunt Mara is and can maybe help you get out of this whole mess. I crossed my fingers for the best case.

"He died," I said. My eyes locked on his face.

Surprise, confusion, and sympathy followed in quick succession across his face, and I exhaled, more certain I could trust him.

"You didn't know?"

"N-no," he said. "I didn't really know the guy. Only in passing. How do you know this?" He adjusted his bag strap again.

I slowed my pace. We'd made it past Miss Whittle's without incident and were almost at Aunt Mara's gate.

"He came around to the cottage yesterday afternoon wanting to pick up a package Mara had put aside for him." I swallowed, knowing how bad the next part of my story was going to sound. I focused on my feet, nervous of his reaction.

"Aunt Mara wasn't home, and he was really insistent, so I went on a hunt through Aunt Mara's things for it. And I found a bag, made up, with his name on it, so I gave it to him."

"Okaaay ..."

We arrived at the gate. I still couldn't bring myself to look at him.

"What was in it?" he asked after a pause, his voice squeakier than normal.

Holy cheese, this was hard. "I don't actually know. I didn't check." Guilt ricocheted through me.

"Yeesh. So what? Did ... did Mara's stuff ..."

I looked up, trying to gauge if I was doing the right thing by telling him. His eyes had grown wide.

"... kill him?"

I nodded slowly. "I think so. Or the sheriff thinks so, anyway."

"Whoa," he said, running a hand through his hair, making it stand on end. "That's ... messed up."

No kidding, I thought.

"What do you think was in the bag?" he asked.

"Something herbal, I guess. Maybe a tea. I didn't look. But there's no way Aunt Mara would give someone poison ... would she?" As much as I wanted to think the best of Aunt Mara, I didn't know her.

Jaystar was silent, chewing on his lip. It did nothing for my nerves.

Please don't let my only living relative be a murderer, I prayed.

Come on, Alice! Mom wouldn't have left you in the hands of a killer.

"Nah, of course not," he finally said, his voice light. "I mean, she can be a little scary and all. And she might threaten people sometimes, but ..."

"Threaten people?" I asked. This wasn't what I wanted to hear.

"Well, yeah ... but I don't think she'd actually *do* anything. Like with Mrs. Whittle. Mara's always making threats that one day Mrs. Whittle might wake to find Brucey missing and a freshly dug flowerbed ..."

I swallowed.

"She'd never really do it though!" he added quickly.

Yikes. I hoped not.

"So back there"—he gestured in the direction we had just come—"you were avoiding the sheriff?" he asked.

"Yeah," I answered sheepishly.

"But she can't think *you* did anything wrong, can she?"

I guess my face said it all.

"Oh," he said.

"Also, I really did think I saw Hades." I didn't want Jaystar to think I was a liar.

"Well, he is a cat. Cats wander, don't they?"

"I guess," I said. I didn't really know what cats did if I was honest. I'd never had a cat before. I still didn't. Hades and I cohabited, that was all. I suspected dragging home ghost men probably wasn't normal cat behavior though, but I wasn't ready to divulge that to Jaystar yet.

"What's your aunt got to say about all of this, anyway?" He shuffled his satchel again.

It took me a moment to realize I'd left out a crucial piece of information.

"She'd be able to set the sheriff straight, wouldn't she?"

"Aunt Mara's missing."

Confusion swept over Jaystar's features again. "What do you mean?" he asked, taking another swipe through his hair.

"She went out yesterday afternoon and ... never came back." It sounded more ominous than I had wanted it to sound. "I went to Christo's in case he had seen her, but I guess Christo's not working today." I wasn't going to tell him I would probably never be allowed into Christo's again.

Jaystar's jaw had dropped.

"I'm sure it's nothing to worry about," I said, trying to fake some optimism. "She's probably back at the cottage right now, wondering where I am." My smile fell flat.

We stood there in an awkward silence for a while. I had to give Jaystar credit; he was taking his time with running for the hills.

Jaystar worked his bottom lip with his teeth. I didn't need the witchy power of peering into someone's brain, to know his was working overtime right now.

"Do you want me to come with you?" He nodded toward the path leading up to the cottage.

My first instinct was to say yes. I liked Jaystar, and who knew what awaited me back at the cottage. But because any number of things *could* be waiting for me, I said no. Jaystar was my first friend in Widdershins. I'd already hit him with a lot.

"I'll be fine," I said, trying a more believable smile.

He seemed reluctant to leave.

"Wait." Jaystar rummaged in his bag and then pulled out his phone. After tapping the screen twice, he handed it to me. "Put your number in there."

I did as he asked and gave it back to him. Almost immediately, my phone dinged with a message from Jaystar.

"Now you have my number. In case of emergency," he added.

I wasn't altogether sure what help he would be in an emergency, but I was grateful all the same.

"You wouldn't know Christo's number, would you?"

"Christo's?" he asked.

"Yeah. In case Aunt Mara's not home yet. Maybe he'll know where she is."

"Umm ..." Jaystar said, scrolling through his phone. "Nah, but I know who will have it. My mom. I can call her and find out?"

Maybe I was overreacting. A wave of self-consciousness hit me. "There's no rush," I said. "Aunt Mara's probably at home waiting for me." *With Mr. Tall-Dark-and-Serious and a dead man the cat dragged home.* "I'll let you know if she's not."

Jaystar hesitated and then gave a one shoulder shrug. "Alright. Well. If you really think you'll be okay ...?" He eyed the pathway to the cottage.

I smiled reassuringly.

He looked disappointed. "I'm heading off to Mom's anyway, so I'll text you Christo's number when I get it."

I gave him a small wave and watched as he started back past Mrs. Whittle's, head down.

Right, time to face my fears. Chin up, Alice. Positivity begets positivity!

Just call me Little Miss Sunshine.

I unlatched the gate and stepped onto the cobbled path leading to Hollyhock Cottage. After shutting the gate behind me, I straightened my shoulders and took a deep breath. Whatever was waiting for me, I could handle it.

Bad luck, be gone, I told myself, as I headed to the house.

Chapter 13

On reaching the cottage, I exhaled with relief. I saw no sign of Mr. Tall-Dark-and-Serious, nor were there any new accusations graffitied on the door. Fingers crossed, I'd walk inside and find Aunt Mara.

Just as I reached out to unlock the door, a shuffling sound came from inside. I paused and pressed my ear up to the solid wood panels. Yup. Someone was definitely moving around in there. My pulse quickened. It had to be Aunt Mara. She'd returned, which meant she could talk to the sheriff and Eli and get the whole messy saga of murder allegations cleared up.

Or, it was someone intent on doing me or Aunt Mara harm. My brain whirred. What if it was the person who had scrawled "Witch" on the door? Or maybe it was whoever had framed Aunt Mara—the person who really killed Man-Bruce. Or ... my mind was on a roll ... what if it was Aunt Mara, and Aunt Mara had deliberately poisoned Man-Bruce? Holy cheese!

Or, Alice, it could be Hades?

That was a reassuring thought. I could handle a cat. Except, of course, if the cat really had brought home a ghost. I didn't even know where to start there.

Deliberation wasn't going to get me anywhere. Better to act.

Feel the fear and do it anyway. Right, Alice?

As quietly as possible, I unlocked the door and pushed it open. The hallway was empty, and everything was quiet. A sudden noise came from the other end of the house. Someone else was here. No doubt about it.

"Hello," I called out, holding a cupped hand to my mouth, hoping it would carry my voice farther and also maybe muffle the quaver in my voice.

Nothing. No noise at all.

"Hello. Aunt Mara? Hades?" Like a cat was going to answer me.

"Aunt Mara?" I tried again. Nothing. I took a few steps into the hallway. Everything appeared the same. Nothing out of place—that I knew of anyway. I paused and listened. It was quiet but for the lup-dup of my heart in my ears.

"Hello?" My throat had constricted, and my voice came out as a strained whisper. I straightened my shoulders, hoping it would inspire some courage, and then I took a few more measured steps into the hall.

A louder crash sounded this time. Undeniable. My heart leaped into my mouth, making me choke back a scream. I froze. What to do? Run? My legs had turned to jelly, so I wasn't sure that was an option. All my senses were heightened. The shuffling was back. It seemed like it was coming from behind the stairs. In the laundry room, maybe, or else ... I swallowed. The basement?

Okay, that would make sense, I told myself. If Aunt Mara was back, she might very well be in her basement apothecary. And it would be completely reasonable for her not to hear me calling out from down there.

But just in case it wasn't Aunt Mara, I'd take a weapon with me. For peace of mind.

The truth was, I wasn't a violent person. I doubted I'd be able to hurt someone, even if my life depended upon it. The best I could hope for was that a weapon of some sort might allow me to put some distance between myself and anyone meaning me harm.

I scanned my surroundings as I approached the staircase for any-thing that might fit the bill. As I approached the doorway to the living room, I remembered the broom I had seen in the corner. A quick detour, and I had a broom in hand. It was a straw broom with a thin wooden handle, the kind I guess you would expect a witch to have. Aunt Mara certainly kept true to the clichés.

If I was a witch, some good old-fashioned witchy powers would have certainly been helpful right about now.

"Alright, Aunt Mara, I'm coming in," I called out as I opened the door under the stairs. Every few steps, I paused, listening for any more clues about who was in the basement. The house had fallen eerily silent.

I clasped the broom close to my chest for comfort. "Okay, I'm coming in," I called out again. Nothing.

The laundry was empty. The light was on, but I might have left it on when I was last in. A bottle of fabric softener had been knocked off the shelf and was lying on the ground in the center of the room. That was probably Hades, I solaced myself. I jabbed at the bottle with my broom.

Yup. It's dead, Alice.

Right.

Keeping the broom in my right hand, now considered my fighting hand, I picked up the bottle. It was pretty light. I'd have to add fabric softener to the shopping list. I made a mental note I knew I would soon forget, applauding myself anyway for my willingness to "adult" in the face of potential danger. I placed the bottle up on the shelf next to the laundry detergent.

So far, nothing supernatural or murderous. I wiped my forehead with my free hand, where cold beads of sweat had broken out. I should check the garage, I told myself, but I couldn't pull my gaze from the door to Aunt Mara's workshop.

Courage, Alice.

I took a step toward the basement, every fiber of my being on edge. I clutched the broom tighter in my hand and counted down from five as I approached the door. Five, four. I wrapped my fingers around the doorknob. Three, two. I turned it slowly, unable to remember if the door squeaked. One. I took a deep breath and pulled the door toward me.

Silence. I exhaled with relief.

The stairwell was pitch-black. My pulse hitched. If someone was down there, they were sitting in the dark. I found the light switch and flicked it on.

"Aunt Mara, are you there?" My voice shook despite my best attempt at feigning courage.

No response came.

Gingerly, I put my weight onto the first step. Like every horror movie I had ever seen, it creaked. My insides curled.

The shuffling sound was back. Oh lordy. I held the broom horizontally in front of me. It made me feel a little braver despite knowing the worst damage it would do was poke someone with the rounded end.

Goosebumps rose on my arms. The temperature had dropped. Considerably. I tried to remember if I had seen windows when I had last been down there. I couldn't remember. I gritted my teeth so they wouldn't chatter. Slowly, one step at a time, I crept my way down the stairs, pausing and listening every few steps.

What exactly is your plan, Alice?

I had none.

I came to the bend in the stairwell. A few more steps and I'd know who was making the noise. My heart hammered and my breath was shallow. This was it.

Steeling myself for whatever was waiting for me, I drew myself up, lifted the broomstick vertically and held it with both hands, ready to whack any unwelcome trespasser. Taking a breath, I rushed into the room, then stumbled backward in fright, landing on my butt on the bottom stair.

What in Hercules?!

A wall of cold air hit me, like needles in my flesh. Three people stood together on the far side of the room, held hostage by a small black cat.

Hades paced back and forth in front of the group, hissing and clawing at air every few steps. I didn't understand. Not a single person in the group appeared threatening. If anything, they looked scared.

I scrambled to my feet, holding the broom in one hand.

"Who are you?" My heart raced, the words slurring as I tried to stifle the chattering of my teeth. The worst part was, I knew very well who one of Hades's guests was.

"You need to help us," Spandex-Man said. He pointed a fleshy finger at Hades. His hand shook as he did so, his jowls wobbled as his bottom lip trembled.

"We don't deserve this!" a shrill voice called out. An older woman with purple rinsed hair stepped out from behind Spandex-Man. She glared at me like I'd put Hades up to this.

"The boys are expecting me," a man with a cigarette hanging out of his mouth grumbled on Spandex-Man's other side.

Murmurs of discontent rang out as they all tried talking together. Hades turned around, staring me up and down with indifference. Then, seeming to think his work was done, he went about relaxing and cleaning his nether regions.

Well, sugar-sticks!

I scanned the eclectic crew. They looked alive enough, although I knew that wasn't the case. Spandex-Man was shaking, eyeing Hades like he was some sort of possessed demon. Possibly he wasn't too far off.

The elderly woman appeared to be in her seventies. She wore an old-fashioned floral nightdress with a string of pearls around her neck. Her hair was near perfectly coiffed in a short, purply-tinted perm.

"I am supposed to be with my husband right now, but this ... this ... *heathen* is holding me hostage. I didn't live eighty-six years, and a good eighty-six years mind you, to spend my afterlife in some motley basement, guarded by this ..." She pointed a heavily ringed finger at Hades, who peered up from his grooming long enough to yawn and flash his canines, before returning to his duties. The woman drew a sharp intake of breath, quickly retracted her finger, and hid partially behind Spandex-Man again.

I had to give it to her—she looked good for eighty-six. And dead.

"See here, girly!" said the guy with a cigarette hanging out his mouth. He was middle-aged but from a different era altogether. He wore a flat cap and suspenders and spoke with a drawl.

"I don't know what's going on here, but I've got responsibilities, ya know? I mean, I get it. These 'uns, they all want the pearly gates and all, but me, I had me little piece of paradise right here, and I ain't doing no one no harm, you understand? I had a good thing going at Pete's. I mean, what other tavern in town gets to claim they're 'aunted? It's good for business, it is. And I get all the free drinks I want. And a good peep at all the dolls too."

Beneath my goosebumps, my skin crawled.

"All we're asking is for you to let us go," Spandex-Man said.

"I'm sorry," I said. "I don't know what you're doing here, but I'm happy for you to leave whenever you want."

Now, would be good, I thought.

Hades's ears pricked up. Then he sat up straight and turned around and glared at me.

"Look, girly. It's not like we ain't tried. Even if we can get past that little devil, we can't leave this room. It's got us stuck here."

"Why did he even drag us here in the first place?" Purple-Perm asked, her voice pitching.

"I really don't know," I said, empathizing with their situation.

My body seemed to be warming up a little too, or else I was getting used to the cold temperature.

I glared back at Hades. Aunt Mara was missing. I had two different law enforcement agencies thinking I might have killed a man. And now, thanks to Hades, I had a basement full of ghosts.

They seemed to be coming around to the fact I had no idea how to help them. Purple-Perm collapsed into one of Aunt Mara's chairs with a sigh, Spandex-Man rubbed his face with his hands in exasperation, and Smoker-Guy started pacing around the room, keeping a wide berth from Hades who watched them all like hawks.

"You!" I said. My eyes finally homed in on a fourth person reclined on the couch by the bookcase, previously blocked by the others.

"You!" I said again, taking a step toward him, broomstick at the ready.

"Oh my!" Purple-Perm squealed. "There's no need for such hostility!"

Man-Bruce peeled his eyes from his phone, finally focusing on me. I had so many questions. How could someone, newly dead, still look so deadpan? And how was it he had a phone?

"Oh. It's you," he said.

"You two know each other, do ya?" Smoker-Guy said.

"No," Man-Bruce replied, turning his attention back to his phone.

"Yes!" I said. "What are you doing here?"

"He's probably 'ere 'cause he got dragged 'ere by that hellion." Smoker-Guy scowled at Hades then spat on the ground.

Spirit spit or not, I made a mental note to get the carpets in here cleaned once the spooks were gone.

"He was the first one of us here," Purple-Perm said.

"But who killed you?" I asked. Man-Bruce was my key to proving my and Aunt Mara's innocence.

"Killed?" Spandex-Man said, shuddering.

"You did," he said, not bothering to look up from where he was furiously tapping away at his phone screen.

With a harmonized gasp, Spandex-Man, Smoker-Man, and Purple-Perm all recoiled. All three gaped at me, aghast.

"I did not!" I retorted. No way was I taking the blame for *his* untimely demise.

"Well, you gave me the tea," he said matter-of-factly.

"Yeah, but only because you insisted."

Another collective inhale came from the group. Even Hades focused on me, as if he were trying to figure out how I planned on getting out of this one.

"I didn't even know tea was in the bag," I said.

"You gave this young man pharmaceuticals without checking first?" Purple-Perm shook with indignation.

"They weren't pharmaceuticals—they were herbs," I said, gesturing to the drying herbs hanging across the room and the jars of various dried plants lining the shelves.

"Ah, so you did know what was in the bag," said Smoker-Guy, before giving me a wink and taking another drag on his cigarette.

My lungs shriveled just from seeing the smoke. "No!" Holy cheese, this was going badly.

"Look, I'm really sorry. I am," I said, trying a new tact with Man-Bruce, who still seemed completely unbothered by the whole thing. "I'm sorry for all of you ..."

"Why? Did you kill us too?" Smoker-Guy asked.

"They said it was my heart condition," Purple-Perm said, her voice rising. "What will this do to my family? My daughter? My grandchildren? How will they react when they find out I've been murdered?" She gasped and held her chest as if I were killing her all over again.

Only, I hadn't killed her in the first place, I reminded myself.

"I didn't kill any of you!" I glanced from face to face, pleading with my eyes that they believe me.

"Well, law enforcement seems to think you killed me," Man-Bruce said, shrugging his shoulders.

At this point, if I were to have a hit list, Man-Bruce was certainly heading to the top of it. "How do you know law enforcement thinks I'm responsible?" I asked.

"Last night, while I was being harassed by that cat of yours, I saw the sheriff leaving. And a tall guy— he said you weren't to leave town."

So Eli had been right; there had been someone else in the house with me.

Man-Bruce remained focused on his phone while I tried to quell the rising tsunami of annoyance bubbling inside me. Did he not realize how much trouble I was in?

"That's all you've got? You were murdered and you can't think of anyone who might actually want you dead?" I was losing my patience. The other three watched our conversation with apparent interest.

"I've got an idea," Man-Bruce said.

"Wanna share?"

He ignored me. I resisted stomping my foot like a toddler.

"When will you be letting us go?" Purple-Perm asked.

"Yeah. I can't stay here, not with him staring at me like that." With a shiver, Spandex-Man pointed a shaky finger at Hades.

"I told you—I'm not keeping you captive. You're free to leave whenever you want."

"Not a smart one, are ya?" Smoker-Guy said. "We already told ya, we're stuck here. Something 'bout this room—it won't let us out."

Right. I'd forgotten about that. My mind cycled through solutions. I assumed being able to see ghosts was a witchy thing, and having them trapped in Aunt Mara's workspace seemed a little witchy too. Which meant that, without Aunt Mara, Mr. Tall-Dark-and-Serious was probably my best bet. My heart dropped.

Hades jumped up on one of the tables and curled up in the middle of a pile of books, unconcerned by the chaos he'd caused. He appeared almost angelic when he was sleeping. How could one small cat cause so much trouble?

I was at a loss.

The doorbell rang. Of course it did. Its timing was always impeccable. I groaned out loud. I was failing miserably at the being "positive" biz. The sheriff couldn't help me with a basement full of ghosts, but she could put me in jail for murder. Eli possibly could help with my ghost predicament, but he also made my head hurt. Not to mention he might also arrest me. It was a good bet it was one of the two of them at the door.

The doorbell rang again, making me jump. I had to do something. Quick.

I glanced at Hades. He was sleeping without a care in the world. Fine then.

"I need you all to be quiet," I said, turning back to the crowd. "Please. And when I get back, I'll work on getting you all to where you need to be."

Purple-Perm and Smoker-Guy raised an eyebrow at me. Spandex-Man slumped in a chair. Man-Bruce was still ignoring me.

What exactly was he doing on his phone? Candy crush? Updating his social media status? I could just imagine: *Srsly. Held hostage in a basement by some chick and her cat. BTW—she killed me. Bummer. Afterlife sucks, man. Dn't recommend. 1 star.*

The doorbell rang.

"Please," I begged again. "Don't move. Don't make a sound."

I took their grumbling for reluctant agreement.

I turned on my heel, broomstick in hand.

"I'm coming!" I called out.

Reaching the front door, I paused for half a second, shutting my eyes tightly and taking a deep breath.

Okay, Alice. You've got this.

Plastering a smile on my face, I opened the door.

"Jaystar?" He wasn't at all who I was expecting.

"I need to talk to you," he said, his energy rushing at me. He was practically fizzing. Then he took a step back, puzzlement crossing his face. "Why are you holding a broom?"

My eyes darted to the solid oak handle in my hand. Oh. "Umm ... I was cleaning?" I said, recognizing too late I had said it as a question.

Very convincing, Alice.

I needn't have worried. Jaystar was bouncing up and down on the balls of his feet, his interest in the broom fleeting.

"Can I come in?" he asked.

I stole a glance over my shoulder, checking no one had followed me into the hall, and then realized immediately how suspicious that looked.

"Now might not be such a good time." I chewed on my lip.

His face fell.

"Oh," he said. "Do you have visitors?"

He peered over my shoulder, and I instinctively went to block him. I was a horrible liar. There was a good chance he wouldn't be able to see my guests even if they were standing behind me.

"No. No, I'm alone. I was just ..." I searched for a better excuse. Oh yeah, the broom. "Like I said, I was just cleaning. Sweeping, you know." I held the broom up to emphasize my point.

Smart.

"Oh, good! Because I think I know what happened to the dude from Christo's."

My jaw dropped. Without thinking, I moved back. Jaystar took it as an invitation, stepping inside.

"So Mara's not here yet?" he asked.

I shook my head.

"Right. Well, I think you'll want to see this." He patted his bag.

Cool, I thought. I'd finally get an insight into what he carries around in that thing other than art supplies. He gestured down the hall for me to lead the way. As I leaned behind him to close the door, I heard the very determined gait of heels on cobbles and a lot of huffing and puffing going along with it.

Oh, sugar-sticks. Another visitor. My brain raced with indecision. Did I close the door and pretend I wasn't home? Whoever was stomping toward the cottage certainly wasn't bringing with them a "Hey, let's be friends" sort of energy. I wasn't sure how I knew this, but I did.

I looked at Jaystar for help. His whole body was signaling he was waiting for me to make a move.

Close the door, close the door! something in me screamed.

Spurred into motion, I took a step to do so, just as a woman's figure came clearly into view. The moment was lost. Jaystar and I grimaced at each other.

Mrs. Whittle, with Dog-Bruce in her arms, was marching up the path, her hair still in curlers. She wore a pink button-up jacket, much warmer than the temperature warranted, and stout pink pumps. Her cheeks were crimson with exertion, anger, or—guessing by the scowl on her face—both.

"Where is he? Where is he?" she shrilled, Dog-Bruce barking in unison.

Jaystar sighed audibly beside me.

"Hello. It's Mrs. Whittle, isn't it?" I said, putting on a light, cheery voice, in the hope it might diffuse whatever had her knickers in a knot. *You catch more flies with honey than vinegar*, I reminded myself.

"Yes, it is," she said, harrumphing and pulling herself up short at the doorstep.

She clasped Dog-Bruce closer to her chest. I noticed he wore a pink dog collar with diamantes. I didn't think I had ever seen anyone so in love with the color pink before, and it made me wonder what the inside of her house was like.

"And who are you? Where's Mara?" Her voice was like acid.

"Mara's out. I'm Alice," I said, automatically holding out my hand in greeting. "Mara's niece."

Mrs. Whittle kept both her arms wrapped around her canine. Dog-Bruce growled, and I quickly retracted my hand.

"Why are you holding a broom?" she asked.

Again, I had forgotten I still had it. "Cleaning." I'd said it enough times, I was almost beginning to believe it.

"Hi, Mrs. Whittle," Jaystar said, peering over my shoulder.

"Yooouu!" she growled by way of acknowledging him.

"Nice to see you too, Mrs. Whittle," Jaystar said, his voice light and slightly mocking.

I choked back a guffaw and pretended to clear my throat.

"Where is he?" Mrs. Whittle demanded, stamping the toe of her shoe.

"Who?" I asked, feigning innocence. From what Jaystar had previously told me, I could guess who she was after.

"That little hell-cat of your aunt's," Mrs. Whittle spat. Dog-Bruce barked to stress the point.

"Oh. Do you mean Hades?" I stopped myself from batting my eyes. *Be the honey*. "I have no idea. I haven't seen him." Behind my back, I crossed my fingers. I hated to lie, but in this case, I wasn't sure telling the truth was much better.

"He's here somewhere," she accused.

Dog-Bruce growled again, and I suddenly felt a little protective of Hades.

"Where is he?" she tried peering around me into the hallway. Jaystar blocked her view.

"Maybe you could tell me what he's done exactly, and I can pass it on to Aunt Mara."

Mrs. Whittle murmured something under her breath before diving into a full foot stomping tirade. "That little devil! He did it again! Destroyed my geraniums. And my petunias!" she added, her voice pitching, with Dog-Bruce yapping for effect.

Jaystar stood so close, I could feel his body quivering with silent laughter. I had seconds before he set me off. As it was, I was having to bite my lower lip to maintain my composure.

I cleared my throat. "I really am sorry, Mrs. Whittle. I'll talk to Aunt Mara about it."

"No! No!" she shrieked. "You don't understand! That cat is possessed. And your aunt probably put him up to it. You let Mara know I'm on to her. I'll be taking it to the sheriff if it happens again. It's all recorded."

Yikes. I didn't like the sound of that. The last thing I wanted was the sheriff involved. And if she had it recorded …

"You've recorded it?" Jaystar asked from over my shoulder.

"I have cameras now!" she huffed. "I told Mara she wasn't going to get away with him running rampant and destroying people's property. And I have the whole incident saved on the inter-webby thing. He ran all through my garden, he did. Back and forth, like it was a right game. Tore up my plants, took a branch off my cherry blossom tree, and near destroyed my fence!"

Oh lordy. Even for Hades, that seemed like a lot.

"I came over here to be nice. To give her one last warning. But you know what? I think enough is enough! Something has to be done. I'll stand for it no longer!"

So much for diffusing the situation, Alice.

She'd worked herself into a real state. I wasn't sure how a cat could do such harm to a tree and fence, but then again, I'd just seen Hades drag home a three-hundred-pound dead man.

Oh no! The thought hit me with ferocity. Could that be what she'd filmed? Surely not? Could a ghost be seen on camera?

"I'll be taking this up with the sheriff now. I've been nice for far too—ahh!"

Her scream made me jump. Hades has chosen that opportune moment to materialize between my feet.

Mrs. Whittle shook a finger at him, her mouth quivering with anger. Dog-Bruce growled and yapped as Hades sat there, nonplussed. Jaystar vibrated with stifled mirth behind me, while my mind reeled: if Hades was here, the spooks weren't being guarded. They said they couldn't leave the room, but if they had been wrong and it was Hades holding them hostage, then ... The thought of them appearing in front of Mrs. Whittle made my heart race.

"You lied! He's here! I should have known. The apple never falls too far from the tree."

Jaystar lost it. Raucous laughter had him doubled over. Mrs. Whittle's face flamed, and her whole body shook with anger.

"That's it!" she said, stomping her foot. "I won't put up with this anymore! You and Mara can expect a visit from the sheriff." Her voice had risen an entire octave, while my stomach simultaneously sank. I was already expecting a visit from the sheriff. Having Mrs. Whittle lodge a complaint would only complicate things.

"I'm very sorry, Mrs. Whittle. I'll let Aunt Mara know you dropped by," I said, trying to take control of the situation. I passed the broom to Jaystar. He paused mid-bellow to look at it in confusion before resuming his hysterics. I scooped up Hades, then stepped back into the hall and pulled the door closed while Mrs. Whittle sputtered from the other side.

I dropped Hades to the ground and he sauntered off again, likely thinking his job was done. I leaned back against the door and sank to the floor. That had been something. Jaystar wiped a rogue tear from under his eyes with his thumb.

"I'm not sure what you found so funny," I said to him in disbelief. "You weren't much help back there."

"Oh, come on," he said. "The woman is a pain in the butt to most people in Widdershins. Seeing her all out of sorts because a cat destroyed her garden ... it's funny. And for Hades to just turn up like that." He chuckled, sniffed, and then took a deep breath in what I guess was an attempt to regain his composure.

Oh boy, what a day this was turning out to be.

Jaystar looked at the broom in his hand like he was surprised he was still holding it and leaned it against the wall beside the sideboard. Then he held out a hand to me.

I placed my hand in his and he pulled me to my feet. A surge of electricity zapped through me and again I found myself weightless, above a scene I was not a part of.

Aunt Mara and Jaystar were in the kitchen of Hollyhock Cottage. Jaystar pulled a brown paper package from his messenger bag and put it on the island between them, where Hades sat watching. Aunt Mara undid the string on the package and pulled the paper back to reveal an assortment of freshly harvested plants, their stalks wrapped in damp tissue paper. Herbs, I assumed, though I couldn't tell what. Aunt Mara beamed at Jaystar and seemed to thank him although I couldn't hear her words. Then she paused, her body stiffening, consternation crossing her face. She held a finger up and said something to Jaystar that I took to mean her telling him to wait, and she left the room.

Jaystar looked around him until his focus landed back on Hades. Hades stared back, eyes wide, and Jaystar started sneezing. Then, it was as if Hades's attention had turned to me. I swear he was staring straight at me as I floated somewhere near the ceiling. *Not possible*, I thought, weakly.

While Jaystar continued sneezing and wiping his nose on the back of his hand, Aunt Mara returned. She had something clutched in her fist, but I couldn't see what it was.

Aunt Mara glared at Hades, and immediately Jaystar stopped sneezing. She leaned in close to Jaystar and whispered in his ear. Clasping his hands in her own, she transferred whatever she had been holding to him. Confusion marked his features while Aunt Mara held his gaze, all the time nodding and speaking. I wanted to get closer to hear what she was saying, but Hades's attention had returned to me, and he bared his teeth in a snarl, quickly drawing the attention of both Aunt Mara and Jaystar. The surrounding air shimmered, and the scene dissolved, but not before I recognized what Aunt Mara had given Jaystar—a small vial of blue-black liquid.

Chapter 14

My blood rushed to my ears. What did it mean? I remembered the vial from my first meeting with Jaystar when it had fallen out of his bag and I had gone to retrieve it. He had been so possessive of it. I had thought the vial contained pen ink, but now I wasn't so sure. The expression on Aunt Mara's face before she collected it had me unsettled. What was Jaystar not telling me?

With the image completely faded, there came something altogether different. It took me a moment to place what was happening. Instead of an image, it was a feeling. Intense and consuming, filling my being. Then, full clarity hit. Oh, my world, Jaystar was crushing on me. I could feel the cheerful lilt of his heart, the warmth in his chest as he held my hand. I even felt rather than saw the curve of his lips and a lightness on his features. Holy cheese! I had not been expecting that!

"Alice? Are you okay?" His voice broke through whatever weird daydream I was in. I opened my eyes, having no recollection of closing them. I was standing in the hallway with Jaystar's hand still in mine.

I quickly dropped it, the strangest mishmash of emotions coursing through my veins.

Okay, Alice. No need to be awkward. You don't know anything for sure.

My eyes settled on his face. Confusion had settled there, and I blushed.

Nice one, Alice. That's not weird at all.

I glanced away. Whatever in Hercules had happened had left me feeling horribly disoriented. The experience had been much like the one at the coffee shop with Lucy. Was this some form of fandangled witchy skill I'd suddenly inherited? And what did it mean, if it even meant anything at all?

I wasn't sure what troubled me the most: Jaystar, whom I'd known for not much more than a day, having feelings for me or the strange vial of liquid Aunt Mara had given him. Man-Bruce had been poisoned. Aunt Mara was a suspect. Strange vials of liquid no longer seemed so innocent.

"Alice?" he asked again.

"Oh, yeah," I said, wiping my hands on the side of my jeans to brush off my lingering misgivings. "I'm fine. What is it you wanted to show me?" I asked, remembering the purpose of his visit.

"Right! Let's sit down and I'll show you."

I led the way into the living room, avoiding the kitchen so I wouldn't have to think about what I'd just seen.

Jaystar plonked himself down on the sofa with space for me to join him, but I took the nearest chair instead. I had a bit of sorting through to do in my mind first before I put myself in any more awkward positions.

"I was on my way to Mom's, right, and I thought I'd check into Man-Bruce."

It was kind of cute to see my descriptor for Bruce had caught on.

"I mean, the guy seemed pretty into his phone when we were at Christo's, right?"

I nodded. If only Jaystar knew just how much he was into his phone outside of Christo's too.

"So it makes sense he'd be on social media, right?"

"Makes sense." I nodded again.

"Right! Well, here ..." He opened his bag and pulled out his phone.

My shoulders drooped. I don't know what I was expecting, but I was hoping for something more exciting than his cell phone. Of course, we were living in the days of status updates, likes, and accumulating followers. Why I hadn't thought of doing my own research, I wasn't sure. I guess my phone was more of a "call in an emergency" type deal.

"So, it turns out Bruce Maximilian—that's his real name," Jaystar said, unaware I'd already learned as much from the man himself, "was an orphan." He paused for dramatic effect.

"Okaaay," I said slowly, not sure why this was important, though it dawned on me, I was now an orphan too. The thought made a lump form in my throat.

Jaystar tapped away on his phone. "Here, look," he said, handing it to me.

He had pulled up a news article dated ten years prior. I took the phone and scrolled down as I skimmed it. It was about a car accident. A family of four coming back from holiday. Mom, Dad, and two kids. A logging truck had taken a corner too wide, crossed the center line, and there had been a head-on collision. In the article, the investigation was still open as to whether drugs, alcohol, or technical malfunction had been to blame.

The truck driver had died on impact, as had the two adults in the other car. The boy and girl were rushed to the hospital in critical condition. A few days later, the girl passed away. The boy was the only survivor: Bruce Alan Maximilian. A photo was underneath. A much younger picture of Man-Bruce peered out at me. It was definitely him, even though this picture was of a twelve-year-old child. He was smiling, and I suddenly felt ill. It was so tragic. The poor boy had lost his whole family. A footnote to the article said a distant relative was being contacted to make arrangements for the child.

My eye prickled with tears. Seeing Man-Bruce as a child and now knowing a bit of his backstory, I could almost forgive his surliness.

"Jeeze, I'm sorry. I didn't mean to ..." Jaystar's voice petered off.

I blinked hard and looked away. It was easy to forget that the person on the other end of a tragedy was a real, living, breathing person who had been a kid once. A kid with a family.

"I don't understand what this has to do with his ... murder." I nearly choked just saying the word.

"Nothing, I guess, when it's taken alone, but then I went hunting. Searching for clues, you know, on social media and the like."

I didn't know. I was one of the few without an online social account.

"I tried to get an idea of who his friends were, what his interests were, and ... who might want to kill him."

Oh boy.

"And guess what I found." He took the phone from me, gave the screen a couple of taps, and handed it back.

"Look familiar?" he asked.

Lucy.

"Hmm." I didn't have the heart to tell him I'd stumbled upon their connection on my own.

"Lucy's worked for Grams for a few months now, but I never knew they were connected in any way."

I continued scrolling through Man-Bruce's social media feed. It was full of moody black-and-white photos of abandoned houses and graveyards, interrupted now and then by photos of Lucy, smiling and laughing—and occasionally photos of the two together. They stood out in complete contrast to the gloominess of the photographs before and after. Two things got me. Man-Bruce was a pretty talented photographer, for one, even if his style was a little too gothic for my taste. And two, it was more than obvious he was completely, utterly enamored with Lucy. I felt another pang of sadness. Poor Lucy.

"See here?" Jaystar pointed to the top of the screen.

It wasn't Man-Bruce's name at the top of the feed. It took me a moment to realize the account was set up under a pseudonym: Max B.

"And this is where things get really weird." Jaystar reached over and opened a new tab. It looked like some kind of comment board with people going back and forth in discussion. Jaystar pulled up a comment written by MB. My eyes skimmed over the text. Holy cheese!

"What is this?" I asked, my mind reeling.

"Good question." Jaystar was almost vibrating with excitement across from me. "He's obsessed! Listen to this: "It happened again.

I'm seeing them, but not just when I'm sleeping. When I'm awake too. Anyone else have this happen to them?'" Jaystar scrolled down some more.

"Seeing who?" I asked.

"He doesn't say, but I think I can guess. He goes on about seeing these people, for literally pages, right, over about six weeks, and then here"—he slowed his scroll and pointed for me to read again—"he's asking for tips on controlling it, so he can see certain people. And further down here, it sounds like he's talking about his family. He wants to see his family!"

My stomach dropped. This wasn't making sense.

"But his family's dead!" Jaystar said, reading my mind—and sitting so far on the edge of the couch to lean in close to me, I thought he might fall off. "And so there's people giving all this advice, right? About how to summon the dead. It goes on for a while, like people saying they know someone who can help, mediums, or tips on using a Ouija board, crystals and everything. And then we get to the fun part."

Fun? None of this was fun.

"Look! Here, this person goes into different herbs, right, ones that can help you reach other planes and talk to the dead, or something like that. Hallucinogens. Some of which, most in fact, are highly toxic, even lethal in different doses."

"How do you know that?" I asked, examining Jaystar's face.

The corner of his mouth quirked, and he looked abashed. "My mom," he answered, raking a hand through his hair. "She's an herbalist, remember?"

Of course. She was Aunt Mara's supplier.

"Do you think Man-Bruce accidentally poisoned himself, then, while he was trying to connect with the spirits of his family?" I guessed it was plausible, and it sure would take the heat off Aunt Mara and myself.

"Maybe ..." he said. "Do you think Mara was helping him by supplying him with some special ghost-seeing concoction?"

If she was, that put her right back as a suspect for his murder. "I don't know," I said. "I barely know Aunt Mara." That hit me with another jolt of sadness. I'd been so hopeful about reconnecting with family in Widdershins, but then Aunt Mara had just upped and vanished. "Did you really find all this out on your way to your mom's?" I asked. It seemed like he'd done a lot of work in a very short time.

Jaystar nodded and shrugged a shoulder. "I'm pretty good with tech," he said.

I'd add it to my list of things that weren't my forte.

A loud crash came from downstairs.

Oh, sugar-sticks! I needed to check on things in the basement. I still didn't have any idea how to help Hades's hostages, but I didn't want them to think I'd abandoned them, either. Also, if I could get Man-Bruce talking a bit more, maybe I could find out what really happened to him.

"What was that?" Jaystar asked.

"You heard that?"

He drew his brows together, puckering his forehead.

I guess I had assumed if a ghost had made the noise, Jaystar wouldn't have heard it. Before I could say anything else, another commotion drew my attention. A bang this time. Whatever was going on down there, it sounded like things were getting broken. Holy cheese, I hope I didn't have a riot on my hands.

Jaystar leaped from his seat, swung his bag over his shoulder, and promptly left the room.

"It's probably only Hades," I called out to him, stunned by his reaction. On reaching the doorway, I saw he'd already grabbed the broom he'd left in the front entrance and was heading back up the hall toward me.

"Stay there," he said as he passed me.

I don't think so, I thought. Part of me admired his quick reaction to facing danger. Another part of me found it kind of funny. His hair was standing on end from running his hands through it, and he was holding the broom like it was a weapon. He looked rather comical.

Not much different from when you took the broom with you downstairs to protect yourself.

Damn, I was right. Another small part of me was terrified of what he might find if he made his way down to Aunt Mara's workspace. Though I assumed he wouldn't be able to see the ghosts, Lucy had, so maybe he'd be able to as well. And if he could, then I'd need to explain why I was harboring souls in my basement.

Jaystar pressed his ear to the door under the stairs. "Is someone there?" he called out. He tried to mouth at me to get back.

I ignored him. "No one's here," I said.

A shuffling sound came from below. If Hades was stirring things up down there, I was going to be so mad!

"I mean no one besides you, me, and Hades," I said, attempting a smile.

Not buying it, he put his hand on the doorknob.

"No, really, Jaystar. It's nothing."

He turned the doorknob and slowly opened the door. I panicked. I wasn't supposed to tell anyone Aunt Mara and I were supposedly witches, but if he found Aunt Mara's room, what would he think?

Maybe that she's an herbalist, like his mom. Right, maybe I was overreacting. *Unless, of course, he could see ghosts too.*

"Where are you going?" I asked, trying the best to keep my voice neutral, so I didn't draw suspicion.

"I think it's coming from down there," he said.

"Down where?" Beads of sweat broke out across the back of my neck. I tried to wipe them away with my hand.

"I think it's coming from Mara's apothecary."

My jaw dropped, and I could almost imagine Aunt Mara telling me I'd be catching flies. If Jaystar knew about Aunt Mara's secret room, then I guess it wasn't very secret. I'd just assumed it was.

"Jaystar, I really think we should stay up here," I said, but he wasn't listening.

He headed into the laundry and stood in front of the door to the basement. "Maybe you should stay up here," he whispered to me.

My heart galloped, a million scenarios playing out in my mind.

"You can't go down there," I said, throwing myself in front of the door, just as he was about to grab the door handle.

A mixture of emotions swept across his face.

"Alice? What's going on?"

Oh gosh. Knowing now how he felt about me, and seeing an element of hurt in his eyes, overwhelmed me with guilt. He knew I was keeping something from him, but I wasn't sure what to do about that. I wasn't allowed to tell him I was a witch, which suggested I should probably keep the whole "seeing dead people" thing quiet too. And as hurt as he might be feeling, I wasn't one hundred percent sure I could trust him. I didn't know what Aunt Mara had given him in the vial of liquid he kept in his bag, but it had seemed suspicious. And I'd known him no longer than I'd known Aunt Mara.

"I'm sorry, Jaystar, it's just …" I struggled to think of what to say. "I don't think we should go down there until Aunt Mara's back. I mean, it is her space."

For a second, he seemed to mull it over; then just as quickly, the hurt returned to his features. I couldn't bear it.

"Alice?" His voice was barely a whisper.

I sighed and stepped aside. I had tried to warn him. From this point on, whatever he saw or conclusions he came to were out of my hands.

Jaystar reached past me and twisted the door handle. Everything was dead quiet. He found the light switch right away.

"You *have* been here before?" I asked, my voice wavering a little.

"Well, yeah. I'm Mara's supplier, remember? I mean, my mom is," he quickly corrected. "I'm the delivery person, I guess," he whispered before putting his finger to his lip and raising the broom in front of him, much like I had.

I took a sharp intake of breath. If Man-Bruce had been poisoned, Jaystar could also be a suspect. He knew about Aunt Mara's apothecary, and the bag Aunt Mara had left Man-Bruce looked like someone could have tampered with it. But what would the motive be? Miss Maisy had teased him that he made Lucy flustered. Could Jaystar have a crush on Lucy too? I didn't know how I felt about that. But it would give him a motive for murder—to get Man-Bruce out of the picture. My insides flip-flopped.

Jaystar crept down the stairs ahead of me. I did my best to be as quiet as he was, although I was confident it didn't matter. I knew what awaited us at the bottom of the staircase.

A hissing sound down below made us both jump.

"Whoever's down there. Show yourself," Jaystar said, his voice surprisingly fierce.

I hadn't pictured Jaystar as being so take-charge. Was that an attribute of a murderer?

Come on, Alice. Innocent until proven guilty. The most frightening monsters are usually those that live in our minds.

Jaystar had paused at the twist in the staircase, his breathing jagged. Maybe he wasn't as fearless as he seemed.

"One, two, three," he whispered, before flying down the last few stairs to the apothecary. I gripped the banister, closed my eyes, and waited for whatever bedlam was going to break loose.

"Meeeooooow," a perturbed voice whined. Hades.

Then the sneezing started.

My eyes flung open, and I quickly went to join Jaystar in the room.

"Me-ow!" a high-pitched cry blasted me.

Sugar-sticks! Was I really being told off by a cat?!

Hades glared at me, his golden eyes flashing. Jaystar was doubled over, sneezing into his armpit. In front of him, three of the freaky foursome were glowering at me, much like the cat. Spandex-Man still looked flushed and upset. He was shuffling side-to-side and wringing his hands. A lamp lay on the ground near him. Purple-Perm sat in her chair, back rigid, hands crossed on her lap, and eyes narrowed on me like all of life's wrongs were my fault. And Smoker-Guy, blowing clouds of blue smoke into the air, shook his head at me like I'd let him down. The fourth member of their little group was less interested. He remained reclined on the couch, playing on his phone. My empathy for him waned.

"Hades! Stop it!" I yelled as Jaystar succumbed to another onslaught of sneezes, and my frustration with Man-Bruce came to the fore. He could be helping us to find his murderer, not playing on his afterlife phone.

Hades's eyes narrowed, and to my surprise, Jaystar's sneezing diminished until he was left a little red-eyed but none the worse. Aunt Mara had said Hades wasn't a witch, but I disagreed with her that he was *just* a cat. There was more than a little weird with that feline.

"I can explain," I quickly said to Jaystar, knowing full well there was no good explanation for why ghosts were in Aunt Mara's basement.

"What do you mean?" Jaystar said, sniffing again, and leaning on the broom. "I guess you were right. It was just the dumb cat, knocking things over."

I sent Hades a warning look so he didn't start up any more sneezing pranks on Jaystar.

"What took you so long, and what is he doing here?" Purple-Hair pointed a bony finger at Jaystar. "It's one thing to be held captive but for you to bring voyeurs here like we're animals in the zoo for casual viewing ...!" She harrumphed and crossed her arms. I glimpsed Hades, who now seemed to smirk at me.

"It's not like that," I said. "None of you are captives! And I tried to be as fast as I could getting back here."

"Who are you talking to?" Jaystar reeled on me, confusion again settling on his features.

Well, now you've done it, Alice! It's probably best you just tell him the truth.

I sighed aloud and covered my face with my hands.

"Alice?" Jaystar said quietly. "What is going on?"

His voice was steady despite the nervous energy pouring off him in waves. I had never thought myself good at sensing people's feelings this way. Things were definitely changing.

"And why is it so cold in here?" he asked, making me drop my hands.

I hadn't noticed the cold this time around. Jaystar rubbed his arms with his hands. Was it possible I had somehow acclimated to the weird temperature drop that accompanied my houseguests?

"You might want to sit down," I said. I wasn't sure if I could trust him, but I wanted to. My mom used to say the best way to find out if you *could* trust someone was to trust them. I had to take the chance. The secrets were piling up and becoming too heavy to carry alone. Aunt Mara seemed to have trusted Jaystar, so maybe I could too. Whatever trouble I might get in for telling a Non-Magical, it couldn't be worse than being accused of murder. I hoped, anyway.

Jaystar made a beeline for the sofa. Smoker-Guy grinned and blew out another cloud of blue smoke.

"Not there!" I said, stopping Jaystar in his tracks.

Man-Bruce took a moment to look up from his phone and eyed Jaystar, then went back to whatever he was doing. Every time I caught sight of that man, my hackles rose.

"Maybe over here?" I said, rushing over to a stool by one of the shelving units. I picked up the pile of books on top of it and placed them on the ground.

Giving me a worried look, he made his way over to the stool. His limbs were too long for the seat. His knees reached up to his chest, and he seemed unsure what to do with his hands. After leaning the broomstick against the shelves, I watched as he tried hanging his arms at his sides, putting both hands on his bag, and then trying to rest them on his knees.

"So what are ya gonna tell 'im, girly?" Smoker-Guy asked, as I paced back and forth, wondering the same thing.

"Shh! I'm trying to think," I said automatically in response, before grimacing at my mistake.

The color had drained from Jaystar's face, and his eyes darted around the room as if he were expecting to see another person.

"Alice?" Jaystar said cautiously. "What's up with Hades?"

I turned around and sure enough, Hades was strutting up and down an imaginary line that placed Jaystar and me on one side of the room, and the freaky foursome on the other. Spandex-Man was back to cowering on one of the wingbacks as best as he could. Every now and then, as Hades walked past the chair, he'd take a swipe at Spandex-Man's leg, making the poor man squeal in fear.

"Stop it, Hades! Leave them alone!"

Hades glowered at me and haughtily sashayed across the room to the staircase before disappearing upstairs.

"Did you see that? He tried to kill me!" Spandex-Man wailed. His hand clutched his chest, and he was breathing heavily despite being dead.

I gritted my teeth. If I didn't fill in Jaystar soon, he was going to think I was off my rocker and leave before I could explain myself. I shot a pleading glance his way. He'd resorted to wrapping his arms around himself to try to minimize his shivering, but by some miracle he didn't look to be going anywhere. I closed my eyes for a second and took a deep breath before turning back to the disgruntled ghouls in front of me.

"Okay," I said, trying to keep my voice calm. "I'm sorry you're here. I want you to all move on as much as you do. I have no idea why Hades gathered you here—"

"Gathered us? He dragged me through the coffee shop!" Spandex-Man moaned.

"He woke me up in the most undignified fashion by slapping me in the face with his paw." Purple-Perm sniffed and lifted her chin indignantly.

"I was 'aving a drink with the boys. He owes me, that cat," Smoker Guy said before taking another drag on his cigarette.

"Alice—" Jaystar said behind me. I automatically put a hand up to shush him.

"You're all just going to have to be patient," I said to the freaky foursome, although I doubted Man-Bruce was actually paying any attention. He seemed the least perturbed of the bunch. "I'm working on a plan. In the meantime, just sit back and,"—I really didn't know where to go with that—"relax..?" I said, more as a question than a statement. It sounded weak even to me. There was more harrumphing. I turned around to address Jaystar. Holy cheese, this was going to be tough.

"Jaystar. I'm so sorry. I have to tell you something, but it's ..." Again, I had no words. "You don't see them, do you?" I asked, stating what I knew to be the obvious.

"See who?" Jaystar asked. "I see you and I saw Hades." He kept his voice quiet and made no attempt to leave. My admiration for him was growing.

I took a deep breath before letting the words roll out. "There are four other people down here with us right now."

Other than shivering and rubbing his arms, Jaystar stayed put. I wasn't sure I would have done the same in his situation.

"This isn't going to make any sense. It doesn't make any sense to me either. But somehow, Hades has been bringing home ghosts." I felt queasy even as I said it. It was ridiculous. No one in their right mind would believe it.

"Ghosts?" Jaystar asked in a squeaky voice.

"Yeah, I guess," I said. "I mean, they're dead." I paused.

Jaystar was staring at me with wide eyes.

Courage, Alice. You might as well tell him everything.

"This morning I went to Christo's trying to find Aunt Mara," I said. "Not long after I got there, Hades showed up and started tormenting a customer."

Jaystar looked like he wanted to say something but worked the inside of his cheek instead.

"He was chasing Spandex-Man—"

"Spandex-Man?" Jaystar asked.

"My name's Gerry," Gerry, aka "Spandex-Man," whined.

I'd forgotten his cyclist friends said that. "Sorry. Gerry," I corrected. "He's a cyclist, so he's wearing spandex."

Jaystar nodded slowly.

I was doing such a terrible job of explaining things. "Hades was chasing Gerry all around the café, and I realized no one else could see Gerry, just me. Everyone else just saw a crazed animal trashing the place, and they blamed me."

"Okay," Jaystar said, leaning forward a little on the stool.

Maybe he believed me. I felt some of my anxiety ebb at the thought.

"Somehow—and honestly, I know how ridiculous this sounds—but somehow Hades dragged Gerry out of the café by the ankle and I guess brought him here."

"So, there's a ghost wearing spandex here?" Jaystar asked.

That was what he was getting from this? I nodded.

"Wait," he said, quickly catching on. "You said there are four ghosts here?"

"Yeah." My stomach tumbled. I hadn't told him one was Man-Bruce. Or that I was apparently a witch, which I guessed was the reason I was seeing them in the first place.

A chime cut through the room.

For the love of Hercules!

"Nooo," I moaned. I'd reached my limit of people just showing up at the cottage.

"Maybe whoever's up there will know how to get us out of this mess," Purple-Perm said, pursing her lips.

My lordy, I hoped they did too. Other than Aunt Mara, who would have no need to ring the doorbell, Eli was my next best shot at solving my ghost problem. He was also just as likely to arrest me and send me to witch-prison. Or else, it was the sheriff—also intent on sending me to prison.

The doorbell rang again. "I need to get that," I said.

"Okay," Jaystar said, jumping up, broom in hand. "I'll come with you."

"No," I said, thinking quickly. "I need you to stay down here."

"What?" Jaystar said incredulously.

"I'm sorry, but you believe me, don't you?" I was sending him all the "believe me" vibes I could. It was still a big ask.

"I believe in ghosts, if that's what you're asking?"

It was my turn to be surprised.

"And you're saying you've got four otherworldly beings right here that Hades has rounded up and held captive. One wearing spandex. And only you and him can see them?"

I cringed. It was true—and the most ridiculous thing I had heard. I nodded.

"Is this some kind of witchy thing? Are the rumors true? You and Mara? Your whole family—you're witches, aren't you?" Jaystar bounced on his toes with excitement again. His face lit up, and he wasn't shivering as much anymore.

The doorbell rang again, and my pulse sped up.

"Coming!" I yelled, knowing whoever it was wouldn't be able to hear me. "Look, Jaystar, I really need your help. It might be the sheriff. She's suspicious enough as it is, and I really don't want her down here until the spooks have gone and Aunt Mara is back."

"Hey!" a chorus of outrage interrupted.

"Sorry." I turned back to Jaystar and lowered my voice. "I know you can't see them, but if they get noisy, can you please try to talk to them to keep them quiet? I don't know what else to do." I was desperate. My words stuck in my throat as I said them. I really hoped Jaystar could help me out.

Jaystar's eyes searched mine. I could feel how torn he was. He wanted to help but babysitting four ghosts was a stretch.

"I'll try not to be long, and then I can tell you everything. I just need to get rid of whoever's here."

Banging had replaced the chime of the doorbell.

"Okay," he said, grabbing my hand and giving it a squeeze. "But be careful."

Holy cheese! A jolt of electricity shot through me, this time without a vision, just a flutter in my chest.

There'll be time to explore that later, Alice. Go answer the door.

I gave Jaystar a weak smile and pulled my hand from his. And, for the third time that day, I went to see who was calling at the cottage.

Chapter 15

Boy oh boy, whoever was at the door sure had their knickers in a knot. A quick slideshow of *Guess Who* played in my mind. Mrs. Whittle. Mrs. Whittle and the sheriff. The sheriff and Officer Jonas. Eli and Tweedledee and Tweedledum.

Aunt Mara, if you can hear me… I mean, if she was a witch and she could read my mind, maybe I could send thoughts to her too. *Aunt Mara,* I tried again. *I need your help. Please, please come home!*

"Open up!" a male voice called out.

Sugar-sticks. I knew exactly who it was.

Think good thoughts, and good things will happen. Think good thoughts, and good things will happen. I looked down at my shirt. Now would be a great time for Bad Luck Be Gone to kick in if there was any way it worked like that.

Again, on reaching the front door, I took a moment to ground myself with a deep breath. I needed to have my wits about me. And I needed to keep him out of my mind!

Smile, Alice! Think happy thoughts. Think happy thoughts.

I opened the door, and sure enough, there stood Mr. Tall-Dark-and-Serious. Eli.

"Wonderland," he said, nodding at me.

Right. He was still going with that, then.

I peered around him, looking for his minions, but couldn't see them. He raised an eyebrow, and I swear he laughed at me with his eyes. If he was reading my mind again ... I wasn't sure what I'd do, but I certainly wouldn't be happy about it!

"Hi," I replied, keeping my tone as neutral as possible. He was maybe the only one who could help with my ghost problem—except he also had me down as a murder suspect.

"I don't suppose Mara has returned, has she?" He said it as if he already knew the answer.

"You suppose right," I said. *That's it, Alice. Stand your ground!*

"Too bad," he said. "Any more information on when she'll be back?"

Though I tried to think of something to tell him, I came up blank.

"Do you mind if I come in?" He was acting more gentlemanly than I had expected. It made me uneasy.

"Where are the other two?" I asked, suddenly suspicious they were scouting other ways into the house while he was the decoy.

"Who?" he asked, face puzzled for a moment. "Oh," he said, realization dawning on him. "You wouldn't mean Tweedledee and Tweedledum, would you?"

My jaw dropped in unison with his lips quirking upward. He was teasing me.

"You called them that when I was last here."

It took me a moment to realize what he was saying. Could I trust him, then, that he wasn't poking around in my thoughts right this moment? I wasn't sure. But I wasn't so confident anymore about letting him inside the cottage either. I'd need to find another way to get rid of my downstairs houseguests.

"Look," I said. "I'm rather busy right now, so like I said yesterday, I'll get Aunt Mara to call you when she returns."

I went to close the door, but he stuck his foot into the gap, blocking the motion. Then he pushed it open farther, making me take a step back. My heart leaped back into my throat. Mr. Tall-Dark-and-Serious had turned all serious again.

"Wonderland, I don't think you quite understand the gravity of the situation you and your aunt are in." His jaw clenched, making me take another step back.

"At the moment, I am the only thing that's keeping you from being tried at the High Council. Trust me, that's not something you want right now. Especially seeing how green you are. I'm going out on a limb for you, but you could make things a lot easier by cooperating."

I stared at him blankly. I thought I had been cooperating. Mostly.

"What do you mean by green?" I asked, the image of Dorothy's Wicked Witch of the West springing to mind. Right away, I noticed how small my voice was. My confidence was waning.

"Right," he said, massaging the line between his eyebrows. "It means you're new to this. You probably don't even know what your gifts are yet. It's why I can get into your head so easily. Don't worry, I'll stay out!" he said, holding his hand up so I wouldn't protest. "Unless it's absolutely necessary," he added, making me grit my teeth. "Will you let me in?" he asked, his voice becoming husky.

"No," I said, surprising myself with my assertiveness. I tried to close the door again. Any goodwill or hope I'd had that he might help had passed. Friend of Aunt Mara's or not, he irked me.

Eli glared, his eyes like ice. Oh boy. He slipped a hand into the inside of his jacket breast and for a moment I thought he might pull out a gun or something. My legs wobbled under me.

Instead, he withdrew a piece of yellow paper folded in thirds and passed it to me. I took it with a shaky hand and began unfolding it. What I hadn't expected was Eli to wave a hand at me and for me to go sliding backward, out of the way of the door and him, until my back hit the wall.

"Whoa!" my voice pitched. I was beginning to believe magic was a real thing. "You can't just come in here," I argued.

"I'm afraid I can," he said. "Ideally, I'd have permission. Hades gave it last time. But when I don't have it, that paper will do the trick." He pointed at the paper in my hand before walking past me and heading down the hall.

Hades? How was it Hades could give permission? He was a cat. The number of things I didn't know about my new life was overwhelming.

Thankfully, whatever Jaystar was doing downstairs was working a treat. The house was dead quiet.

"What is it you're hiding, Wonderland?" Eli said, as I rushed past him to block him from moving further down the hallway. Again, he waved me out the way, and I was powerless to stop him as I slipped across the slate tile.

"Mara!" His voice boomed, and I flinched.

"I told you she's not here," I whispered, my voice shaking.

He ignored me and bellowed at the ceiling. "If you care an ounce for your niece, I suggest you get your butt back here now. I can only hold off the Council for so long. A Reaper is dead, and someone has to be held accountable. If you're not here, they want me to bring her in!"

I moved toward the stairs and plonked myself down on the bottom tread before my legs gave out. None of that sounded good. I had no idea what a Reaper was, so maybe there had been a second murder and this wasn't just about Man-Bruce. But how was it I was involved? Could Aunt Mara have actually killed someone and now be in hiding? A heaviness landed in the pit of my stomach.

A crash drew both of our attention. Oh, sugar-sticks!

Alice ...

The voice was a whisper, barely audible at all. At first, I thought I'd imagined it. And then it came again.

Alice. Tell him, child. He can help.

Aunt Mara?! Was it even possible? I was sure it had been her voice, but it had been so quiet, not at all like when Eli had jumped into my head.

Aunt Mara? I tried to send her the thought as strong as possible, hoping she could hear me. *Where are you? What's going on?*

Nothing.

Eli stood at the door under the stairs, his body rigid, as if he were listening.

"What was that noise?" he asked, his eyes narrowing back in on me.

I shrugged my shoulders and tried to play cool. "Hades, I guess?" Tears were prickling behind my eyes, and I blinked them away, hoping he hadn't noticed. Had that really been Aunt Mara? Should I really trust Eli? I didn't know who to trust anymore. Why would Aunt Mara leave me in this situation? It was all becoming too much.

Eli was scanning my face. I guess he didn't trust me either.

"Who else is here, Wonderland?" His voice was low.

I went to answer, but no sound came out.

He turned back to the door and, in one fluid movement, twisted the doorknob and swung the door open. I jumped up from where I was sitting, just in time to hear Jaystar cry out and then see Eli twisting his arm behind his back.

"No!" I yelled, grabbing Eli by the arm and trying to yank him off Jaystar. "Let him go!"

"Ow, ow, ow!" Jaystar yelped, struggling under Eli's vice grip.

"Who is this, Wonderland?" Eli growled.

"My friend! Now let him go." Eli grunted and released him, making Jaystar stumble, his legs near giving out under him. He turned to face us, rubbing his arm and shoulder with one hand.

"Alice?" he said, looking the giant up and down.

"This is Eli. He thinks I killed Man-Bruce or a Reaper or something. I don't even know anymore." I glared at Eli but felt the prickling of tears all over again. Eli's eyes darted back and forth between Jaystar and I.

"You're law enforcement?" Jaystar asked, shock making his face pale.

"What's going on, Wonderland?" Eli ignored Jaystar and focused in on me.

I didn't know where to start.

Trust him. Tell him. The voice again was just a whisper, but I was so sure it was Aunt Mara's.

"Do you hear that?" I asked Eli.

"Hear what?"

Both men stood silent, heads tilted, senses on alert.

"That voice?" I breathed. "I think it's Aunt Mara."

Jaystar's eyes went wide, and Eli's jaw clenched.

"I don't hear anyone," Jaystar said, still rubbing his shoulder.

Eli looked at Jaystar warily. "Is there a reason your friend is here?"

"Moral support," I said, not knowing what else to say.

"You need to leave." Eli turned on Jaystar.

Jaystar flinched and swallowed. I couldn't say I blamed him.

"He's part of this," I said and then cringed. Implicating my friend in a murder investigation probably wasn't the smartest thing to do, but I really didn't like Eli bossing people around, either.

Jaystar raised an eyebrow at me. "Alice is right." His voice wavered a little. "I was with Alice yesterday when we first met Man-Bruce—"

"Man-Bruce?" Eli asked.

"I'm also in business with Mara. I'm her graphic designer and drop off supplies to her." Jaystar pulled his shoulders back and shifted his bag strap. He had to tilt his head upward to meet Eli's eyes as Eli still stood a head taller than him.

"You know you've just implicated yourself in a murder investigation?" Eli said, his jaw tight.

I was getting tired of the macho-intimidating thing Eli had going on. Time to turn the tables and level the playing field, I thought. Then maybe we could work together to find Aunt Mara and solve whatever murder she and I were being accused of.

I knew Eli wouldn't like it, and I was sure I was breaking a rule, but I did it anyway. I had faith that if Jaystar could handle ghosts, he could handle witches. I crossed my fingers behind my back just in case and turned to Jaystar. "Eli is from the Witchy Bureau of Crime or something." I waved my hand in Eli's direction.

Jaystar's eyes went wide, and his jaw dropped just as a long, low growl erupted from Eli.

"Whoa! Hold up! You're a witch, too?" Jaystar faced Eli in awe.

"What in damnations do you think you're doing?" Eli's eyes flashed. "You told him? You told him you're a witch?" He balled his hands into fists at his sides.

Maybe I had gone too far. I swallowed hard.

"Okay ... so it *is* all real, then? Witches exist? Whoa! The town gossip was right for once." Jaystar bounced up and down on his toes, excitement coming off him in waves. "How many of you are there? I mean, it was never too hard to believe Mara was a witch. I mean, she lives here ..." He waved his arms around to take in the cottage. Momentarily, pain contorted his face, and he grabbed his shoulder. It didn't curb how animated he'd become, though. "And you're a witch, too, right?" He looked at me for confirmation without allowing me time to give it. "I knew it! I mean, I didn't, but I suspected it. And when you said dead people were in your basement, I mean, it makes sense, right?"

Holy cheese, what had I done? A deluge of emotions flooded Eli's face, and I felt a spark of satisfaction that he had been the one to tell Jaystar I was a witch, not me. Eli's expression finally settled on fury.

"Dead people?!" Eli bellowed. "What in damnation is going on, Alice? Do you have any idea the kind of trouble you're in?!"

Not the good kind, apparently. It was possible I'd made things much worse though I couldn't help being thrilled that Jaystar now knew my secret, and he'd taken it better than I could have wished. Eli, I hoped, would come around in his own time.

Alice… The voice was like a sigh in my head. Why was Aunt Mara's voice so weak when Eli's had been so loud?

A pounding on the front door made us all jump and fall silent. My heart thundered in my chest. What if whoever it was had heard Eli's outburst? How could I explain dead people in the basement? Jaystar and I exchanged a glance. It was possible he was thinking the same thing. The knocking came again.

Eli closed his eyes for a moment and then opened them. "It's the sheriff," he whispered. "I need to get you out of here. We'll get you into some safe housing until I work out what to do with you."

"How do you know it's the sheriff?" Jaystar whispered to Eli. "Did you just do a spell or something?"

Eli shot him a murderous glare. Jaystar raised both of his hands as if to ward off an attack.

"Jaystar comes with me, right?" I squared my shoulders, knowing what Eli would say before he said it.

"Not possible," Eli stated.

Jaystar's jaw dropped. He mouthed the word "What?!" at me.

"It's not a negotiation," I said, feeling braver than I felt. "If Jaystar is found here alone, it opens up a whole other can of worms."

The banging on the front door continued.

"Miss Lovell, it's the police. We have a warrant. Open up!"

"There are rules, Wonderland," Eli growled. "No Non-Magicals."

"Well, I'm staying here, then." I crossed my arms and glared at him.

"Well, fortunately I don't need your permission," Eli growled at me, reaching out to grab my arm.

"I'm coming!" I yelled as I darted out of his way and dashed toward the front entrance. The banging was growing to a crescendo.

"What are you doing?!" Eli snarled.

I figured if I let the sheriff know I was here, he couldn't take me. It would seem even more suspicious for me to suddenly disappear. I reached the door and turned back to Eli and Jaystar. Eli looked like he was fizzing with anger. I pulled my shoulders back.

"Just a sec!" I called out. Aunt Mara had said I could trust Eli. I hoped she was right. I gestured for Jaystar to take Eli downstairs. Jaystar's face paled, and he looked like he wanted to argue. Instead, he whispered something to Eli. Eli's expression made my breath hitch. I really hoped I was doing the right thing by sending him down there with Jaystar. I waited a moment for Eli to close the door behind him before I reached for the doorknob.

I'm with Christo... tell her to find Christo... It was Aunt Mara's voice again—barely above a whisper.

Christo? I thought back. No answer came.

I turned the doorknob. The door was shoved open from the other side, making me lose my balance. I grabbed the sideboard to steady myself. Sheriff Markson stood in the doorway. Behind her, I could make out Officer Jonas and another officer I hadn't seen before. He was a short, stocky man with a boyish face and blond hair. He tugged at his collar, and my first thought was how nervous he appeared.

"Good morning, Sheriff," I said, my heart racing.

Saying nothing, she thrust a piece of paper my direction before pushing past me into the hallway.

The second piece of paper issued by law enforcement today. I hadn't checked the one Eli had given me, but this one, I assumed, was a search warrant. Officer Jonas stepped past me, giving me a skewed smile in greeting. The other man seemed reluctant to enter. He lingered on the bottom doorstep, shuffling from foot to foot.

"Jensen! Get in here!"

The sheriff's voice slapped him out of his paralysis, and he hurried up the steps, trying to keep as wide of a berth from me as possible. His eyes never left mine as he side-stepped past me. Beads of sweat glistened on his brow, and I got the distinct feeling he was scared of me. Maybe he was one of the residents of Widdershins who thought Aunt Mara—and maybe me by association—was a witch.

I didn't even bother opening the warrant, choosing to leave it on the sideboard where I'd placed Eli's. Nothing I said was going to stop the sheriff from looking for whatever she was looking for. I only hoped that she might disregard the door under the stairs, thinking it a linen cupboard or something. Aunt Mara's apothecary and Eli and Jaystar might be hard to explain to the sheriff. I had the horrible suspicion, though, that Sheriff Markson wasn't the type to cut corners.

Officer Jensen headed upstairs, probably eager to put as much distance between the two of us as possible. Officer Jonas turned right into the kitchen. The sheriff hovered for a moment at the bottom step of the staircase. Maybe she had her own sixth sense; it seemed like she was listening for something. She was far too close to the doorway under the stairs for my comfort. I needed to get her out of here.

Aunt Mara's words danced around my mind. "I think I know where Aunt Mara is," I blurted out.

The sheriff turned to face me, her right hand resting on her holster.

"*Now* you know where she is?" the sheriff snarled while taking a slow step toward me.

"Maybe," I said. My voice sounded hollow in my ears. Sugar-sticks. What if I was making a mistake and setting Christo up for trouble?

"Well then? Where is she?" The sheriff took another step toward me and my breath hitched.

"What will you do when you find her?" I asked. Stalling, in case I had made the wrong decision and any moment now, Aunt Mara's voice would pop up in my head and have me recant.

The sheriff raised an eyebrow, her steely blues barely blinking.

"Nothing up here," Officer Jensen's voice called down.

What were they were even searching for? I wondered.

"Obviously, we have some questions for her. We have reason to believe it was one of your aunt's teas that poisoned Mr. Maximilian. You wouldn't know anything about it, would you, Miss Lovell?" Her eyebrow was raised, scrutinizing my face the whole time she was talking.

My throat had gone dry, and I desperately needed to swallow but was scared she'd read too much into it.

"So, where *is* your aunt, Miss Lovell?"

"Okay ..." I said slowly, choosing my words carefully. "I don't know exactly *where* she is ..."

The sheriff's jawline stiffened.

"But I think I know *who* she's with," I said, hoping that would be enough.

"You think, or you *know,* Miss Lovell?"

Tough customer.

"I know." Which wasn't true. I was going on what some disembodied voice that sounded like my aunt whispered to me in my mind. It sounded weak even to me. "She's with Christo," I said.

"Christo?"

"Yeah ..." I realized I didn't actually know Christo's last name. "Christo. The owner of Christo's Café," I tried to clarify.

"I know who Christo is," the sheriff barked. "Why do you think Mara is with Christo?"

"I remember her saying something like that before she left the house yesterday." Another untruth. But if I were to tell the sheriff the truth, I'd have to tell her I heard Aunt Mara talking on the phone to Marion before she disappeared. I suspected the fact that Marion died this morning wouldn't help Aunt Mara's case.

"Mara provides teas for Christo's Café. Maybe it was a business meeting?" I added, hoping my voice hid the way my heart was racing in my chest.

"Hmm." The sheriff said nothing for a moment, as if she were thinking. "Jensen," she called.

"Here," Officer Jensen said, already on the staircase behind her.

"Take Jonas and go check out Christo's Café. If Christo's not there, you need to find him. Miss Lovell here seems to think Mara is with him." Her lip curled in a growl as she glared at me. "I'll meet you back at the station," she said. Her eyes never wavered from my face.

I exhaled with relief and felt my shoulders loosen. She was leaving. Jonas joined Jensen, having overhead the sheriff's instructions. The two of them filed past me, Jensen again giving me as wide of a berth as possible, before they headed out the front door.

"Miss Lovell, you're coming with me."

My jaw slackened and my stomach dropped.

"What do you mean?" I asked, my voice pitching with panic.

"You need to come with me to the station. Until we find your aunt, you're our primary suspect. I want you where I can see you."

"You're arresting me?" My voice was barely a squeak.

"I'm asking you to accompany me to the station, Miss Lovell." The sheriff's voice was steel. She scared me almost as much as Eli.

My mind raced ahead. I needed to stall. Let Jaystar and Eli know. But how? I couldn't very well go down to the basement and tell them without giving it away.

"Okay," I said, gulping back the lump in my throat. "I just need to grab my things." I pointed toward the kitchen, hoping she wouldn't follow—and hoping she didn't notice the bulge in my back pocket where my phone sat.

The sheriff crossed her arms and tapped a foot impatiently, jerking her head in the direction of the kitchen as permission.

I'd leave a note. It was too risky to text Jaystar, in case they confiscated my phone at the police station. My best bet was to leave a note addressed to Aunt Mara saying I was at the station. I could pretend it was in case Aunt Mara came home and was wondering where I was. My fingers would just stay crossed that Eli or Jaystar would find it, and maybe one of them would have an idea of how to get me out of this mess.

Chapter 16

The police station was a single-story, red-brick building situated off one of the side roads from the town square. A sign above the main double-glass doors, spanning the length of the wall, read simply "Police Station." One marked police car was parked outside on the road. The sheriff pulled in beside it.

My lip felt raw from chewing on it. Never in my life would I have anticipated that in just two days of meeting Aunt Mara, I'd be a murder suspect sitting in the backseat of a cop car parked outside the Widdershins Police Station.

I'd spent the brief trip mulling things over in my mind. Had Eli and Jaystar found my note yet, and did they have a plan to get the sheriff off my case? Had Eli sent the freaky foursome haunting the basement on their way to the afterlife or wherever it was they were meant to go? Of course, it depended whether he could see them. I assumed seeing ghosts was a witchy skill, so my hopes were high that he could. I regretted not having more time to fill Jaystar in on everything better before Eli had turned up. He would have been able to fill in Eli as needed. Wondering whether Officers Jensen and Jonas had found Aunt Mara and Christo was also gnawing away at me. I hadn't heard anything more from Aunt Mara's voice inside my head since I'd left the cottage.

Tears welled in my eyes, and I sniffed, willing them to disappear. This was all a big misunderstanding. I just knew it was. From what Jaystar had found, it was more than possible Man-Bruce had accidentally poisoned himself.

The sheriff came around to the passenger door and opened it for me. She said nothing. I guess I should have been thankful she hadn't handcuffed me. I slid across the seat and stood up, blinking hard against the sunlight, as if I had been sheltered from the world, a hardened criminal, for longer than the five-minute drive. I guess she didn't see me as a flight risk.

She led the way, pulling open the glass doors and entering the building.

The station was small. I guess crime wasn't much of a thing in Widdershins. Six plastic chairs lined a wall opposite the reception window. A man and a woman sat spaced out upon them. A small table was set up for coffee and tea in the corner, next to a couple of doors looking like they might lead off to other rooms or a corridor. Posters hung around the walls, relating messages like: "Do the Crime, Do the Time," and "Speed Kills."

The sheriff made a beeline for the reception window while I hung back, not knowing what to do with myself. A woman in plain clothes manned the counter. She and the sheriff spoke in hushed tones for a moment before she slipped the sheriff a clipboard. While she went about writing something on the clipboard, the office lady turned her attention to me. From the waist up, she was dressed in a blue-and-pink floral shirt and appeared to be in her sixties. She had an ash-blonde, shoulder-length perm. Thick-rimmed glasses perched on the end of her nose. She was also beaming a huge smile my way.

"Aww. Well, don't you look just like your mother?" she exclaimed while tilting her head at me.

This woman knew my mother?! My pulse sped up. Mom had never talked about Widdershins. The first I had heard of the place was in learning about Aunt Mara from the executor of her will. I gave the office lady a weak smile while the sheriff mumbled something I couldn't hear with her back to me. She pushed the clipboard across the counter back to the woman, then turned to me with a gesture to the nearest closed door.

I followed her directions and opened the door into a small room. It looked like it might be the sheriff's own office. A police diploma hung on the wall beside a small bookcase. A desk took up most of the space, with a filing cabinet to one side of it. Behind the desk sat a comfy-looking swivel chair. A computer faced away from me on the edge of the desk, beside which, pens and pencils stood in a desk caddy. On the side closest to me were two cheap plastic chairs, like the ones I saw in the waiting area.

With a gesture from the sheriff, I took one chair nearest the door. I tried to appear as relaxed and innocent as I could sitting in the chair. The truth was, I was scared.

"Stay here," the sheriff growled, before turning away and heading out of the room again.

My foot tapped nervously under my chair, and I mentally tried to stop it.

"Here we are, my dear."

She had snuck up like a ninja. The office lady was suddenly standing beside me, holding a Styrofoam cup of hot, black liquid out to me. "I thought you might need a bit of a pick me up." She placed it down in front of me.

"Thanks," I said. It was nice to have someone not growl their words at me for a change.

She plonked herself down in the chair beside me and patted my hand. "Now don't go letting Carissa intimidate you. She might come across all scary and tough, but she's really a pussycat underneath," she said.

Holy cheese. Was she talking about the sheriff? A pussycat was not how I would describe the woman. A mountain lion maybe.

"Thank you," I whispered again, thoroughly confused. She'd caught me off guard with her kindness. "Did you know my mother?" I asked, swallowing hard as I said it.

"Oh yes," the woman said, her eyes becoming shiny.

"Maggie was a pretty wee thing. Looked a bunch like you. We used to see a lot of her on account of Mara always being in trouble." She giggled, then pulled a tissue from a box on the desktop and dabbed her eyes.

My shock must have shown because the woman quickly continued on.

"Oh, no. It's not like that. It's just ... there've always been people who've taken a bit of an aversion to your aunt on account that she's a"—she leaned forward and cupped a hand around her mouth to whisper the end of her sentence—"witch."

She pulled back and studied my face. No amount of self-control would have hidden my surprise, and she giggled again, dabbing at her eyes.

"Your mom and your grandmother spent a good deal of time having to collect her from here. She was always upsetting someone." She shook her head, chuckling at the memories. "Mara's in much less trouble nowadays, thankfully. We went through a good number of officers simply because they couldn't keep up with the paperwork!" She gave my knee a pat.

"It's so dreadful what happened to your mom," the woman said gently. "It's been a good couple of decades since I'd seen her and all, but you don't go forgetting sweet little things like her. And although Mara would never admit it, I know it near broke her heart when your mom moved away. But now you're here ..." Her face relaxed into a grin again. "Mara must be thrilled. I've got a sense for these sorts of things." She leaned toward me, this time tapping her temple and giving me a wink.

Oh boy. She obviously didn't know Mara was missing and a murder suspect. I chewed on my lip again, then, finding my senses, introduced myself.

"I'm Alice," I said. "Thank you for your kind words ..." I meant to say more, but just thinking about my mother made my eyes water.

"Oh, my dear." She twisted in her seat and then wrapped her arms around me in what I imagined was a grandmotherly hug, pulling me hard against her bosom. "Now, now," she cooed.

I blinked feverishly to stop tears from falling. Finally, I pulled away.

Her gaze searched my face. "I'm Betty Borjeson. And you know, my dear, if you need anything, you come to me. If it weren't for your aunt and her *special* teas ..." She air-quoted the word special and gave me another wink. "Well, I'd be a lonely old widow, wallowing in self-pity, I would. But your aunt, she set me up with Cupid's Kiss, and now I'm getting married!" She wriggled in her seat and waved her hand in my face. A big emerald surrounded with small diamonds sparkled on her finger. "It's the tea that did it, I swear by it. Cupid's Kiss. You know, if you're looking for love, my dear, you ask your aunt about it. I recommend it to all my friends now. I owe Mara. When I think what a sad, lonely woman I was turning out to be—"

A bell dinged loudly from the waiting room.

"Helllllooo? Hello! Where is the service around here?" a shrill voice called out.

Betty's face fell immediately into a grimace, and she shook her head. "I suspect I would have ended up much like that!" she said, gesturing toward the door.

The bell rang another few times, accompanied by a yappy, high-pitched barking. My stomach sank. The voice had sounded familiar, but the dog had cinched it.

Betty rolled her eyes at me, heaved herself out of the chair, then left to deal with Mrs. Whittle and Dog-Bruce.

There was still no sign of the sheriff. Maybe this had been her plan all along—to make me wait so I'd break and tell her everything in a flood of anxiety when she came back. Well, the joke was on her. The more time that went by and the more people told me, the less I felt I knew.

It had been a comfort meeting Betty. In the few moments I'd spent with her, it was obvious she was team Aunt Mara and about as fond of Mrs. Whittle as I was, so we had something in common.

"I demand to see the sheriff!" Mrs. Whittle's voice carried through the building. A muffled voice joined hers, which I assumed was Betty.

After a moment of dithering, I moved closer to the door to listen better. I poked my head around the corner just enough to watch the spectacle, ready to hide if she dared turn my way. The two people sitting on the chairs at reception seemed just as riveted by the woman in the bright pink velour track suit as I was.

Mrs. Whittle had changed her appearance a little since storming up the path at Hollyhock Cottage that morning. Her hair was now free from rollers and perfectly coiffed into waves. Large pearly earrings hung from her ears, and a matching pearl necklace adorned her neck. A diamante studded dog leash ran down to the Dog-Bruce's collar. She had white wedged slides on her feet. I suspected her toenails were painted to match her track suit.

"I demand to see the sheriff! This is a matter of trespassing and destruction of private property!"

Holy cheese. I had no doubt in my mind why she was here.

Mrs. Whittle waved her cell phone back and forth in front of Betty, whose lips were tightly pursed, eyes peering over her glasses in disdain, hands clasped in front of her. She let Mrs. Whittle rave on without a word, but even from where I peeked, I could feel Betty's hand itching to lash out and slap some sense into the woman. Maybe my witchy powers *were* manifesting and somehow heightened my senses. It explained how I would know this. Although I would never condone violence, I was mesmerized by these two older women facing off.

"As I have told you," Betty said, her voice steady and firm, "the sheriff is busy right now. If you take a seat, she'll see you in due course."

Mrs. Whittle looked around her, focusing on the plastic seats on the far wall. A tall, gangly man, unshaven, dressed in tight black leather pants and a leather jacket, with a leathery complexion, leaned forward, elbows on his knees, and stared back at her. Beside him, a few seats away, a middle-aged woman in a pencil skirt and tucked-in blouse, holding white gloves in her hands, perched on the very edge of her seat, taking it all in.

Horror showed on Mrs. Whittle's face as she turned back to Betty. "I don't think you understand!" she said, her voice rising an octave higher. Dog-Bruce growled to emphasize the point.

"Look at this! Look!" She pushed the phone up close to Betty's nose, making Betty grimace and pull back a little. She adjusted the glasses on her nose and after a few seconds, she settled a steely glare at Mrs. Whittle.

"Mrs. Whittle! Let me get this straight." The ice in Betty's tone almost gave me goosebumps. Mrs. Whittle dropped the phone to her side, and even Dog-Bruce fell quiet for a time and sat on his haunches. "We have a murder *and* an unknown cause of death being investigated at this time. Widdershin's entire law enforcement team consists of the sheriff and two *very* young reserve officers. The state police are severely understaffed. And YOU would like everyone to drop everything because some cat got high on catnip and tore up a few flowers in your garden?"

Holy cheese! Betty was good! I swelled with admiration for this woman I'd just met.

Mrs. Whittle's mouth opened and shut like a fish's for a few beats, her face flushing the color of her tracksuit. Leather-Guy beamed from his seat behind her. He pumped a fist in the air, and I swore I saw the corner of Betty's lips twitch.

Finally, Mrs. Whittle found her voice again. "Of course not!" She looked around nervously.

Though I pulled back as she glanced in my direction, I instantly knew I'd been too slow.

"There! Over there!"

I leaned against the office wall, taking deep breaths, trying to figure out what my next move was going to be. I'd been seen. I could continue hiding or face my accuser.

"This is all her fault!" Dog-Bruce started yapping again.

I sighed. I might as well face Mrs. Whittle. I'd be interested to see the footage of Hades. No mention had been made of an overweight spandex-wearing guy being dragged through her garden, so that, at least, was a positive. But part of me was curious if I could see ghosts on film, even if other people couldn't, and as the sheriff still hadn't shown up …

I stepped out from the doorway and made my way to where Mrs. Whittle, Dog-Bruce, and Betty stood in the center of the waiting room.

Betty rolled her eyes at me.

"This woman"—Mrs. Whittle pointed a fleshy finger with a manicured pink nail at me—"and her aunt are to blame for this! They've been sending their cat to destroy my property. And I've tried to be nice! I've asked them to stop!" Mrs. Whittle's voice rose another octave. "But look! Look! That cat is obviously possessed, and they refuse to do anything about it." She stomped her shoe, making Dog-Bruce woof. She was working herself up into another fit, waving the phone again wildly in all directions, making it impossible to actually see. Betty grabbed the phone from Mrs. Whittle's grasp and held it out so we could view the footage. Mrs. Whittle grew silent again. Leather-Guy's curiosity must have been piqued too, because he quickly joined us as we crowded around Mrs. Whittle's phone.

Betty tapped the screen to play. The footage was in black and white and grainy, but it was easy enough to see the camera was aimed at a garden along the fence line between Mrs. Whittle's and Aunt Mara's. The cobbled wall was recognizable, being the same as I'd seen from walking down the path to Hollyhock Cottage. On Mrs. Whittle's side, it too was covered with ivy. A tree stood at one side of the screen, and the foreground showed a garden of various flowers. Everything was still. Until it wasn't.

From offscreen, a streak of black came into view. It was one hundred percent Hades.

"Look! Look!" Mrs. Whittle cried again.

"Shh!" Betty snapped at her, although there wasn't any audio in the footage.

Hades certainly appeared possessed. His back and tail were arched, fur on end, and he was leaping all around Mrs. Whittle's flowers, flattening them as he did so. Sometimes he'd stop and his ears would go back, and he'd lash out with his paw.

I chewed my lip. No one was commenting on the large man in cycling gear Hades was trying to herd over the fence. I guessed Hades had given up dragging Gerry for shepherding him to the cottage. Poor Gerry was huffing, sweating, and flailing his arms, looking terrified and on the edge of having a heart attack. Coincidentally, what had killed him in real life. Most of the time, Gerry had no impact on Mrs. Whittle's garden. When he slipped and face-planted, Mrs. Whittle's geraniums seemed none the worse. But other times, like when he was trying to scramble up and over the wall, it was as if he *could* touch the physical. It wasn't Hades who broke a branch off of Mrs. Whittle's tree although for anyone else it might have looked that way. Gerry had been trying to hoist himself over the top of the wall.

Poor Gerry, I thought. His friends at Christo's had said he'd been terrified of cats while living. And now here he was being harassed by one in his afterlife.

I could almost empathize with Mrs. Whittle too. She was a victim of Hades's strange obsession with bringing home ghosts, and Hades really shouldn't have been in her garden.

The footage ended with a new reel of footage starting up. It must have come from another camera because this was a different view. This shot was directed at what I guessed was another part of the boundary line between Aunt Mara's and Mrs. Whittle's. The cobbled fence had transitioned into a wooden one with old planks, looking loose and askew. Over the fence, I was sure I could make out the roof of Hollyhock Cottage. But it was what lay at the base of the fence that had me draw a sharp breath. Half-hidden by overgrowth, a couple of spray cans peeked out.

Mrs. Whittle snatched her phone back from Betty and furiously tapped the screen. Well. If that wasn't suspicious, then I didn't know what was. It was a strange thing to fathom. Mrs. Whittle sneaking through the fence, spray cans in hand to graffiti Aunt Mara's front door. Although, I'd just watched a dead man being chased through her garden by a cat, so at this point, anything was possible. It was certainly something to ponder.

I tried my best to keep my expression neutral as I slowly raised my eyes. Leather-Guy was beaming, like he'd just watched the most entertaining thing he'd seen in a while. Betty had her eyes raised to the ceiling, her face twitching as if she were trying to compose herself. I guess even if they couldn't see Gerry, Hades acting like a goon was rather amusing.

"I want a trespass notice and charges rendered for destruction of private property!" Mrs. Whittle demanded.

"A trespass notice against what? A hopped-up cat?" Leather-Guy guffawed loudly and slapped his thigh with one hand.

Mrs. Whittle's mouth dropped. And I felt a sense of relief.

"Alice wasn't even there," Betty said calmly from beside me.

"Well, it's her cat! Or her aunt's at least. The whole family needs to be locked up!"

"And maybe you'll get your way." A sharp voice crept up behind us. Sheriff Markson.

Chapter 17

"**M**rs. Whittle, we're law enforcement, not animal control. I suggest you take up whatever problem you're having this week with them." The sheriff's words cooled the temperature in the room fast.

Leather-Guy raised an eyebrow at Betty and returned to his seat. The woman sitting on the far side of the room was openly watching us. Dog-Bruce let out a small whimper, and Mrs. Whittle's bottom lip quivered for a moment, before she lifted her shoulders and jutted her chin into the air.

"Well, then! This would never have happened if my Frankie were still alive. This town has gone to .... has gone to ..." She seemed to be searching for the right words.

"To Hades?" Betty said, winking at me again.

I stifled a snort.

"Well, I never!" Mrs. Whittled huffed. She tugged on Dog-Bruce's leash and turned on her heel. As she left, Leather-Guy grinned broadly at Betty. I glanced back and forth between the two of them. *Could it be ...?* I wondered. The way they were looking at each other, I would bet money that Leather-Guy was the purchaser of the big green rock on Betty's engagement finger.

"Miss Lovell. I asked you to stay in the room."

Yikes. If looks could kill ...

"No!" a woman's voice cried out. "No, no, no, no, no!"

What in Hercules?!

Behind the sheriff, the woman with the gloves was standing on her chair, wobbling on her high heels, staring at the floor in horror.

"No, no, no!" she screamed again. All color had drained from her face. Her eyes were wild. I couldn't see what had her so spooked.

"Are you okay?" I asked, stepping around the sheriff, ready to rush to her aid. Whatever was going on, she certainly didn't appear okay.

"I'm good," Leather-Guy said, giving me a weird look. "Hi, kitty-kitty," he said, bending down to pat Hades, who, like magic, had again appeared from nowhere to stir up trouble. Hades ignored him and paused in front of the woman on the chair. Standing on two legs, he reached up with a paw to swat her ankle. She tried to jump out of his way while keeping her balance on the plastic seat.

"What is that cat doing here?" the sheriff growled, turning to Betty, who glanced at me.

"Here kitty-kitty," Leather-Guy cooed, trying to pull Hades's attention from batting at the seat beside him. "He's just like the cat on the security cam," he mused.

Heat seared my cheeks. This was going to be hard to explain.

"You can see me!" The woman on the chair turned her attention to me. "Help me! Please! Help me!"

I looked around. I'm not sure why. No one else could see her. I took a deep breath.

"Hades! Come here!" I pleaded with the cat, knowing the likelihood of him paying any attention to me was low.

"He's yours?!" the sheriff's voice cut through.

Leather-Guy guffawed again.

"No," I replied. My mind cycled through ways to pick the devil up without suffering my own very real mauling in doing so. "He's Aunt Mara's."

Maybe Betty hadn't been kidding when she said she *knew* things, because within seconds she was standing beside me with a cat-sized box. She placed it on the floor.

"What is he doing? He sure is acting strange," she said. "Good thing Mrs. Whittle isn't still here. She would have skinned the poor thing alive."

Bracing myself for an onslaught of hurting, I grabbed Hades around the middle. His legs went rigid, his claws exposed, and he let out a deep throaty yowl worthy of a jaguar. I held him as far away from me as I could, while the woman on the chair shot me an appreciative glance. I lowered Hades into the box. He struggled, but somehow, miraculously, I got him in and closed the lid. With me holding it secure, he calmed down relatively fast. A golden eye glared at me through a gap in the lid. Well, he could be as peeved with me as he liked. Attacking a woman in a police station was really pushing at my limits of magnanimity, even if the woman was dead.

"You need to get that thing out of here, Miss Lovell." The sheriff scowled at me. Not a cat-lover, obviously.

"So, I can leave, then?" I asked, wondering if my luck was changing.

"No. I still have questions for you. I wasn't joking when I said at this point you and your aunt were in a serious amount of trouble. But I want that thing out of here. Let it go outside or something."

I swallowed. I knew I couldn't do that. If I let Hades go, he'd just find another way inside to harass the woman on the chair. I looked back and forth between Leather-Guy and Betty. It was Betty who spoke first.

"Thomas and I can hold onto him until you're finished, if you'd like?" she said, gesturing to Leather-Guy. I dithered for a moment. Could I trust Hades to behave for them? He could just as likely bite his way out of the box and create chaos again. I wished I knew why he was so set on collecting ghosts. And for a small town like Widdershins, there seemed to be an awful lot of them. If I could just have a moment to talk to the woman on the chair, maybe that would help.

"Miss Lovell, I don't have time to wait for you to decide what to do with your cat! Unless you weren't listening before, we now have two deaths on our hands, and I'm not altogether convinced that you're not somehow involved."

Oh lordy!

"Hades! Hades, you dumb cat!" With a flapping of limbs and messenger bag, a ruffled, red-faced Jaystar almost fell through the front doors to the station before coming to a sliding halt on the tile. He'd obviously been running a distance. He had his hands on his thighs and was sucking in mouthfuls of air.

"Hades ... he ... took off." Jaystar panted between breaths. "Wh-where is he?" He peered around the room. The box at my feet rocked violently, as if to answer his question.

"Get. It. Out. Of. Here. Then I expect to see you back in my office, Miss Lovell!" The sheriff threw her arms in the air and stormed into her office, slamming the door behind her.

For a moment, I contemplated doing a runner. Now would be the perfect time. I hardly thought Betty or Thomas would try to stop me, and Officers Jonas and Jensen were obviously still out tracking down Christo and Aunt Mara. But I suspected running from a police station wouldn't help me with a pending murder charge.

"Jaystar! Is that you? My word you've grown! It's been a time and an age. How's your mother doing? Is she all good?" Betty didn't let him get a word in, which probably suited him fine, as he was still gasping for air.

"Are you okay?" I asked, searching his face for intel on what was going on. Like, where was Eli? Had Eli been able to get any information from the basement ghosts, or, better yet, sent them on their way? And why had Jaystar been chasing Hades?

"Hi, Betty." His breathing was returning to normal. Jaystar stood up, wiped the sweat from his forehead with his hand, and straightened his messenger bag. "Mom's good," he said, forcing a polite smile.

Betty eyed the two of us. She seemed to think hard for a moment and then, making her mind up, she moved to Thomas, grabbed his hand, and pulled him toward her. "Let's leave these kids be, eh?" she said, sending me a wink over her shoulder as she led him into her office.

As soon as I thought them both out of earshot, I leaned into Jaystar. "What are you doing here?"

"He just took off. Like lightning. And your *cop-friend*—"

I noticed a hint of sarcasm in his voice.

"—sent me out to get him. He figured Hades was off to retrieve more ... you know. We found your note, so it didn't surprise me when Hades headed this way."

"Why didn't you just let him go?" I asked.

"I don't know," Jaystar said with a one shoulder shrug. "*Mr. Cop-Guy* seems to be fond of the beast. I don't get it."

It was true. I had noticed the same.

"So where's Eli?" I asked.

"He wanted more time to talk to the—" He peered around the empty room. "You know? The ... ghosts."

I guess it made sense. I had wished Eli might just let them go. Wouldn't that have been a win-win for everyone? The dearly departed could continue on their journeys to who knew where, and Aunt Mara's basement would be spook free again.

"Excuse me," a voice from a few feet away drew my attention.

I had totally forgotten about the lady on the chair. She was sitting now, prim and proper, on the edge of the seat again.

"Did you say there are more of us?"

"Um ... I'm not sure how to tell you this," I whispered to Jaystar, "but we've got company." I pointed to what would appear to be an empty chair to him.

Jaystar looked over my shoulder and squinted. "I don't see any-one— Oh!" he said, understanding dawning. "So that's who Hades was after?"

I nodded and took a few steps toward the woman.

"Hi," I said, softly. "I'm Alice Lovell."

"Marion," the woman said. "Marion Marigold."

"Nice to meet you, Marion Marigold," I said.

"Marion Marigold?" Jaystar asked from behind me. "That's the woman who died at the Tea Shoppe this morning." Jaystar's face paled.

Holy cheese! She could be the woman who last called Aunt Mara.

"Marion, would you mind if I asked you a few questions? I don't have much time, but it would really help me out."

"Do you promise to keep that fleabag away from me?" She pointed to the box by Jaystar.

"I'll certainly do my best," I said.

She nodded.

"How did you die?" I asked.

Her face fell, and I couldn't really blame her. She'd only been dead a few hours. I could only imagine how disorienting that might be, but I didn't have time to beat around the bush. At any moment, I was expecting the sheriff to come storming back in, wondering why I was taking so long.

Marion sighed. "I was having my usual specialty tea at Miss Maisy's, and then I guess ... something just wasn't right about it. I ... started feeling weird. And then, I'm looking down at myself sprawled on the ground with a crowd of people mulling around. It was all very strange." She shook her head, disbelief on her face. "I'd expected there to be a bright light or a distant family member waiting to take me to wherever it is you go when you die, but there was no one. So I came here." She sighed a full-body sigh. "I know it makes no sense. Obviously, no one besides you and that beast seem to see or hear me. However, I'd always been taught to seek the police when you're in trouble or need help."

"What's she saying?" Jaystar whispered at me.

"She was poisoned," I said, looking for confirmation from Marion as I said it.

She nodded.

That made two poisonings in less than twenty-four hours. But at least this time, I was nowhere near the scene, and Aunt Mara had been missing at the time.

"Poisoned? At Grams?" Jaystar balked. "It's not possible. Marion only ever orders tea and it's specially ordered. She's the only one Grams lets drink—Oh damn!" he said, eyes widening.

"What? Ooh." My stomach dropped. "It was Aunt Mara's tea, wasn't it?" already knowing the answer.

"Ask who served her," Jaystar said, trying to hold the box closed while Hades threw himself around inside.

"It was a young girl," Marion said without missing a beat.

I relayed her response to Jaystar, my stomach sinking further.

"Susie and Bronwyn were working today. Neither of them seems the type to poison someone," Jaystar said.

I felt a flicker of relief. My mind had instantly honed in on Lucy, but of course, she had been with me at Christo's. How had that only been this morning? So much had happened since.

"One last question," I said to Marion. "Did you call my aunt yesterday afternoon?"

Marion looked puzzled for a moment.

"Mara," I said. "Mara Lovell. She got a phone call, and I overheard the name Marion. She's been missing ever since." My heart sped up as I wondered what her answer would be.

"Oh my," she said. "I didn't put it together. You're Mara's niece! And you said Mara's missing?" Her eyes grew wide.

I nodded.

"I'd been led to believe Mara and Christo were going into a partnership together. I'd invested a large amount of money into the venture. It was all signed off on. But yesterday, as I was walking to my car, I overheard an argument between Christo and a young man in the backroom. I wasn't eavesdropping. My office is next door to Christo's Café, and I park my car close by. Christo was furious. He accused the other party of backstabbing him, poaching Mara for his own gains, and that was why she wouldn't sign off. I panicked, thinking it meant Mara was no longer going into business with Christo. She was the whole reason I was making an investment and taking a chance on the start-up. So I called her to check for myself, and she confirmed I'd been duped."

I relayed it back to Jaystar as quickly as I could.

Jaystar's eyes grew wide again. "Ask her if she knows where Mara might have gone?"

I didn't need to. Marion answered straight away. "She didn't say she was going anywhere, but I can guess. I bet you can too," she said.

I stole an anxious glance at the sheriff's door. It was still closed. She was being more patient than I had expected her to be, but I didn't want to take my chances with spending any more time in the waiting area.

"Thank you, Marion," I said. "My condolences for your passing." I wasn't sure it was the right thing to say, as I hadn't ever been in this situation before. "Jaystar," I said, turning to him. "I need you to take Hades back to Hollyhock Cottage in the box." I shot him an apologetic smile.

Hades yowled from inside. He wasn't going to make it an easy task.

"And Hades, you need to play nice. No making Jaystar sneeze!" I whispered to him.

Jaystar looked at me strangely.

I turned back to Marion. "You need to go with Jaystar," I said to her. "He'll take you back to Aunt Mara's cottage, where there are more of you. Eli's there. He's working on a way to get you all back to where you're supposed to be." I hoped he was, anyway.

Marion stood up and smoothed her skirt. I admired her. She was handling things remarkably well for someone who'd recently been poisoned, harassed by Hades, and found herself earthbound.

"Alice, dear," a kindly voice from the reception desk startled me. "I just thought I'd warn you. It's probably not the best time to keep Carissa waiting." Betty gave me a warm smile.

Right. Time to face the music with Sheriff Markson.

"Thank you," I whispered to Jaystar. Boy, did I owe him one. He lifted the box up and juggled it in his arms before sneezing. Oh jeeze. "Hades!" I growled a warning at the box.

I opened the door for Marion and Jaystar and watched them leave before quickly making my way to the sheriff's office. I stole a glance in Betty's direction as I did so, and she gave me a thumbs up. The sheriff's a pussycat, Betty had said. I sure hoped she'd calmed down enough to be a more amicable one than Hades. I somehow doubted it. I knocked on the door anyway.

Chapter 18

"**R**ight, Miss Lovell. So you're sticking to your story? You don't know where Mara is?"

I gulped and nodded. It was true. I didn't. But I still felt like I was holding out on the sheriff. And I guess I was. I wasn't sharing a lot of details. Where Mara was wasn't one. My life would have been a lot less complicated if I knew the answer.

The sheriff sat on the edge of her desk, with one foot touching the ground and the other dangling. She towered over me as I shifted in my chair, trying to find a pose that would make me look as innocent as possible. Sheriff Markson was petite. Shorter than me, but also probably one of the most terrifying people I had ever met. She glowered at me with such intensity I felt brain cells dying as if they were being lasered.

"Yet you said she was with Christo?"

"Mm-hmm," I nodded. I had said that. I wasn't going to tell her Aunt Mara's disembodied voice said as much. With everything Marion had told me, I could believe Aunt Mara might have sought Christo after their phone conversation. I didn't imagine she'd take kindly to him lying to Marion about her. However, that didn't explain why she hadn't come home.

"What exactly is Mara's relationship with Christo, Miss Lovell?"

Relationship? I'd known both of them for a couple of days. The sheriff likely knew more about them than I did, but I relayed the small amount I'd learned.

"They're friends. I think. I mean, Christo said they were yesterday. And they had a business arrangement. Mara sold some of her teas at Christo's Café." I didn't share what Marion had told me. Mainly, as she was dead at the time we met. That would be hard to explain. But also, because she suspected she'd been poisoned, and I didn't think the sheriff had made the connection yet. When she did, it might not work in my or Aunt Mara's favor. Marion's words made me believe Christo was somehow involved. I chewed my lip. I had liked Christo. I hoped there was an innocent explanation for everything.

"It seems Christo never showed for his shift at the café this morning, nor is he at his house. It's strange that both Mara and Christo, the two people who might get you off the hook for Mr. Maximilian's murder, are missing, don't you think?"

I swallowed. My mouth had gone dry. Did the sheriff know I had been the one to give Man-Bruce the tea?

"You forgot to mention you'd been at Christo's Café this morning, Miss Lovell." Her eyes had narrowed in on me further.

Bad luck, be gone! Bad luck, be gone! I chanted to myself. Maybe that's how it worked? What was the use of being a witch if I couldn't magic my way out of trouble?

"Jonas and Jensen relayed an interesting story about you causing quite a ruckus there. You and your cat." She raised an eyebrow and the corner of her mouth lifted in a sneer.

Holy cheese. She was enjoying this. I was close to having a heart attack from the way my heart was racing, and the sheriff was relishing the moment. No wonder they only needed a small police precinct in Widdershins. I suspected even hardened criminals would cower around Sheriff Markson.

The thought crossed my mind—was it a felony or a misdemeanor for owning a cat that trashed a café? While my judicial knowledge was limited, by the way the sheriff was looking at me, it wouldn't have surprised me if it was a felony.

"So, Miss Lovell, now I'm wondering why you didn't mention going to Christo's Café this morning, asking for Christo? And why do you think Mara is with him? I'm beginning to think you might be lying."

Don't faint! Don't faint! Lights danced in my periphery. Would fainting be an admission of guilt? I sucked in a deep breath and said nothing. Maybe I should ask for a lawyer? Isn't that what they do on TV? Oh, jeeze.

"You were home last night, weren't you, Miss Lovell?" The sheriff stood up and walked around the desk.

I nodded. I didn't like where this was going.

"And yet, you said you recognized Mr. Maximilian from Christo's Café."

My mind raced ahead, trying to anticipate her next question.

"I've had an anonymous tip that Mr. Maximilian might have paid a visit to your aunt's cottage yesterday evening, after you said Mara had left the house."

I sucked in another deep breath of air. I'm sure it made me look guilty, but I also thought that ship had sailed several questions ago.

Aunt Mara? If you can hear me ... help!

The sheriff eyed me for a moment longer before opening a drawer in her desk and pulling out a file. She slammed it down on the desk between us, making me jump in my seat. Tears threatened, and I blinked hard trying to stay them.

"How well did you know Marion Marigold?"

This was going from bad to worse.

Aunt Mara! I screamed as loud as I could in my mind. If she could communicate once, surely she could do it again?

"Who's Marion Marigold?" I asked, my voice trembling.

The sheriff pursed her lips. "While you were talking to your boyfriend out there, I got to thinking about an unfortunate incident that took place this morning. Now, we're still waiting on a toxicology report, but it's the second death in two days where the victim was found drinking your aunt's tea. Tell me again when you arrived in Widdershins, Miss Lovell."

I couldn't win. I worked my lip with my teeth in the hopes it would stop me from bursting into tears or fainting. I was on the cusp of both.

"Do you recognize any of these people, Miss Lovell?" The sheriff's lip curled ever so slightly as she opened the file and slid two eight- by eleven-inch glossy photos across the desk toward me.

I tentatively leaned forward to see better. The first one was of Marion. It looked like a professional headshot or something taken from advertising material.

The sheriff tapped a finger on it, and I shook my head. I'd never met Marion when she was alive, so in a way, I was telling the truth.

The sheriff tapped the second photo. "Well?"

It was a photo of the crowd I'd seen gathered in front of Miss Maisy's Tea Shoppe that morning. I was relieved it didn't show the other side of the street where I might have been seen poking my head out around the corner of the building opposite. I swallowed and hoped my voice would work.

"There's Mrs. Maisy," I said, pointing to the figure in the center of the photo. "And Mrs. Frieda. I met them both yesterday when I went in for a drink and something to eat." I cringed. Much like this morning's fiasco, it hadn't ended the way I had hoped.

"And?" the sheriff inquired.

I scanned the rest of the picture. It was possible I'd seen a few of them in passing but no one jumped out ... until ... almost hidden at the back of the crowd, I saw Jaystar.

"There's Jaystar," I said, pointing to him.

Jaystar. An ugly thought crossed my mind. He had been at the scene of the crime. He'd said he'd been out the back when Marion passed, but that wasn't to say he hadn't done something to the tea. I assumed he knew about herbs. His mom was a supplier, and he made deliveries to Aunt Mara. He'd been in Aunt Mara's apothecary before. In fact, he'd made a delivery to Aunt Mara yesterday. He'd also been super guarded about the strange vial of liquid he carried around with him. What if it was poison?

No. Jaystar couldn't be a suspect. And if my vision had been right, Aunt Mara had given the vial to him. And anyway, what motive could he possibly have? Sure, if he had feelings for Lucy, then getting rid of Man-Bruce might make sense. But why Marion? No. A strong enough motive didn't exist, I consoled myself. Plus ... he was Jaystar. He didn't seem like the killer type. But then neither did Aunt Mara. Or Christo. Or anyone else I had met, for that matter. Except for maybe the sheriff. And ... maybe Eli. Oh, sugar-sticks. Nothing made sense.

Three knocks on the door behind me made my heart leap to my throat. Even the sheriff jolted in surprise. The door swung open without an invite, and an all too familiar giant filled the doorway.

Eli.

"Afternoon, Sheriff Markson." His voice and stance were all business. He didn't even glance my way. "I'm Special Agent Eli Fisher, from the FBI. I can see you've been talking to Miss Lovell without her having representation. Miss Lovell is presently under my protection and helping with an out-of-state investigation. Miss Lovell, if you can please go outside, I need a word alone with the sheriff."

No way would the sheriff buy it. I was certain of it.

Eli kept his attention solely focused on the sheriff. Who, as if by magic, or maybe it *was* magic, suddenly turned into a syrupy teen. Her scowling, uptight façade disappeared. In its wake, she flashed Eli a smile, batted her eyelashes, and wound a loose strand of hair around her finger before demurely taking up the chair behind the desk and crossing her legs. I couldn't tear my eyes away. What had he done to her?

"Of course, Special Agent, come in. Please, take a seat," she purred, gesturing toward me. Noticing I hadn't moved, her features became sharper and her voice a little more venomous. "You can leave, Miss Lovell. I'll be in touch at a later time if I need more information."

I'd been dismissed. I was both relieved and flabbergasted. I'd barely left the room when the door slammed behind me. Who knew the way to the sheriff's heart was a good-looking man? Even as I thought it, I kicked myself. What if Eli was listening in to my thoughts? The last thing I wanted was him thinking I thought he was good looking. Sugar-sticks. That fire didn't need stoking.

The waiting room was empty. Thomas must have left. The clicking of nails on a keyboard suggested Betty was behind the counter.

"Hi, Betty," I said, finding her as I expected.

"You're free, are you?" she enquired with a warm smile.

"I think so," I said. "Mr—" I struggled for a moment, trying to remember what Eli had called himself. That's right. "Special Agent Fisher is chatting with the sheriff now, so I'm hoping that means I'm done for the day."

"Oh, yes, I'm sure you are. She doesn't really have anything to hold you with. I told her you weren't a murderer. I have a way of knowing these things. Just like I knew, one look at Mr. Handsome there and the sheriff would be putty in his hands. Carissa likes to act all hard-nosed and such, but I tell you, she really is a pussycat."

She had said so already. I still wasn't sure I believed it.

"I hope she wasn't too hard on you, dear? Let's just say her people skills need a little fine-tuning."

I couldn't argue with that.

"Betty, I was wondering if you could help me with something." I had to try. I wasn't ready to believe that Aunt Mara was behind Man-Bruce's death. And if she was in trouble, I needed to help her.

I also wasn't convinced the sheriff and her two minions were doing enough to track her down.

"I met this woman earlier today—Lucy? She works at Miss Maisy's Tea Shoppe, although she wasn't there today. Would you know her last name?" It was a long shot, but Widdershins was a small town. And with the police force being as small as it was, maybe Betty helped with the paper side of the cases. Surely, if the sheriff suspected foul play with Marion's death, there had to be a list of employees from the Tea Shoppe somewhere.

"Oh, yes. Lucy. She's a quiet one, isn't she? There's something unusual about her though I've never been able to put my finger on it. Keeps to herself a lot. I can't remember her last name off the top of my head, but it'll be around here somewhere. After this morning's incident—poor Marion, she was such a doll—I made sure to get a list of everyone who works at Miss Maisy's."

I'd been right. I gave myself a mental high-five. Maybe my thing was solving mysteries?

Oh gosh. I hoped not. The last two days had severely frayed my nerves, and I still didn't know where Aunt Mara was or who killed Man-Bruce or Marion.

Betty tapped away on her keyboard for a second.

"Here we are! Lucy Andrews is her name. Let me guess," she said, giving me a wry smile, "you'd like her address too?" She winked at me, and my cheeks warmed. Maybe she was a psychic?

"Umm ..." I wasn't sure how to answer. I did want it, but I also realized it was probably all sorts of wrong for her to give it to me. The thing was, Man-Bruce might be able to help me find out who really killed him, which might lead me to Aunt Mara. And as Man-Bruce wasn't talking to me, maybe he'd talk to Lucy. If she could see Gerry being chased by Hades, I suspected she'd be able to see Man-Bruce too. And it might be a good thing for Man-Bruce and Lucy—one last chance to say their goodbyes.

Betty chuckled. "Here we are." She scribbled an address down on a Post-it Note and pushed it into my hand. "Now just don't go telling Carissa what I've done for you. She gets a little tetchy when I give out personal details from our database."

I could imagine. Giving out information from a police database sounded like a big no-no. Though I also felt like Sheriff Markson was guilty of playing a bit loose with the rules too. I probably should have been offered a lawyer before she interrogated me. Or been read my Miranda Rights. Shouldn't I have?

And then we had Eli, who'd just marched in and assumed the identity of an FBI agent. I would bet money there were laws against that. And what was it Eli had told me the first time the sheriff had shown up at the cottage? Oh yeah.

"If I have to intervene and put the WBI at risk, Wonderland, you can bet things are going to get a whole lot more complicated for you!"

Yikes! How much more complicated could things get?

Chapter 19

"**G**et in."

Eli still hadn't looked at me. Anger wafted off him in waves.

He opened the car door for me, and I slid inside. I wasn't sure how I thought Eli got around, but it wasn't in a black BMW sedan. I guess the whole witch thing had me envisioning broomsticks or nose twitches.

He'd walked out of the sheriff's office with a smile on his face. The sheriff appeared in the doorway after him, almost hugging it to keep herself upright, a love-struck expression on her face. Whatever he'd done, he'd spelled her good.

But then, Betty, too, had nearly swooned when he gave her a smile and a nod. Color rose in her cheeks, and she fanned herself with her hand.

When he reached me, he'd turned into Mr. Serious again, grabbed my arm, and escorted me out of the police station without a word.

He slid into the driver's seat, turned on the ignition, put the car in gear, and pulled out from the curb. He was still silent.

Right. Well, two could play at that game. I'd ice him out too.

Nope. I couldn't do it. Too much was at stake, and I had too many questions.

"Where are we going?"

He ignored me, turned left, and pulled over beside a park with tall oak trees and a sign reading "Mystic Ire Park." He shut off the ignition.

Oh. This wasn't good. I glanced around. In the distance, a young woman with a small child on her hip pushed a toddler on a swing, but besides them, no one was around. No other witnesses. Oh lordy.

Eli clenched the steering wheel momentarily, then relaxed his grip, dropping his hands to his lap. He twisted in his seat to face me.

"Right, Wonderland. There are some things we need to get straight."

I swallowed. His jaw was tight, and conflicting emotions showed in his eyes. Definitely anger, but something else as well. Maybe fear?

"What I just did in there broke more rules than I can count. Up until now, I've tried to protect you, but if you don't start talking and helping me out, by Zeus ..." His voice trailed off, and he clenched his hand in a fist on his lap before relaxing it again.

Even though he was scary when he was angry, Aunt Mara—or her disembodied voice anyway—had said I could trust him. Maybe now was the time.

"I think I heard Aunt Mara's voice in my head," I said. "Back at the cottage."

He scanned my face, and I made sure not to glance away.

"What did she say?" he said slowly, obviously trusting I was telling the truth.

"That she was with Christo. And ... that I could trust you."

He exhaled loudly, his shoulders lowered, and relief settled on his features.

"You can," he said in a soft voice.

Fireworks went off inside. Finally, I felt like I might be getting somewhere.

"Christo's gone missing," I said. "Not even the police can find him. I think ... I think ..." The words stuck in my throat. "I think Aunt Mara might be in trouble. Her voice was weak. It wasn't strong like yours was." I hadn't wanted to admit it to myself, but now that I had, a wave of emotion threatened to drown me. I wiped at my eyes where a few tears were already escaping.

Saying nothing, Eli leaned over me and opened the glove compartment. He pulled out a thin box of tissues and handed them to me. I gratefully took a handful and dabbed at my eyes.

Pull yourself together, Alice. You don't know for sure anything has happened to her.

I sniffed and sucked in a big breath, balling the tissues into my hand. "What's a Reaper?" I asked, remembering back at the cottage him saying a Reaper had been killed.

"You really don't know anything do you?" He shook his head and sighed.

I shrugged. I really didn't.

"Reapers are the people who help souls cross over to the other side. It turns out that the guy you might have killed was a Reaper."

"Man-Bruce?!"

"Why do you and your boyfriend keep calling him Man-Bruce?"

"Jaystar's not my boyfriend! He's a friend!" I retorted, my cheeks warming.

He arched an eyebrow at me.

"And I call him Man-Bruce so I don't confuse him with Dog-Bruce." I realized how stupid it sounded as soon as I said it.

"That's a problem for you, is it? Confusing men and dogs?" The corner of his mouth twitched, and my face teetered on the cusp of full combustion from both embarrassment and irritation.

I tried to rein in my emotions and steady my breathing. I still had questions.

"Did *Bruce*," I said, leaving off the Man part of his nickname, "know he was a Reaper? Does that give him magical powers or something?" He didn't look the type to have magical powers, but I probably didn't either, and in theory, I had them even if they hadn't yet made themselves known.

"I don't think he knew. I couldn't get much out of him. That guy has a weird thing going on with his phone. And no, Reapers aren't magical. They're normal humans whose destiny it is to be a conduit for helping people cross over. They're essential to keeping order in the universe. When it's their time to pass, there's normally another one waiting in the wings. But when one dies suddenly—well, the next one might not be ready, which can create real havoc for the dead and the living. Hades is actually doing everyone a favor. Rounding them up and keeping them at Mara's until the next Reaper is ready was smart thinking."

Ha! Who knew there was a reason for Hades's ghost collection?

"The thing is," Eli continued, his face growing serious again, "the Council doesn't go easy on Magicals interrupting the balance like this. Killing a Reaper is one of the gravest of crimes. Mara's experienced with using special herbal concoctions to help Reapers through their transition. For some Reapers, suddenly seeing spirits can do a real number on them. But if she's killed a Reaper, even if by way of trying to ease the transition – well—that's a misuse of magic. Another major felony. It was only by pulling in some pretty big favors I was able to get on this case. If we can't figure things out soon, or find Mara, you're the scapegoat, and you'll be wishing the sheriff *had* locked you up on a murder charge. Things won't be so golden for me either. I was supposed to bring you in yesterday."

Yikes. It was a lot to take in, and yet part of me felt lighter—reading between the lines, I was beginning to believe Eli thought I was innocent.

I wondered how someone transitioned into being a Reaper. Maybe Man-Bruce's fascination with the afterlife, which Jaystar uncovered online, was a clue. If he was beginning to see spirits, I couldn't blame him for wanting to reach out to see his family again. I'd give almost anything for another chance to see my mother.

"Two more things, Wonderland, just to save us any more trouble: You don't go telling Non-Magicals you're a witch. There are some serious penalties if you do."

"What kind of penalties?" I asked.

Eli grimaced. "I think we'll leave that discussion for after we find Mara."

I gulped.

"Second thing, you need to get better at hiding your thoughts. You're an open book. It means anyone with even the slightest bit of ability, Non-Magicals included, can see and hear exactly what you're thinking."

That explained a lot. The taxi driver. Aunt Mara. Maybe even Betty.

Well. Can you see this? I thought indignantly, sending him a not-so-nice hand gesture with my mind.

The corner of his mouth quirked upward.

Sugar-sticks!

"It's new," he said. "Whatever you were doing to keep me out earlier, practice that. It's a good skill to have."

I didn't get it. Having my innermost thoughts broadcast to the world didn't seem like a great skill, and I wasn't really sure how to stop it from happening.

"You'll find magics are usually two-edged. Eventually, you'll be able to see into other people's minds and read their emotions just as easily."

So this was supposed to be one of my witchy talents? I couldn't help feeling a little disappointed. I tried to climb into Eli's mind for a moment to see if I could get a glimpse of what he was thinking.

"Nice try, Wonderland. I've been doing this for a lot longer than you. You're on a need-to-know basis."

I resisted poking my tongue out at him.

Eli started the engine. "Now, I'm taking you back to the cottage. I want you to stay in the basement. Mara spelled it so no one outside of The Lovells can use magic in it. That means if the Council grows tired of waiting and they send someone else to collect you, their magic won't work. You can hang out with Hades's haunts down there and entertain them until I've found Mara and maybe the next Reaper too.

The sheriff shouldn't be hassling you for a while. I've got her looking into something else."

My brain was working overtime. I couldn't go back to the cottage now. If everything Eli said was true, then I needed to clear Aunt Mara's name, as well as my own, as soon as possible, which meant finding Aunt Mara. And if something bad had happened to her, I couldn't just sit in the basement listening to angry ghouls complain because their afterlife wasn't living up to their expectations.

"I'm coming with you," I said.

"It's not going to happen, Wonderland." Eli shot me a look that might have made my legs give out had I been standing.

I will not let him intimidate me. Aunt Mara is the only family I have. I squared my shoulders and sat up straighter in my seat. Then I felt around in my pocket until I found the Post-it Note Betty gave me. I handed it to Eli.

"What's this?" he asked.

"Man-Bruce's girlfriend—and maybe the next Reaper."

"You surprise me, Wonderland," he said before pulling out from the curb.

Chapter 20

We pulled up alongside a tiny bungalow. Paint flecked off its pale lemon siding. The front yard was bare except for a narrow, cracked concrete path leading from the chain-link gate to the front porch. There was no fence. The gate stood alone, a pathetic attempt at gatekeeping if ever there was one. The lawn was dehydrated and tinged brown.

Don't judge a book by its cover, I reminded myself.

I checked the address with the number on the metal mailbox, which stood at a strange angle beside the gate. Forty-nine. This was it.

Eli and I sat there for a moment in silence. I was wondering what to say to Lucy. She'd been beside herself when I saw her last, made worse by Hades and Gerry's sudden appearance. I assumed that seeing spirits was new to her, and here I was about to tell her she might be a Reaper, a person whose job it was to help spirits cross over. On top of which, she needed to come to my aunt's house with me, a stranger, into the basement, where her first act of Reapership, if that was even a word, was to do away with the spooks my aunt's cat was hoarding, one of whom was her boyfriend. Deceased boyfriend.

It made my head hurt just thinking about it. But if she could get Man-Bruce talking about how he died, his information might help Aunt Mara. And who knew? Maybe Man-Bruce knew where we might find Christo. They certainly hadn't seemed very close, but they'd worked together, so it was definitely a shot.

"Right. Are you ready?" Eli said, killing the engine and unbuckling his seatbelt.

"You're not coming in with me," I said.

His eyes narrowed. "Of course I'm coming in with you."

"No way!" I said, holding my ground. "You haven't met Lucy. She's been through a lot. And no offense, but you're a little ..." I searched for the right word. "Intense."

He ground his teeth. "If you're sure about her being a Reaper, then you just need to get her back to the car so we can at least put a stop to another potential Armageddon," he growled.

Another? Armageddon? I had far too many questions, but right now, getting her back to Hollyhock Cottage was exactly what I wanted. Even if she wasn't a Reaper, she might still get Man-Bruce talking.

I climbed out of the car and made my way toward the small gate. For a second, I considered opening it and walking through, but I could feel Eli's eyes following me, and knew how ridiculous it would look. I walked around it instead, my eyes on the house, searching for any sign of life. As I drew closer, I could see around the side of the house. I glimpsed what might have been a flower bed with freshly turned over soil. The drapes were pulled in the windows, making it even more mournful and bleak. I crossed my fingers, willing Lucy to be home.

There was no doorbell by the front door. I knocked and held my breath, waiting for the sound of footsteps from inside. No one answered. I fought against turning around to check if Eli was still watching. If I did, he might want to join me, and I wanted a moment with Lucy alone. I lifted my fist and knocked again. This time, I heard a shuffling inside.

"Who's there?" a small voice called out from the other side of the door. I stayed myself from fist-pumping the air. Lucy was home.

"Lucy, it's me, Alice. From ..." Oh sugar-sticks, this could go poorly. "From Christo's," I finished, cringing as I did so.

"Alice?" she said, her voice wavering.

"I was hoping we could talk," I said. "I might be able to help you." A few seconds passed, and the lock clicked on the other side. My heart hammered in my chest.

The door opened slowly until I could see the pale, drawn figure of Lucy. Her hair hung limp around her face, and her cheeks were pink and blotchy. She had changed since I saw her earlier that morning, now wearing a shapeless green dress with buttons up the front.

I gave her a weak smile, conveying, I hoped, the empathy I genuinely felt for her.

"Can I come in?" I asked gently.

She nodded and opened the door wider to let me in.

The house, although worn, was marginally better on the inside. Twinkle lights hung down from the molding in the hallway. Oak planks made up the flooring, and the walls were painted pale green. A couple of pastel-colored paintings hung on the wall. The air held a strange elixir of warmth and sorrow.

I followed Lucy down the hall into a living area. It contained a couple of armchairs, a small two-seater couch with an array of embroidered cushions, a coffee table, a small bookcase with books, a reading lamp, and an oval rug. Everything looked like it had been sourced from a thrift store, yet somehow the aesthetic worked.

She eased herself down onto an armchair as if she were an old lady and not someone in her early twenties, if that. She appeared more wraith like than her actual deceased boyfriend. I pushed aside a few cushions and sat on the couch.

"How are you doing?" I asked softly.

Lucy sniffed and wiped her eyes with her palm. "You said you could help me?" she said, getting right to the point.

I nodded. "At Christo's," I started, "you saw him, didn't you? The man that my aunt's cat was chasing?"

Lucy shifted in her seat. Her bottom lip trembled, but she nodded. "You saw him too?" she asked, her voice barely a whisper.

"Yes," I said. "He's the first ghost I've seen. His name is Gerry," I said. "Am I right in guessing he's not the first ghost you've seen?"

Just ripping the band-aid off, eh, Alice?

The little bit of life left in her face drained away. Her eyes grew wider. She nodded again. So far, so good, I thought.

"What was your cat doing?" she asked, her voice wobbling.

I had to give her kudos for holding it together better than I'd expected. I hoped it continued, because things were only going to get weirder.

"Hades is my aunt's cat," I said. "He has a strange way of going about things, but he was actually trying to help Gerry." No one who had seen the pandemonium Hades caused in the café would have believed that, and yet, Lucy sat there, unmoving, like she was taking it in. "Lucy, I know you're going through a lot right now, but I need to ask you about Bruce."

"Bruce?" she repeated, her bottom lip trembled again. She wrung her hands in her lap.

"The police think he was poisoned. Have they talked to you about anything?"

She shook her head. "No one knew about us until yesterday," she said.

"No one knew you were in a relationship?" My heart broke for the woman in front of me. She was grieving the loss of her boyfriend all alone.

She shook her head. "No one in Widdershins," she said. "He wanted to keep it quiet. He didn't think his family would approve. But he loved me. I know he did." She sniffed loudly.

Family?! It took me a moment to remember the note at the bottom of the news article Jaystar had shown me about Man-Bruce having a distant relative. Could that relative be in Widdershins?

Stay focused, Alice, I reminded myself. I needed to get Lucy to the cottage.

"Lucy, could Bruce ... you know? See things like you?"

It took her a moment.

"At first he was excited," she said. "He read every book he could find on the subject. Mediumship. Occultism. He said he'd wake up and just see someone standing there at the end of his bed. Sometimes it would freak him out, but then he got to thinking that maybe he had a special gift. Maybe if he could see dead people, one day he'd be able to see his family again." She let out a small sob, pulled a scrunched-up tissue from her pocket, and blew her nose. "Other times, it got so overwhelming, he thought he was losing his mind."

I stab of guilt hit me in the chest. Maybe I'd done Man-Bruce an injustice. Being suddenly confronted by the paranormal was overwhelming. The unfairness of being able to see other people's loved ones but not your own ...

"Did he ever see his family?" I asked.

Lucy shook her head. "No. He tried everything he could to communicate with them, and got nothing. Instead, all these other random people showed up. And they all seemed to want something from him, only he didn't know what. I didn't believe him at first. I thought maybe all the stress he'd been under at work was getting to him."

He certainly hadn't seemed stressed when I saw him at Christo's. Disengaged and lethargic, yes. Stressed, no.

"He worked at Christo's, right?"

Lucy nodded. "They were going into business together."

Alarm bells started going off in my head. Business together? That didn't seem like the relationship I had witnessed. Last I had seen of Christo and Man-Bruce together, Christo was making plans to get rid of him. Oh lordy.

"They wanted it hush-hush until everything was signed off."

Was Man-Bruce who Marion had overheard arguing with Christo?

"Was Bruce getting help with handling his ghost sightings? Seeing anyone? Taking anything?"

She nodded and blew her nose again.

"Lucy," I asked, my heart hammering in my chest. "Do you know Mara Lovell?"

She sniffed, and her eyes locked onto mine.

"Yes," she said. "She killed my husband."

Chapter 21

Holy smokes, that had not been the answer I was expecting. She, too, thought my aunt had killed her ... her *husband*?! She didn't have a ring on her finger, but that didn't mean anything. My mind raced in several directions at once, competing with the speed of my heart.

I tried to think of what to say next. While I wanted to defend Aunt Mara, the truth was I couldn't be sure of anything anymore. Had Christo and Man-Bruce gone into partnership behind Aunt Mara's back, so she killed Man-Bruce as revenge? Or had Christo killed Man-Bruce and framed Aunt Mara because he thought the two of them were in cahoots? But then, didn't every murder-mystery show on TV link it back to the husband or wife? In which case, Lucy was now a suspect. And where were Aunt Mara and Christo?

I glanced around the room, half expecting another surprise. Someone to jump out and attack me, or better yet, clues to help any of this make sense. She didn't even have wedding—or regular—photos of herself and Man-Bruce together. Nothing to suggest Man-Bruce ever lived there, except for maybe something in the bookcase. Books on spirit communication, mediumship, and the afterlife were mixed among others on homeopathy and crochet.

My eyes traveled back to Lucy while my brain scrambled for something to say. A tear rolled down her cheek, and she wiped it away with the back of her hand.

"I'm not scared of you," she said.

Which was good, I guess. I was trying to work out if I should be scared of her.

Wonderland. What's going on in there?

Eli had somehow snuck into my mind. I wasn't sure whether to try to push him out or allow him to be there in case I needed backup. I chose to ignore him.

"Aunt Mara's gone missing," I said, trying to keep my voice steady. "I'm not sure what happened to Bruce, but I want to find out, and I think you can help. You can trust me. I promise." I scanned her face for a reaction. Lucy showed little sign of anything beyond grief. Other than dabbing at her eyes, she barely moved.

"How long have you been seeing spirits?" I asked.

"Since Bruce died. I've been seeing them. And other strange things too. I feel like I've been losing my mind."

"Were you with Bruce when he died?" I asked. Something I couldn't quite put my finger on wasn't making sense.

"I was in the shower," she said, a fresh wave of emotion hitting her. "I'd just got back from work. I'd had to go back because I'd forgotten something. Bruce must have arrived while I was in the shower. I found him …" Her voice broke and tears streamed unrestrained down her face. "He … he …"

My own grief threatened to break free. Losing someone was horrible, and there was no doubt in my mind how much Lucy loved Man-Bruce. I leaned forward and put my hand on her knee.

"It's okay," I whispered. "I'm so sorry this happened."

"He was at the kitchen table. Your aunt's herbs were beside him. He'd made a tea." She broke down fully and covered her face with her hands.

I left my seat and moved to put my arm around her. While losing my mom had devastated me, I'd had time to say my goodbyes. I couldn't imagine losing my soulmate so suddenly.

I tried to put the pieces together while Lucy sobbed. She must have called the sheriff, herself. And if all the evidence had been there, leaving no suspicion around Lucy, it made sense for Aunt Mara and I to be on the suspect list. Seeing poor Lucy like this, I doubted even the sheriff would question Lucy's innocence.

When the sobs started to fade in intensity I moved back to my chair.

Wonderland. What's going on? If you don't answer me, I'm coming in.

I'm fine, I thought back at Eli. *Just give me a moment.*

I swear I could hear a low growl in the recesses of my mind.

"Lucy?" This was a delicate question, but I had to ask. "Have you seen Bruce since he passed?"

She eyed me for a moment and then slowly nodded. "Texts," she said.

I didn't understand, and she must have seen it on my face.

"He texts me. All the time. I haven't seen him, but I get his texts. Except they disappear. I've gone back through my phone, and there's nothing."

"Text messages?" I asked, trying to put it all together.

She nodded. "Sometimes it's him telling me he loves me. Other times it's about the business he was starting with Christo. I started writing them down in a notebook. The texts—they fade so fast. It's like he's wrapping up loose ends. Bruce never took out life insurance. Everything was wrapped up in this business. So he texted me bank account numbers. Where to find all the paperwork. Addresses. Everything.

He'd always talked about how this business was going to set us up for life. We could pay off our student loans. Buy a house. That sort of thing. I never asked much about it when he was alive. It was something he was doing with Christo. He wanted to bring me into it, but he was choosing his time. He said Christo was acting strange. Paranoid, even. Accusing him of going behind his back and working with Mara. Which wasn't true. Bruce sought Mara out to help him with the spirits he was seeing. He couldn't even tell Christo we were married. He thought it would cause more trouble. I think Bruce wanted to pull out, but everything, his and my savings, it was all tied up in this herbal supplement and tea business." Lucy took a deep breath and wiped her nose again.

I'd been listening open-mouthed. Man-Bruce was dead and yet somehow he'd been able to text Lucy. It explained why he was always glued to his phone. It also eliminated Lucy as a suspect. Didn't wives kill their husbands for their life insurance? Lucy said Man-Bruce had none, and his and Christo's business had barely gotten off the ground.

Unknown to Christo, she might be his new business partner, but that didn't mean she'd be rolling in money right off the bat.

What surprised me the most, I guess, was Christo. He had come across so friendly and lively when I met him. And yet there was another side I'd been hearing about from Marion and now Lucy. A paranoid, angry side. And wherever he was, Aunt Mara might be with him. My stomach flipped.

Before I could say anything, a loud knock thudded on the door. We both startled. Lucy's eyes widened.

"Alice! Open up!"

Eli. A wave of relief washed over me. Not so much Lucy though, whose hands gripped the arms of the chair like she was trying to decide whether to run.

"Just a minute!" I called back.

"Who is that?" Lucy asked, her voice trembling.

"That's Eli. He's a ..." I actually wasn't sure what Eli was. "A friend," I finished. "He drove me here. He thinks he can help. I know this is going to sound really weird ..." Understatement of a lifetime. "But we can take you to Bruce, so you can see him. In person."

"But he's dead," Lucy whispered.

"He is," I said. "But he hasn't crossed over. He's still here. I think that's why you've been getting messages from him. He needs to see you first."

"Alice?!" Eli's voice rumbled from outside the door.

Give me a moment! I said as loudly as I could in my mind. This was a precarious situation and somehow I didn't think him banging on the door and yelling was helping any.

"Do you trust me?" I asked. Witchy or not, I did my best at trying to send calming, trustworthy vibes her way. Astonishingly, it seemed to work.

"You're telling the truth? I'll get to see Bruce again?" Her eyes pleaded with me.

"I promise," I said. I stood up, relieved to see her do the same.

"I ... I just need to grab something," she said.

I gave her a smile as she made off down the hall in the opposite direction. I headed to the door ready to face whatever temper was waiting on the other side.

Opening it, I came face to face with the towering intensity of Eli, his face a mixture of emotions—fear, anger, worry, and, dare I say, relief.

"What took you so long?" he growled under his breath, glancing down the hall behind me.

"What were you doing in my head?" I hissed back.

"I was worried about you."

Sugar-sticks. He looked like he'd meant it. Something fluttered in my chest, and I pushed it down.

"Hi," he said as Lucy took a step out from behind me. "I'm Eli." He stood there, all awkward for a moment. "I'm sorry for your loss," he mumbled.

Lucy said nothing, but I glanced at her out the corner of my eye. A hint of a blush showed high on her cheeks. Eli certainly had a way about him.

Eli led the way to the car. I let Lucy sit in the front while I sat in the back. She'd brought a small bag with her. Crocheted by the looks of it. She clasped it tightly on her lap.

None of us said anything. My brain was too busy trying to predict what was going to happen next. Lucy and Man-Bruce would say their goodbyes, that was one thing. But maybe Man-Bruce might share something else about his death or about Christo or Mara. And if I was right, then Lucy, as the new Reaper, could happily send the rest of the spooks crowding the basement, on their way.

I felt a growing panic that time was running out. If Eli had been telling the truth, and if we didn't clear things up soon, the High Council, whoever they were, might just swoop in and take over the case—charging me for the murder of a Reaper and for misuse of magic. Magic, that I still didn't believe I had.

Something else suddenly dawned on me.

"Lucy. You said something about Bruce texting you an address?"

Eli raised an eyebrow at me in the rear-view mirror.

"Yeah," she said.

"Do you remember what the address was?"

Where are you going with this, Wonderland?

I'm not sure, I replied. *I'm going to call it intuition. And get out of my head!*

Eli pulled the car over on to the side of the road.

"I noted it down here," Lucy said, scrambling in her bag to find something. She pulled out a small pocket-sized notebook and flipped through it until finding what she was after. "36 Greenacre Place."

Eli tapped the address into the GPS.

"It sounds fancy," I said.

"It's on the industrial side of town," said Eli.

"Any idea why Bruce gave you this address?" I asked Lucy.

"No," she said. "But it seemed important. We *are* still going to see Bruce though, right?" she asked, swiveling around to face me, her eyes welling again.

Eli pulled the BMW back onto the road.

"One quick detour first," he said.

I reached out and gave Lucy's hand a squeeze. She didn't argue.

It didn't take long to get there, which I supposed was a perk to living in a small town. Everything was close by. It helped that Eli had his own sense of what the speed limits were. I suspected he had his own rules for most things.

On the way, streets of bungalows and leafy trees had given way to corrugated iron façades and large graveled lots with sprawling block buildings. Overgrown grass grew on the berms lining both edges of the road. Another five minutes, and buildings were even sparser. We'd made it into the country.

Eli slowed the vehicle. The GPS was indicating for us to turn right. At first glance, the side road was invisible, hidden by overgrown grass and a few tall trees on either side. When we took the turn, I realized we'd hit a gravel road. On the left stood empty paddocks of long grass. In the distance on the right stood a big block storage unit surrounded by a tall chain-link fence, topped with rolled barbed wire. Were they trying to keep people out, or people in? I wondered. It was a blemish on what could otherwise have been beautiful country land.

Eli pulled up to the front gate. Also, chain-linked but with metal bars reinforcing it. A sign read "Trespassers Will Be Prosecuted." Two cameras angled down from the top of the fence to where we had pulled up. I thought I could see more around the building and fence line in the distance. The red corrugated iron façade met a gray angled roof.

While I couldn't see any people or vehicles, there was every possibility they were hidden around the back of the building.

"Why would Bruce give you this address?" Eli asked Lucy.

"I don't know," she whispered.

"Is this the site for Bruce's and Christo's business?" I asked.

Eli's eyebrows shot up. "Christo and Bruce were working together?"

"Herbal supplements and the like. It's why they wanted Aunt Mara on board, I guess."

Eli's eyes grew dark. I wished I could read his mind.

Lucy said nothing.

Do you think Mara is in there? he asked.

Possibly, I thought back. *Aunt Mara said she was with Christo.*

My heart sped up. *Please, please let Aunt Mara be inside*, I thought, knowing in all likelihood Eli was still listening in.

"Are we going in?" I asked no one in particular.

Lucy shifted uncomfortably in her seat.

A phone rang, making me jump. It took me a moment to realize it was coming from my back pocket. I had forgotten it was there.

"Alice?" the voice said as I answered. "I think we have a problem." It was Jaystar.

My chest fell. Now was not the time to be adding more problems to the list.

"I can't find Hades," he said.

"What do you mean?" I asked. Hades was supposed to be helping guard the people in the basement. I couldn't very well expect Jaystar to do it, considering he couldn't even see them.

"I mean, he just disappeared. He was down here, I guess guarding our guests, and so I thought it would be alright to go upstairs and make a sandwich. I came back down, and he's gone."

"What's going on?" Eli asked.

"Hades has disappeared."

"So?"

"So, Jaystar can't very well ..." I tried to think of how to choose my words carefully. I finished the sentence in my mind. *He can't very well guard people he can't see!*

He doesn't need to, Eli retorted. *I've already told you, for whatever reason, your aunt has a binding spell set up on the apothecary. It means no magic besides Lovell magic works down there. It also has the side effect that without a Reaper, those spirits can't leave even if they wanted to.*

It didn't make any sense to me, but our basement guests had said as much, I remembered. They'd tried to leave and couldn't.

"Alice. Some weird stuff's going on. I don't think our *guests* are very happy."

I didn't realize Jaystar was talking again.

"What do you mean?" I asked.

"I mean, lights flickering, furniture rocking. I feel like I'm in a poltergeist movie. It's all a bit freaky to be honest."

Right, so now we also had a room of upset ghosts on our hands. As long as no one turned up at the front door, like the sheriff, it would probably be okay.

Eli killed the car's engine and opened his door.

"What are you doing?" I asked, my mind flying to the thought that Eli was going to go in without me. If Aunt Mara was in the warehouse, I needed to be there.

"Stay here. I'll be back soon," he said stepping out of the car.

"I'm coming too," I said.

"If this place belongs to Bruce, I want to go too," a small voice said. I had almost forgotten Lucy with everything else.

A scratching sound came from the trunk making me jump.

"No way! You two stay here!" Eli's orders made my hackles rose.

Since when was he the boss?!

"Alice? What's going on? I can hear Eli, but who else is with you? Where are you?"

"That's Lucy," I said. "Man-Bruce's wife."

"Man-Bruce?" Lucy asked clearly confused.

"Wife?" Eli and Jaystar said at the same time.

Sorry, I mouthed at Lucy. Way to disrespect the dead, I reprimanded myself.

Eli's eye's darted between me and Lucy; then he turned his back to us and headed to the gate. He was not going in without me. I scrabbled to undo my seat belt. The scratching sound increased behind my seat.

"What about the cameras?" I called out to Eli as my seatbelt finally unfastened.

Looking at me, he pointed a finger from one camera to the other. Sparks flew from the white boxes. My jaw dropped. It was both impressive and down right scary. When was I going to get those kinds of powers?

"I'm sorry, Jaystar. I have to go," I slid across the seat and opened the door. Eli was fiddling with the lock on the gate.

"Wait!" Jaystar said. "What do I do about your *guests*?"

"Nothing," I said. "They can't leave, anyway. Just ... I don't know. Have another sandwich?"

"But ... Alice! I think ... I think I'm ..."

I didn't hear the rest; I'd already hung up. Boy, did I owe Jaystar.

I made it outside of the vehicle. I guess Lucy had ignored Eli's requests to stay put, too, because she was already a few steps ahead of me. As I closed the car door, I swore I heard a whine coming from the back of the vehicle.

Sugar-sticks! I was torn—I wanted to run and catch up to Eli and Lucy, but there was something back there, and I couldn't leave it.

Again with the scuffling. A few choice words flew through my mind as I tried to open the trunk. "Eli!" I called out.

He turned and glared at me, a finger to his lips shushing me. He'd gotten the gate open. Maybe it was better to send my thoughts to him.

I need the trunk open. I think we have a stowaway.

Eli's jaw tightened and he balled his fists. Then with an exaggerated sigh he clicked his fingers in my direction and the trunk sprang open.

A black ball of fuzz burst from its confines. What the— How? Hades had gone back to the cottage with Jaystar. He absolutely could not have been in the trunk all this time.

Tail held high, he trotted to Eli, ignoring me entirely.

"Thanks for rescuing me!" I whispered after him sarcastically. Stupid cat.

I quickly joined Lucy, who'd kept a few paces behind Eli. She wore her bag like Jaystar, across her body, and held it with one hand against her side. She seemed not to notice when Eli pointed his finger at the visible cameras around the building. Lucy's gaze seemed entirely focused on the building ahead of us.

Suddenly, Eli turned around to face Lucy and me.

"You two need to go wait in the car." His expression was stern. "We don't know if it's safe."

"Nuh-uh," I said shaking my head. "If the cat goes, I go."

"Hades can look after himself," Eli said through clenched teeth. His anger and frustration made the air around him flicker with orange and red spikes. Well, that was new. Also, scary.

"Bruce wanted me to find this place," Lucy said in a quiet voice. "If this is the business he shares with Christo, then doesn't that make this place part mine?"

She had a point.

A low growl rumbled through my head.

"Keep close!" Eli had obviously given up trying to make us stay behind.

The four of us, Hades leading the way, walked up to the front of the building. A large roller door faced the road. We couldn't get in that way. Hades, strangely enough, seemed to know exactly where he was going. He strutted along, tail up, not a care in the world. Probably enjoying the drama. We followed him to the left along the side of the building. He paused at the corner, making Eli stop too. Lucy and I waited for Eli to peer around the corner of the building before moving alongside it again. We did the same.

When we reached a green door on the side of the building, Hades put a paw up to it, patted it a few times, and then looked at Eli.

Something was off about things. The air around us was almost fizzing. I couldn't put my finger on it, but despite the heat of the day, goosebumps had formed on my arms.

Feel that? Eli asked.

I nodded.

I need you to stay out here with Lucy. One Reaper down is bad, to lose another one is something I don't even want to think about. Eli's eyes held mine a moment longer than normal. My heart sped up.

I nodded again in understanding.

Eli held his hand up to the door. The edges of his hand glowed red. Was Lucy not seeing this, I wondered? Surely a normal person would be freaking out right about now?

The door moved a few inches, and my eyes fell on Hades, standing between Eli's feet. He was like Eli's wingman, a soldier standing at the ready to follow his commander into war. I suddenly felt a rush of protectiveness toward him, toward both of them: Eli and Hades. Sure, they got under my skin at times, but they were here for Aunt Mara. Maybe even for me.

Lucy went to follow Eli and Hades through the door, and I grabbed her arm. "We need to wait here," I whispered.

Her eyes widened. "What do you think's in there?"

"I don't know. What do you know about this business Bruce and Christo were setting up together? How was Aunt Mara involved?" I whispered to her.

"I told you. I don't know a lot. Christo didn't even know Bruce and I were together. Bruce wanted me to be involved, but I didn't pay a lot of attention when he talked about it. It was only when things started to go sideways and Bruce said Christo was acting weird that I started to really listen. We'd invested everything. Our livelihoods were at stake.

"Mara was supposed to be helping them manufacture the teas and some of the herbal concoctions or at least supply them with her recipes or something. Bruce said Mara's teas flew off the shelves at the café. Customers raved about them. Said they were like magic. Christo and

Mara's contract for selling them at the café was ending. Christo wanted to not only extend it but to go bigger. There had been talk about commercializing her teas. Selling them online and overseas. There was a big market for them in China. Bruce already had contacts lined up. Christo had promised he could get Mara on board, but it turned out he couldn't. And for whatever reason he began blaming Bruce."

Holy cheese. The more Lucy told me the more I began to suspect Christo. Why hadn't she drawn the same conclusion?

"Lucy?" I asked. "How did Bruce meet Christo?"

Lucy stared at me for a minute, a small line forming between her eyebrows. She swallowed.

"Christo is Bruce's uncle."

Chapter 22

A   *lice!*

The voice was loud. It rattled the insides of my skull, like someone had screamed though I was the only one who could hear it.

Alice! Get out! The voice was weaker but marked with the same urgency.

It was Mara's! I knew it with all my being. She was close by. She was inside. A loud bang echoed inside the building. It was closely followed by a second. Holy guacamole! That did not sound good!

Lucy flinched at the sound, crouching down and covering her head with her arms.

"What was that?" she asked, her voice trembling.

"I don't know." I leaned against the side of the building, blood thundering in my ears. Mara was inside! I needed to get to her. My head spun. I put my hands against the side of the building to steady myself. The warmth from the sun-cooked corrugated iron heated my palms, until it felt like my hands were on fire, and the sheet metal was melting beneath them. I closed my eyes to block out the near-roaring in my head.

Everything seemed to slip away, and I felt weightless, suspended in nothingness. I was sure my eyes were open again, yet I couldn't see anything. Darkness engulfed me. And then all too soon, I was shocked back into my body, winding me. I closed my eyes tight against the blinding light and felt cool concrete beneath my palms and through a tear in the knee of my jeans. I gasped for breath and blinked hard, acclimating myself to my surroundings, the roaring in my ears fading as I did so.

Holy cow, I was inside the warehouse. How had that happened? It looked like a greenhouse—or the beginnings of one, at least. Aisles divided most of the space. Closest to me were low basins of plants. Herbs at first glance. Farther down the aisles, stood vertical racks of trays. Tubes and piping ran the length of each section and along the ground. Racks of LED lights were suspended from the ceiling, some in between the aisles, and looked as if they could be lowered, lifted and maneuvered to suit. Smaller tubing ran in and out of the basins of trays from plant to plant. The air was warm and moist, and heady with the scent of vegetation. Behind me were pallets with items swathed in plastic wrap, with containers of colored solutions and more tubes and piping. A sticker on one pallet read Nutrient Solution. Large unopened wooden crates were stacked to the side, behind which I could just make out a door. The space was huge.

A low pounding filled my head as I tried to come to grips with what had happened. A noise from the other end of the warehouse made me jolt upright onto my knees. I glimpsed movement dashing between the vertical racks at the far end of the space.

An arm grabbed me around my middle from behind, another hand clasped itself firmly across my mouth. When I tried to scream, nothing but a muffled cry came out. My captor half lifted and half dragged me behind one of the crates. I struggled but still felt so weak and disoriented. A sharp swipe at my ankle brought me back to my senses.

Hades! The beast! I was being assaulted and instead of helping, Hades had taken a swipe at my ankle and was now glaring at me while I struggled to free myself.

"Sshhh!" a warm breath whispered in my ear. "I told you to wait outside," Eli growled, and all at once, relief and embarrassment washed over me.

He released his hand from my mouth, and I shuffled away to make some space between us, as he slid fully to the ground beside me. His face was unnaturally pale, beads of sweat appeared on his brow. The hand that had been locked around my middle now clutched his left shoulder. A red stain bloomed out from beneath his palm.

Eli was hurt!

Nausea swirled in the pit of my stomach. I'd seen enough cop shows to know what sounds like a gunshot and bleeds like a gunshot is probably a gunshot.

A loud bang made me jump and cover my head with my hands.

"It's okay," he said softening, trying to calm me. "It was just a door. He's gone."

I scanned Eli's face, and I bit my lip to stop it from trembling. The pressure of tears built behind my eyes.

Hades was snuggling up to Eli on his good side, head-butting and purring at him, nonplussed by it all.

"It's okay, Wonderland. It's just a flesh wound. Bullet nicked me, that's all. If it weren't for Hades getting under my feet when he did, it could have been much worse."

Hades. Hades might have saved his life. I don't think I had ever loved a cat more.

Tears escaped, and I quickly wiped them away with my hand.

"Good puss-puss," he cooed before grimacing in pain again.

Lights danced before my eyes, and I tried to will myself back into my body. Now was not the time to faint.

Focus, Alice! I needed to help Eli. And Aunt Mara! Was Aunt Mara here? And holy cheese, I'd left Lucy on her own outside. What if she came face to face with the person who shot Eli?

I shook with shock. A tsunami of panic began to take hold.

"Wonderland!" Eli's voice cut through my panic. He grabbed my arm and pulled me closer, making me focus on him. His eyes held mine and my breath hitched as a strange electricity vibrated through my veins, stemming from where his hand touched my skin.

"It is going to be okay." He said each word slowly, his eyes searing it into my psyche until I almost believed it. A strange fluttering in my chest set my senses alight, and for the briefest of seconds it was just Eli and me. No one else. Nothing else. Only the blue of his eyes, the gold flecks that radiated out from his pupils, and my reflection.

All too suddenly he released my arm. The spell broke. He shifted his body, his eyes darting away from me, and clamped his hand back over his shoulder. I instinctively rubbed my arm where he had touched me. The electricity between us gone. I felt calmer, for sure, and my mind was clearer, but the underlying sense of loss was unsettling. Had he spelled me? Was this what he did to the sheriff to make her all smitten with him? The idea came with a sense of heaviness. Another thing to push away. Now was not the time.

"We need to get you fixed up," I said, spurred to action. I scoured my surroundings looking for something. "We need a tourniquet or something." I really didn't know if that was what we needed; I was purely going off the movies I'd seen.

"We don't," Eli said. "It should be safe now, so we need to get to Mara. She'll sort my arm."

"Aunt Mara's here?" I asked my heart leaping in my chest.

Of course, Alice, you heard her yourself! I had. I remembered. Right before I somehow transported myself here. Only she sounded panicked.

I pushed myself to my feet and held out my hand, ready to haul Eli up with me. He went to reach out, then pulled his hand back, as if reluctant to touch me. Instead, he used it to push himself up from the ground.

Was he feeling as weird about things as me?

"Where is she?" I asked, "Where's Aunt Mara?"

"Follow me," he said. "Hades?"

He gave the cat a nod, and Hades stalked around the side of the crate keeping us hidden. He came back in a few seconds, tail high, and gave a short mew.

"Good boy," Eli said.

Hades gave his leg an affectionate head-butt. I took it to mean the coast was clear.

With Hades leading the way, I followed behind Eli. He headed to the door I'd seen half-hidden when I'd first arrived. It opened easily, and I pushed past Eli, mindful of his arm, as I threw myself at Aunt Mara.

"Aunt Mara! Aunt Mara!" My hands scrabbled at the ropes binding her to the chair, fresh tears burning my cheeks. My fingers felt like useless sausages, making no impact upon unknotting them.

"Well, it took you long enough, my girl," she breathed. Her voice was raspy and teasing. "Eli, can you please help me out here?"

Eli moved me aside and bent down to help her. Even with only one arm at capacity he made short work of unbinding her.

I couldn't believe what I was looking at. It was a small office. A desk on one wall. Packed boxes beside it like someone was in the process, I assumed, of moving in. Aunt Mara was in the center of the room. She looked tired. Older than I remembered her. She had a red cut on her forehead with a bruise forming around it. A strange smell hung in the air, one I recognized but recoiled at.

"It's dill," Aunt Mara said, as if—no, most likely—reading my mind.

"Why in Zeus—" Eli started.

"People believe it tempers the magic of witches. He rubbed it all over the rope."

Dill. I'd never much had a taste for it. I guess, now I knew why.

"So he knows you're a witch?" Eli asked, his voice tense.

"No. He *thinks* I'm a witch. There's a difference."

Good to know.

"Are you okay?" I asked, relief and fear competing for my attention.

Eli had found a pack of water bottles on the floor behind the desk. He unscrewed the cap on one and brought it over for Aunt Mara. I kneeled beside her, scanning her with my eyes for any other injuries.

Aunt Mara accepted the bottle and took a long drink. Her hands shook as she held the bottle.

Who had done this to her? And why?

I suspected I knew who, but it made me nauseous to admit it.

"Give me space, child. I'm fine." Her tone was warm despite her words.

Eli handed me a bottle of water too.

"He got away," Eli said. "I hadn't been expecting a gun."

Holy cheese! I'd almost forgotten.

"Eli was shot," I said to Aunt Mara. "I ... I don't know what to do?" My voice wavered.

"It nicked me, I'm okay."

Hades had made himself at home on Aunt Mara's knee. She stroked him with one hand while he purred. Her eyebrow raised in Eli's direction.

"Show me," she said.

Eli shot me a look, and with a sigh, started unbuttoning his shirt. Oh lordy.

Aunt Mara caught my eye and raised both eyebrows. I blushed and glanced away.

"We need to get the two of you to a hospital," I said, refusing to make eye contact with either one of them.

"Nonsense," Aunt Mara said. "We have bigger fish to fry, and we have everything we need here."

I resisted looking around the room in case I caught sight of Eli, but it certainly hadn't seemed to be overflowing with first-aid goods when I'd first walked in.

"Help me up," Aunt Mara said, her tone leaving no room for argument.

Hades stretched and then dropped on to the floor. I knelt down beside Aunt Mara and let her put an arm around my shoulders while I wrapped mine around her waist. Together, we struggled to stand upright. Suddenly, Eli was on the other side of her, helping her up with his free arm. Pain drew his features taut. I was thankful to see his shirt was unbuttoned enough to pull over his shoulder but nothing more.

"Alice, go grab a couple more bottles of water. Eli can help me out."

I did as she asked, Eli taking her weight off me. The two of them slowly moved toward the door and out into the main warehouse area. Hades followed. I searched behind the desk and found another couple of bottles of water left in the pack. I eyed the area for anything else that might be helpful, but as I didn't know what I was looking for, I found nothing.

Eli and Aunt Mara had parked themselves on a pallet of plastic-wrapped gear. I approached them and placed the water bottles on the ground.

"On the wall over there," Aunt Mara said, pointing to my right. "There's a first-aid box."

It was hanging on the far side of the building, just visible behind the basins of plants: a large, white metal box with a red cross painted on it. I hurried over, unlatched it and studied its contents. First aid was another thing on my list of not being my forte. Blood made me queasy for starters. I focused on my hands, my attention following the trail of blood up my left arm where Eli had held me. I blinked back tears. Eli had been shot, and Aunt Mara held hostage and hurt. Who would do such a thing?

The same person who killed Man-Bruce and Marion was the obvious answer.

I guessed I'd need bandages, tape, scissors, gloves, but figured just to take the whole thing.

Once I worked out how to remove it from the wall, I rushed back to where Eli and Aunt Mara waited. Their heads were close together, and they were whispering. Between them a small bunch of herbs with small yellow-and-white flowers were being deftly shredded, mostly by Aunt Mara who was plucking the leaves and flowers off the stems and making a small pile. They stopped talking as I approached.

"What do I do?" I asked still holding the first aid kit in my hands, which were trembling.

Eli took it from me, opened it, and placed it on the pallet between him and Aunt Mara.

"Should I call 911?" I reached into my back pocket for my phone.

"Calm down, child, it's not so bad as that. What we need is to get Eli temporarily bandaged up; then we need to get back to the cottage."

"The cottage?" Right. Jaystar was there. And a basement of spooks. And Lucy ... Lucy was still outside. "I need to go get Lucy!" She was probably scared and wondering what had happened to us. That was, if the shooter hadn't gotten to her first.

"One thing at a time," Aunt Mara said, her voice returning closer to its usual self.

Eli said nothing. He'd barely spoken a word this whole time.

"A bottle of water, please." Aunt Mara gestured to the bottles on the floor. I held one out to her, and Eli took it from my hand instead.

Here he was bleeding, and Aunt Mara was likely suffering from exhaustion, maybe a concussion, and I had no idea what to do. I fidgeted with my fingers and wrung my hands.

Eli eyed me, and I stopped fidgeting.

He pulled open his shirt a little more and poured the water over his wound, his teeth clenching as he did so. The blood made a pink trail down his shirt and chest. Lights danced before my eyes again.

"How did you get in here?" he asked, as he went about making a small pile of the herb on the inside lid of the first aid kit.

"I—" Sugar-sticks. I wasn't sure. I suspected Eli knew better than me and was trying to distract me.

Aunt Mara poured a little water over the flowers and leaves. "Crush it up in your hand," Aunt Mara said to Eli. "It's not ideal, but it'll do until we can get you fixed up properly."

Eli followed her instructions.

"I was outside with Lucy," I said, forcing my mind to replay what had happened. "And I heard a bang. A gunshot." I glanced at Eli, swallowing hard to quell the nausea.

"It's just a graze," he said, not looking at me.

"Good. That looks good," Aunt Mara said, focused on the green mash on the first-aid box lid.

"Alice, can you get a piece of gauze and surgical tape ready, please?"

I followed Aunt Mara's instructions.

Eli picked up a handful of the mushy herbal paste and smothered it over his wound. His jaw tightened, and I swallowed. It hurt to see him in pain.

"Your turn, Alice," Aunt Mara said.

Come on, Alice. You've got this. Gauze and tape. Easy.

Swallowing another wave of nausea, I attended to him the best I could, with him holding the gauze in place as I taped around it. Aunt Mara unpackaged a sling and handed it to me. I helped Eli into it.

"It's yarrow," Aunt Mara said, indicating the paste remaining on his hands. "Also called soldier's woundwort. It's antiseptic and stops bleeding. It's also used in love spells. And for instilling courage and increasing psychic powers. Fortunately, it's one of the first plants Christo has seen fit to grow." She pointed to one of the plant beds.

"Water, please," she said gesturing to the other bottle at her feet.

I picked it up, unscrewed the lid and held it out to her. Eli held his hands out and Aunt Mara poured water over them, giving him a chance to wash the remains of the herb off his hands. After rinsing, he wiped them on his pants. We were a right sorry-looking lot.

"What else do you remember about getting in here?" Eli asked.

"I heard her voice," I said, nodding to Aunt Mara. She seemed to be regaining some of her strength. Color showed in her cheeks. "You were warning me to get out. I thought my head was going to explode."

Eli locked on Aunt Mara's face.

"Then?" she asked.

"I don't know," I answered truthfully. "I think I leaned on the wall, and everything went funny and disappeared, and then it was like I was floating." It made me uneasy thinking about it.

Eli and Aunt Mara exchanged another glance.

"Why? What happened?" I asked in a shaky voice.

"You teleported," said Aunt Mara. "It's a skill few witches are blessed with. Apparently, you are one of them."

My mind fizzed and cycled through every sci-fi movie I'd seen. "Teleported?" I asked.

"Yeah," said Eli. "Let's keep this one between us for the moment, eh?"

I wasn't sure who exactly I would tell. It wasn't like I had done it intentionally.

"The Council restricts teleportation," Aunt Mara said. "It seems your magic is awakening though. That's good. I'm pleased you could hear me, though you need to work on protecting yourself from people accessing your mind."

"I've told her the same," Eli said.

"What happened to you, Aunt Mara?" I bit my lip, unsure I really wanted to know. Hades perked up and jumped onto Eli's lap. Eli patted him with his good hand.

"There'll be time enough for stories later; right now we need to get back to the cottage. Jaystar will be needing us."

"Jaystar?" I asked.

Neither of them said anything. Their silence was infuriating.

"Well, we need to find Lucy first," I said.

"Lucy's gone." Eli scratched the top of Hades's head. The cat gazed up with doe eyes at his man-crush.

"What do you mean gone?" I asked, my blood turning cold.

"I had Hades check while you were getting the first-aid kit. She left with Christo."

Holy cheese. It had been Christo I'd seen behind the plant racks. Which meant it had been Christo that shot at Eli, and Christo that had held Aunt Mara hostage.

My heart raced. We needed to go. Lucy could be in trouble.

"I suspect it won't be Lucy who is needing our help right now. It'll be Jaystar," Aunt Mara said, heaving herself to her feet.

"Jaystar? What does Jaystar have to do with this?"

"Oh, my dear," Aunt Mara said, with a strained chuckle. "If my intuition is right, he has everything to do with everything."

259

<h1 style="text-align:center;">Chapter 23</h1>

"Do you think Christo is heading to the cottage, then?" I asked, my eyes flitting from Aunt Mara to Eli.

Aunt Mara nodded just as Eli said, "I suspect so."

"Well, then we need to hurry!" I wrapped my arm around Aunt Mara's waist, ready to assist her. "We need to get to the car!"

"There's no time," Eli said, scooping Hades into his arms and standing up.

"What do you mean?"

"I mean they already have a head start on us. We'll have to teleport. I'll send Nix and Crowley back for the car later."

My stomach dropped. "Isn't that restricted by the Council?" The idea of going through a repeat of the disorientating whiplash I'd experienced earlier made me feel ill.

"It is."

"But I don't know—"

"Not you, child. Eli will take us," Aunt Mara said, cutting me off.

So Eli could teleport too. He was one of the few Aunt Mara had mentioned.

I barely had time to ready myself. With Hades positioned on Eli's good shoulder, he took two strides and wrapped his healthy arm around both me and Mara. My cheek pressed against his chest. Before I could even protest, it felt like my legs went out from under me. The air fizzed with electricity. I blinked.

"Holy guacamole," I said breathlessly. Eli released me from his grasp, and I took a step back to acclimate myself.

Hades jumped down from Eli's shoulder as Aunt Mara sent me a look.

"Close your mouth, child. You'll catch flies." She sighed.

Right. It took me a moment to realize where we were. The cottage loomed above, but I was seeing it from a new angle. We were in a small yard area. A few hedges stood behind me, and instead of the cobbled wall I was used to seeing there was a worse-for-wear wooden fence. It wouldn't have surprised me if it were the same part of the fence line I had gotten a glimpse of in Mrs. Whittle's video footage. If I were to move aside some boards and climb through, I suspected I'd find a couple of discarded spray paint cannisters. I'd need to tell Aunt Mara about that later.

Just within my line of sight to the left, was the curve of a driveway.

"Why aren't we inside?" I asked.

"Element of surprise," Eli whispered back. "Hades?" he said, looking at the cat lounging on the ground in front of us.

Hades sat up as if a soldier standing to attention. Eli gave a small nod in the direction of the front of the house to our right, and Hades ran off. I assumed Eli had just sent him on recon duties.

A noise came from the left. Before I could even turn my head, I was sucked into the hedge behind me by an invisible force. Sharp twigs and brush tore at my skin. I went to call out and caught myself just in time.

"Hands up!"

My heart leaped into my throat. Between the gaps in the foliage, I saw Aunt Mara and Eli holding their hands in the air.

Stay quiet! Eli's words came at me with force.

I bit down hard on my lip trying not to make a sound. Barely breathing.

"Well! Look who we have here. Agent Fisher and Ms. Lovell, hiding around the side of the house. You know, Agent Fisher, this woman is the lead suspect in a murder investigation. Yet here you two are skulking around the side of the house, covered by the looks of it, in blood." It was the sheriff's voice, but she was still out of view.

"If you let me put my hands down, Sheriff, I could explain. You don't want to be making false accusations against an FBI agent now, would you?"

Aunt Mara and Eli shuffled slightly bringing the sheriff and Officer Jonas into view. They were holding guns. I willed my legs not to give way under me. This was not good. Not good at all. I was sure if Eli or Aunt Mara were able to use magic, they'd be able to get themselves out of this predicament, but of course, there were rules. Stupid rules like not letting Non-Magicals know you're a witch, although Eli hadn't gone out of his way to hide his camera-killing, door-opening skills in front of Lucy. Maybe there were different rules about letting Reapers know.

The sheriff and Officer Jonas were closer now. Their guns still aimed at Aunt Mara and Eli. How long before they saw me hiding in the bushes?

I closed my eyes against the roaring panic building in my head. Pieces of conversation floated through my confusion. Whatever spell Eli had put on the sheriff at the station had well and truly worn off. She was almost as snarky as she'd been with me. I caught something about taking them down to the station and something about Eli's car being seen, leading them here, but my mind seemed incapable of focusing on their conversation. My breathing was labored like I was close to having a full-on panic attack until something cut through the noise in my head. If they'd followed Eli's car here, then Christo must've stolen it. Christo and Lucy were already here, which meant Lucy and Jaystar were in trouble. I had to do something.

Stay where you are, Wonderland! a voice growled in my head. *And keep it together! The High Council takes note of unregistered teleportations. I put you at risk by bringing you here. You've already got a target on your back.*

Eli was eavesdropping. His warning did nothing to quell my rising anxiety. Keeping calm—also not a talent of mine. And it wasn't like I knew how to teleport at will.

A heat rose inside me, sweat broke out along my hairline. Eli was saying something, but I couldn't grab onto it, the roaring in my head had intensified. I needed to get to Jaystar. I needed to get to Lucy.

A weightlessness took over, and my eyes snapped open. It was happening again. I wanted to call out, but I couldn't. I didn't need to. I was on my knees again. Voices spoke behind the static in my head, and I was aware of bodies around me. It had happened so much faster this time. It was still more intense than when Eli did it, and I was still disoriented, trying desperately to focus on my surroundings.

"Alice! Alice! Are you okay?" One voice cut through the rest. Jaystar was kneeling on the ground beside me, his arm around my shoulders. "What the heck was that?!"

"I ... I ... Oh, my gosh, Jaystar! You're alive!" I threw both my arms around him, my joy at seeing him overwhelming any distant thoughts of him being the bad guy.

"Of course I'm alive." He gave a nervous chuckle. "Should I not be?"

I pulled away to look at him properly and wiped away a tear that had escaped. His face was beet red, which in turn made me blush. I might have overdone things in my excitement.

"Wait, Alice! You're covered in blood!" Some of the color drained from his face.

I looked down at my arms and chest. I was. I was a mess.

"It's not mine," I said. "It's Eli's."

"Eli's?"

"It's okay. He's fine. I think. I don't know. The sheriff has Eli and Aunt Mara outside at gunpoint, and Christo and Lucy, they're here. In the house I think." It was a deluge of words. Jaystar's face contorted into a myriad of expressions, ending with him speechless, mouth wide.

"Lucy?" A voice from behind us said. "Lucy's here!"

We were in the basement. We had an audience. Most of whom were regarding me as if *I* were the ghost. Man-Bruce pushed himself to the front of the crowd, more animated than I'd ever seen him.

"Lucy's here?!" he asked, raking a hand through his hair.

"Christo has her. He also has a gun. We need to be quiet." The full extent of the situation was coming into focus again. "She got your texts," I said.

His eyes welled, and my heart went out to him. I really hoped Man-Bruce and Lucy got to say their goodbyes before the day was through.

"Why is Christo here?" Jaystar asked.

"He kidnapped Aunt Mara when she went to have it out with him about lying to their investors that she was on board with his and Man-Bruce's business."

"Man-Bruce and Christo were in business together?" Jaystar asked, standing up and pulling me to my feet with him.

"Man-Bruce?" Man-Bruce's eyebrows shot up. "My name's Bruce."

"Oh, yeah. Sorry. Bruce," Jaystar said, blushing again.

"Wait a minute!" My brain fought to keep up. "You heard him?!" I turned to Jaystar. And he wasn't shivering, I realized. The last time we'd been in the basement he had nearly turned blue.

He nodded slowly and shuffled his bag on his shoulder. "I tried to tell you ... on the phone."

My mind backtracked. Oh lordy. He'd been trying to tell me, and I'd hung up on him.

"I'm so sorry," I said. "But I don't understand. If you're not a witch and not a Reaper, how can you see them? You couldn't see them before."

He gave a one-shoulder shrug. "I don't know." Leaning in, he whispered to me. "And it's really not what it's cracked up to be. Other than Marion, all these guys have done is complain."

"I heard that!" Purple-Perm said, indignantly.

"I'm missing Happy Hour," Smoker-Guy said, blowing a cloud of smoke.

Gerry was sitting on a chair, elbows on knees, holding his chin, looking more glum than ever.

"We've got a plan," I said to the freaky foursome, "but right now I need you to be quiet."

Marion stepped forward. She'd been so quiet in the background I'd almost missed her.

"Your aunt's okay?" she asked.

I nodded.

"Good. We'll help any way we can," she said. She gave each of the freaky foursome a pointed look.

I gave her a smile. It was good to know at least one of our guests had our backs.

I surveyed the room. Furniture had been moved and several things were lying on the ground that hadn't been there when I'd left. It looked like they'd put Jaystar through his paces.

"He'll be here for the book," Bruce said.

Confused, I furrowed my brow at him.

"Christo. If he's here, it'll be for the book. If he can't get Mara onside the next best thing is her book with all her herbal remedies and stuff. He's convinced she has one. And it's not the first time he's come searching for it. If he's here, he'll be seeing this as his last-ditch effort."

I studied Bruce's face, trying to understand why he was suddenly Mr. Helpful. I guess the thought of seeing Lucy again appealed to his good side. I tried to think back if Aunt Mara had ever mentioned a book. Of course! The family's Book of Shadows! That must be it.

Aunt Mara had said something about someone looking for it. And thanks to one of the Tweedles I knew exactly where it was. Not that it mattered. It was blank. I'd seen it with my own eyes. And it had been spelled so it couldn't be taken from the room. Christo wasn't going to be happy. A lightbulb went off in my mind—if Christo had been in the basement looking for it, then he'd had the opportunity to tamper with Bruce's tea.

Footsteps sounded from upstairs. I swallowed hard. Sugar-sticks! If this was Christo, I had zero plan. He had a gun. Sure, we had five ghosts, but I wasn't sure how helpful they'd be against a bullet.

Jaystar must have heard it too. His body went rigid, his eyes darting around the room. He raced over to where Gerry slumped in his chair and grabbed the lamp that had fallen on the ground. It had a heavy base. I assumed he planned on using it as a weapon. Holy cheese!

"Over here!" he mouthed at me, gesturing as he crouched down by the wall shielding the staircase.

I did the same. We wouldn't be able to see anyone until they were in the room, but they'd have their back to us. With nowhere else to hide, it would have to do.

Marion, Bruce, Purple-Perm, and Smoking-Guy stood up, clearly interested in whatever was to happen next. Even Gerry perked up in his chair. All eyes focused on the staircase.

The door opened to the basement, and a sudden thunder of paws clambered down the stairs.

"Damn cat!" a voice hissed from the top of the stairwell.

My heart leaped into my throat. I was sure it was Christo's voice.

I gripped Jaystar's arm. Damn the sheriff. She should have been down here, arresting Christo, not outside with guns pointed at Aunt Mara and Eli.

Jaystar twisted to face me. He lifted a finger to his lips and went about slipping his bag strap over his head, handing it to me. He leaned close, his mouth almost touching my ear. "I was keeping it safe for Mara," he whispered. "If something happens to me, it's in there." He turned away and lifted the table lamp in his fist.

I had no idea what he was talking about. I gripped his messenger bag in my hand and let go of his arm. Blood rushed in my ears. Was Jaystar really going to try attacking Christo? A lamp versus a gun. How in Hercules were we going to get out of this?

Chapter 24

Hades raced into the room. I prayed he wasn't going to give us away. Instead, he leaped onto Aunt Mara's workbench, where he'd have the best view of the basement, and waited. He glanced in our direction and then locked eyes on the staircase.

Two sets of footsteps made their way down the stairs.

The light in the stairwell threw an elongated shadow onto the floor. The footsteps paused at the bottom step. Jaystar blocked my view of who it was.

"How is it so cold in here?" The slight European accent was undeniable.

Jaystar held the lamp upside down, the cord wrapped around its base. It shook in his hand.

"Shh!" Came a hiss from behind. "The sheriff might still be outside."

Christo stepped into the room. I could see him now. Back to us, unknowingly facing a line-up of ghosts.

"Lucy?" Man-Bruce's voice trembled as he stepped forward, spurring Jaystar to action.

He leaped from his crouched position, hefting the lamp over his shoulder like a softball bat.

Time seemed to slow down, and Christo must have sensed something. He partially pivoted in Jaystar's direction just as Jaystar swung. The base of the lamp connected with the side of his head. Thwack! Christo's arms flew up, followed by a leg. Then, with a sickening thud, he hit the ground, sunny-side up.

A squeal escaped from Lucy. I rushed to join Jaystar, who stood stunned over Christo's body, his face drawn of color, mouth open. His eyes traveled down his arms to the lamp, and he released it, letting it crash to the ground.

"Impressive!" Smoker-Guy said, nodding in approval before taking a puff on his cigarette. Gerry had covered his face. Marion and Purple-Perm looked away.

"Is he dead?" I whispered.

"I don't think so," Jaystar breathed.

"Bruce?" A small voice heavy with emotion came up behind us.

I turned to Lucy, then recoiled, grabbing Jaystar's arm and pulling him with me.

"What's going on?" Her voice was shaky, the handgun wavering in her grasp. One moment, she aimed at Jaystar and me, the next, she covered our ghostly visitors.

"Bruce? I can see you! You're really here?!" A sob broke free, but she still pointed the gun with both hands, her eyes wild, unsure who to aim it at.

"She's going to kill us!" Gerry moaned, his mouth and jowls trembling. He'd placed his hands on the chair arms, looking as if he were ready to bolt.

"Oh hush, you nincompoop! You're already dead!" Purple-Perm barked at him.

Smoker-Guy smiled, obviously amused.

Bruce took another step toward Lucy, his arm outstretched, palm down as if to placate her.

"Lucy. It's okay. You're safe," I said. "Christo can't hurt you."

She spun to face me, bringing the gun with her.

"How are you here?!" she asked. "We have your car." The gun shook even more in her hand.

Something wasn't right. My mind raced trying to piece things together.

"It must have been her," Jaystar whispered to me.

"Shut up!" she cried, tears rolling down her face.

Jaystar and I took another small step back.

"Can you do something?" Jaystar whispered to me. "Use your magic?"

"I don't have any magic," I said, my stomach clenching. "I got here by complete fluke."

Sugar-sticks! Sugar-sticks! Sugar-sticks! What use was a witch without magic?

"Lucy, hon. This isn't like you. Put the gun down." Bruce moved toward her. His voice was calm, but he wore his emotions plain on his face. Love, grief, and fear.

"Brucie," Lucy whimpered, her focus back on him. "Who are these people?" She pointed the gun at the group of spooks behind him.

"They're no one," he said, his eyes never leaving her face.

Smoker-Guy and Purple-Perm harrumphed together.

"Put the gun down, Lucy-Bell. You're okay. It's going to be okay."

Not a single trace remained of the moody, apathetic Man-Bruce I'd been acquainted with. Just a man trying to help the woman he loved from doing something she would regret.

I needed to help them but didn't know how.

As Man-Bruce stepped closer, Lucy lowered the gun slightly.

"I'm here, Lucy-Bell. You're going to be okay."

"I'm not!" she said, shaking her head violently. "I did this. It was me. I am so sorry!" Fresh sobs wracked her body. My heart was both breaking for her and terrified of her.

It took me a second to realize Jaystar had taken up my hand in his and held it close to his side. I wasn't sure if it was meant to comfort, or to stay me from doing anything.

"It wasn't you!" Man-Bruce argued. "You're not a murderer."

Lucy shook her head again. Whatever she was thinking seemed to be causing her horrendous pain.

"You used my mortar and pestle," she said, between sobs. "I hadn't cleaned it. You used it for your tea. I hadn't meant to hurt you." She sank down to her knees, head hanging. "I'm so sorry, my love. I'm so, so sorry. I ruined everything."

I looked at Jaystar speechless. Had Lucy just confessed?

A moan came from Christo's direction. He rolled his head slowly side to side. We needed to wrap things up before he woke. Christo had kidnapped Aunt Mara and held her hostage. Just because he hadn't killed anyone didn't mean he wouldn't try.

"And me?" A woman's voice asked. "Was there a reason you killed me?" Marion stepped forward to join Bruce and Lucy. Her face was stern.

My stomach dropped. This couldn't have been what she had in mind when she said she'd do what she could to help. Jaystar took another step backward, pulling me with him.

"I'd invested a good deal of money to help Bruce and Christo with their start up. So why kill me?!" Her hands were on her hips, the air around her tinged with red.

Behind her, Smoker-Guy leaped onto the couch and perched himself on its back, shoes on the seat cushions. He leaned forward, elbows on knees, and rubbed his hands together, cigarette hanging from the corner of his mouth. "Now it's getting good!" he said grinning.

Gerry let out a half-moan, half-sob, and Purple-Perm muttered something under her breath before shooting him a withering look. Smoker-Guy raised his eyebrows in faux surprise and then chuckled.

Purple-Perm stood up from her chair and marched over to where Jaystar and I stood.

"I've had quite enough of this nonsense. You said you were going to help us move on. My husband will be wondering where I am."

Holy cheese! Could she not see this really wasn't the time?

"Lucy's a Reaper," I whispered to her. "She'll be able to help you. Give her a moment." I sent her a look to stress my point.

She swiveled on her feet and stormed over to Marion. Christo gave another moan, his head lolling to the other side, though his eyes remained closed.

"Enough of this foolishness! You apparently have a job to do. We've waited long enough."

Marion gave Purple-Perm a steely glare. "First, I want to know why she killed me."

Man-Bruce, who'd been on his knees trying to comfort Lucy the best he could, glared at the two women.

I took inventory. Now we had three angry ghosts, a grieving woman with a gun, and a mostly-unconscious kidnapper on the ground. And I still had no idea what to do.

I let go of Jaystar's hand. Even without a plan, I had to do something.

"Lucy?" I said as gently as I could while taking a step toward her. Jaystar tried to pull me back, but I shrugged off his hold.

The three spooks and Lucy swirled around to face me. Lucy, to my shock, brought the gun with her. She lifted herself to her feet, the gun aimed at my chest.

"It's your aunt's fault!" she said, taking a step to me. She lifted her arm to wipe tears and snot from her face, not releasing hold of the gun. "She refused to help them. Bruce and Christo were going to bring her on board. Cut her in. But she refused. And she wouldn't share, either! Christo said she has a book here somewhere with all the recipes, everything. It would have set the business apart, but she wouldn't share!"

She stamped her foot like a child. Her hair was damp around her gaunt face. Her dress hung like a sack. She looked like a child, I realized, in more ways than one. Her emotions were unbridled.

"When I overheard *her*"—she turned on Marion momentarily, flashing the gun in her face, before angling back to me—"telling your aunt that she'd be pulling her money, getting her lawyers onto killing the contract, all because your aunt wasn't onboard ... I ... I couldn't let her do that!" She looked in Bruce's direction and choked back another sob. "We had plans. This business was going to set us up for life."

"Lucy-Bell," Bruce cooed. "It's okay. The business will still survive. You and Christo can run it. I texted you all the important stuff. She'll get you the book," he said, indicating me, "and you'll have the recipes."

I wasn't giving them my family's Book of Shadows. Besides, I was pretty certain the High Council would have something to say about me doing so, and I suspected it wouldn't be good.

"You killed me so I wouldn't pull my investment?!" Marion exclaimed.

"Well, I had to do something!" Lucy argued, pointing the gun back at her. "And it was easy. You and your special tea. Every Monday morning! As soon as I finished my shift, I went home. I had monkshood in our garden. I knew what it could do. I used gloves, ground it up, put it in a baggie. I didn't need much. When I got back to the Tea Shoppe, I said I'd forgotten my phone. It was Mara's fault you were pulling out, so it made sense to add it to Mara's tea, especially put aside for you. It was the end of the day. No one knew. No one saw. It took seconds. If anyone took the fall, it would be Mara—and it would serve her right!" She stamped her foot again, punctuating her point. Even now she thought she'd done the right thing.

Both Marion and Purple-Perm looked appalled. Even Man-Bruce appeared slightly taken aback.

Christo groaned again from the floor.

Please don't wake up! Please don't wake up! I pleaded.

"I used that mortar and pestle," Man-Bruce said, quietly. "Mara always said the tea would work better if you ground it yourself. It was supposed to acclimatize me to seeing ghosts, not make me one."

"I didn't know what to do," Lucy sobbed, focusing again on Bruce. "I got home, and you were unconscious, and it was all my fault. You'd left everything out. Mara's bag of herbs right beside the mortar. The empty mug of tea was there on the floor where you fell. I had to act quickly. I pulled the monkshood, the entire flower bed, and buried it all. I showered before I called 911 and told them I found you after my shower. The sheriff believed me. All the evidence was there. Mara killed you. She already has a reputation in Widdershins with her herbs. And I had no motive. There was no big payout. No life insurance waiting for me."

Holy cheese! Lucy may not have killed Man-Bruce, but she was capable of much more than I could have imagined.

"I need the book!" she said, all her focus laser-pointed on me. "I need the book!"

"Shh! You don't want to bring the sheriff," Man-Bruce tried to calm her.

Christo groaned again. This time his right arm jerked.

Oh, I hoped the sheriff had heard her yell.

"When is she sending us onward?" Purple-Perm whined.

"No one's going anywhere until I get Mara's book!" Lucy waved the gun wildly around the room. Even Smoker-Guy put his hands up for a second. Then she aimed it back at me.

I looked at Jaystar. He nodded at me.

The thing was, nothing was in the book. I knew that.

The gun's safety latch clicked off. Holy guacamole. I didn't know what other choice I had.

"Get me the book!" she ordered.

"Do it!" Man-Bruce said.

I was back to disliking the guy again.

Christo's leg jerked.

Lucy had closed the gap between us. She was not much more than arm's length. If she pulled the trigger, I was done for.

Everyone was watching me. I slowly made my way toward the couch where Smoker-Guy was perched. He was the only one unaffected by the emotion in the room.

"Of course the book's in the bookcase," he said as I made my way behind the sofa.

Crowley had found it hidden in the bookcase, and I remembered Eli making him put it back. Oh gosh, I hoped Eli and Aunt Mara were okay. I hadn't heard a word from Eli since being in the basement. I knew the room was spelled so only Lovells could do magic within its walls, so maybe it extended to no magical thoughts being allowed in too.

"Hurry up," Lucy said.

Man-Bruce followed along with her.

I'd placed Jaystar's messenger bag over my shoulder and across my body like how he wore it. He'd said he was keeping something safe for Aunt Mara in there. Something magical, maybe? If I had a chance to look inside ...

I squealed as the gun barrel poked the side of my ribs.

It probably wasn't going to happen, I realized.

I hadn't paid attention to the shelf Crowley had hidden the book on, so I just went about pulling books and allowing them to drop to the floor, feeling guilty that I was messing up Aunt Mara's space.

"Where is it?" Lucy asked.

"I don't know," I replied. "What are you going to do when you get it, anyway? The sheriff is just outside." Oh, gosh, I hoped she was. It was also possible, not knowing anything was going on inside, she'd already stuffed Eli and Aunt Mara into the back of her car and trundled them off to the precinct. "And what about Christo? He's half of the business."

"Bruce gave me all the bank accounts," she said.

Man-Bruce nodded, shaking his phone at me.

"I'll take the book, transfer the money, and set up somewhere else. Bruce will help me."

I glanced at them. Lucy had lowered the gun slightly and was gazing at Bruce in a way that made me uncomfortable. For all their faults, their love appeared genuine.

"Man-Bruce is *dead*," I said, ruining the moment.

Nice one, Alice. I'm sure she knows that!

They both wheeled to face me. Lucy's bottom lip quivered, her eyes—glassy. Man-Bruce scowled.

Lucy jerked the barrel of the gun at me again, and I went back to pulling books from the shelf.

Finally, I glimpsed it, pushed to the back of the deep shelf, half-obscured by a row of books on herbology. The thick leather spine was cast in shadows. As my fingers brushed its surface, my skin tingled. This was my family's grimoire. A beautiful book full of blank pages. I wasn't sure how I felt about that.

"Did you find it?" Lucy asked peering over my shoulder.

Another moan traveled from the other side of the room.

"Alice, he's waking up!" Jaystar said, sounding rattled.

I sent him a look. I wasn't sure how to help him. *The lamp. Can you use the lamp again?* I had no idea if the thought would reach him.

Lucy nudged me again with the gun. I turned back and tried wheedling the book out of its hiding place. It was really heavy. I remembered its size from when I first saw it. I wasn't even sure if I'd be able to lift it to hand it to Lucy, and Lucy was such a waif, herself, I wasn't sure she'd be able to carry it either.

Finally, I pulled it free from the shelf. It rested in my hands, lighter than I had expected, though still of a certain heftiness. Unknown, yet familiar, sigils were engraved into its cover. The book seemed to pulse in my palms. Electricity streamed into my hands and up my arms, like a pleasant form of pins and needles. The certainty hit me: this was *my* book, my grimoire.

"Give it to me," Lucy demanded.

I hesitated, my eyes darting around the room, searching for an alternative. Everyone was focused on me. A streak of black stole my attention. I had totally forgotten about Hades.

Hades flew across the room. He launched himself in the air toward Gerry. Gerry must have glimpsed something in my expression. He twisted in his seat, his jaw dropping, terror tattooing his features as the hellion hurtled his way. A shrill banshee cry erupted as he flung himself from his chair, just as Hades landed on the seat cushion. Gerry belly-flopped onto the ground, sending reverberations around the room despite his spectral mass.

Lucy and Bruce spun around. Lucy squealed, her arms jerking upward, gun still in hand. Hades, limbs outstretched, claws extended, sprang at them. A shot fired, and Lucy yelped in surprise.

Without thinking, I lifted the grimoire above my shoulder and struck Lucy hard against the back of the head. She crumpled to the ground just as Hades slammed into Man-Bruce's chest, pushing him backward through the couch, making Smoker-Guy leap to his feet. Man-Bruce's head and shoulders stuck out from under the couch. I wasn't sure how Hades could physically interact with ghosts, but he crouched there on his chest, ears back, a low growl emanating from deep inside.

Dazed, I held the grimoire in my hand. I'd never hit anyone before. Adrenalin pulsed through my veins. Bruce struggled under Hades, but somehow Hades anchored him to the ground. The gun had fallen out of Lucy's hand, and I gave it a small kick to send it skidding across the floor, just like they did in the movies.

Smoker-Guy clapped a round of applause.

Purple-Perm stood up, her face even more ashen, and hand clutching her chest. "Well, I never ..."

Marion held her hand over her mouth, eyes round. Gerry rolled onto his back, and I swore tears rolled down the side of his cheeks.

A thundering came from upstairs, drawing my attention to the stairwell. Near the bottom stair, Jaystar kneeled beside Christo, the lamp once again clasped in his hand. His hair was standing up at the front, mouth slightly agape, eyes locked on me.

"Lucy ..." Man-Bruce whispered.

Hades answered him with a jaguar's snarl.

Footsteps pounded down the stairs. Eli was the first in the room, followed closely by the sheriff, gun in hand.

My arms shook, the book suddenly feeling so much heavier than moments before.

Eli's eyes swept the room in seconds, then he was there, with me, his hands on my shoulders. "Wonderland!" he breathed. "Are you okay?" His face was close to mine, eyes scanning my features.

I nodded dumbly, then shook my head as tears welled and my legs weakened.

He looked down at the book in my hands, recognition crossing his face. He glanced behind him and I followed his line of sight. The sheriff was checking Christo's pulse, gun still drawn. Her attention going between Christo and Jaystar.

Eli grabbed the book from me. Quickly bending down, he pushed it under the couch where Bruce lay, and grabbed a hardcovered book from the floor, which he pressed into my hands with a severe expression.

Squatting at Lucy's side, he checked for a pulse. After a moment, he wiped his face with his hand and exhaled heavily. Turning, he called out to the sheriff, "We have another one here. She's breathing."

"Alice!" a voice called out across the room. Aunt Mara appeared at the bottom of the steps with Officer Jonas peering over her shoulder. Aunt Mara's jaw dropped as she, too, surveyed the room, no doubt also taking in the spooks in their varying states of shock.

"We need an ambulance," Sheriff Markson barked at Officer Jonas. He seemed not to have heard her. "Now!" she ordered, snapping him to. "This is now an official crime scene. None of you are going anywhere." She stood up, locking eyes with those of us still standing and breathing. "And what the heck's going on with that cat?!"

Hades still growled and hissed at Man-Bruce, who had continued to call out for Lucy.

"Hades," I hissed. "Leave him alone. He can't go anywhere."

Hades stood up, stepped off Man-Bruce's chest, and jumped up onto the couch where he curled up and promptly fell asleep.

"He probably thought he was protecting you," Eli whispered to me.

I almost smiled—he probably had.

Chapter 25

The ambulance arrived and collected Christo and Lucy, both of whom had regained consciousness and, with support, could now stand and walk.

Man-Bruce had tried to stop the paramedics from taking Lucy. But other than the unexplained temperature drop they felt, the paramedics had no way of knowing he was there.

Lucy sobbed, imploring Bruce to stay with her. She struggled against the paramedics' vise grip. Handcuffed, and as weak as she was, it was a dismal effort. From the looks the paramedics and the sheriff exchanged, they thought she was crazy. And she probably was. But she was also grieving. How does a person not go crazy when they've accidentally killed their soulmate?

Bruce tried to console her by telling her over and over again that he loved her and she would be okay. I don't think any of us who heard him believed it.

Christo—escorted out by the sheriff and Officer Jonas—spent the entire time pleading his innocence and arguing that whatever he was being accused of was a big misunderstanding. I don't think anyone bought that either.

Whether it was because the sheriff now deemed Special Agent Fisher trustworthy again, or because an understaffed police department allowed no alternatives, she left Eli to supervise us while she saw Christo and Lucy off.

Man-Bruce had slumped to the floor at the bottom step. His face was blotchy from crying, and his zombie-like apathy seemed to have embraced him again.

Purple-Perm had not stopped whining about returning to her husband since everything had happened. I'd done my best to ignore it, but it was certainly taking a toll.

"What now?" I asked. *Perk up, Alice. Happiness is a choice, remember?* Yet I was all too aware I'd failed. Not in getting Aunt Mara's name cleared of murder—that was looking like a done deal. Jaystar and I had relayed Lucy's confessions to the sheriff about Bruce and Marion's deaths. I was sure they'd find monkshood buried in the side garden at Lucy's, and they could check for that in Marion's tea at Miss Maisy's Tea Shoppe too.

The sheriff already knew Lucy and Man-Bruce were married. Lucy had told her the night Man-Bruce died. But it was news to Christo, and he was furious on finding out. Although he hadn't killed Bruce, it would have made things so much easier, inheriting the entire business as Bruce's only living relative. The sheriff saw first hand his temper, which made it even more believable that he had kidnapped Aunt Mara.

I guessed Eli and Aunt Mara had filled in a lot of gaps when the sheriff was trying to arrest them. Whatever had gone on upstairs while Jaystar and I were in the basement, had to be a story in its own. One I'd hopefully hear about later.

Where I had failed was in helping Hades's haunts.

I'd promised to help them move on to the other side. Also, there was the whole, "messing with the balance of the universe" and "cataclysmic consequences," or whatever it was that Eli had implied would happen if a Reaper didn't do their job. Problem was, as of seconds ago, our Reaper had been hauled out in handcuffs.

Aunt Mara interrupted my thoughts. "We've got a few moments to move these spirits on before the sheriff returns." She placed her arm around my waist, drawing Jaystar in as well, and squeezed us both to her for a moment.

"Don't you need a Reaper for that?" Jaystar asked, thinking the same thing as me.

Aunt Mara gave Eli a wry grin.

"Yes, we do!" she said.

"Our Reaper just left in handcuffs," I reminded her.

Eli massaged his brow. "Lucy's not the Reaper," he said. He leaned against the workbench. Hades nuzzled his arm until he reached out and scratched between his ears.

"*You* are?" I asked. I thought witches and Reapers were two completely different things.

Aunt Mara chuckled. "No, child. Think again," she said.

My brain had done about enough thinking for the day. In fact, I'd had about enough of this day, for the day. I would have been happy to go up to my room, crawl into bed, and start all over again tomorrow.

"Jaystar, when did you start seeing and hearing ghosts?" Aunt Mara asked.

My breath hitched.

He shrugged a shoulder. "I didn't at first. After a while, when Marion was walking with me, I thought I could feel her nearby. And then things just became clearer, I guess. I thought I was seeing glimpses of things while I was down in here and Eli and Alice were out looking for you. And then I could hear them. And then they all got angry at me because I wasn't sending those two "—he pointed at Purple-Perm, and Gerry—"to the afterlife, and that guy—"he pointed to Smoker-Guy—"back to the pub."

Oh sugar-sticks.

"But, Lucy—" I said in protest.

"There are rules, Wonderland. You can't be a Reaper when you intentionally take a life. Lucy killed Marion."

I glanced from Eli to Aunt Mara to Jaystar. His eyes had grown wide.

"Um ... what does that mean?" he said in a shaky voice.

"That means, my child, you—Jaystar—are Widdershins's new Reaper."

Holy cheese!

Jaystar's mouth opened and shut in silent protest. I was as surprised as he was.

"I ... I ... don't understand," he said, running his hand through his hair.

"We'll explain things later. Right now you have a job to do." Aunt Mara was back to being all business. "Normally, there's a gradual transition into a position like this that takes weeks, sometimes even months. You've had a few hours to get used to the idea, but you'll be fine. Reaping itself is all very easy. We'll start with Mrs. Shirley since she's driving us all nuts."

"Well, I never!" Purple-Perm indignantly stamped her foot.

Aunt Mara sent her a withering look before gesturing for her to come forward.

I moved over to stand beside Eli, not sure what I was going to be witness to.

"Mrs. Shirley—hold out your hands. Palms up, please."

Purple-Perm pursed her lips before doing as she was told.

"Jaystar, when I say, I want you to slowly put your hands, palm down, on top of Mrs. Shirley's. Then I want you to center yourself, just as I've been teaching you. Three breaths in, and on the final exhale, Mrs. Shirley will be reunited with her husband—and we get a break from her incessant whining."

With a harrumph, Purple-Perm glared at Aunt Mara. Aunt Mara ignored her.

Jaystar sent me a worried glance. I tried to give him a reassuring smile.

"Ready?" Aunt Mara asked Jaystar.

He nodded.

"Now you don't need to think of anything. As a Reaper, it's in your blood; it'll just happen."

Jaystar took a step forward and held out his hands, hovering them above Purple-Perm's. Then slowly he lowered them until they were touching hers. An aura of golden light encircled their hands. Jaystar closed his eyes and took three deep breaths. On the final exhale, Purple-Perm faded away, and the light left Jaystar's hands. It took him a moment before he opened his eyes. I couldn't believe it was so easy.

"That's it?" Jaystar asked, incredulous. He glanced from face to face.

"Sending souls on their way is the easy part," Aunt Mara replied. "It's the collecting them that can get tricky. Fortunately, Hades did the hard part for you this time around."

Hades was purring and enjoying Eli's attention. He certainly had a fondness for that man.

"Next," Aunt Mara called out.

Marion stepped forward.

"I'm so sorry you got caught up in all of this," Aunt Mara said. "I'll do what I can to make sure neither Christo nor Lucy see a cent of your money." Aunt Mara looked solemn.

"You've always been a good friend," Marion replied. "And I'm getting a good sense of why your teas always worked so well." Her eyes sparked.

Jaystar repeated the process of sending Marion to her afterlife. I admired how much he was taking this in his stride. He even seemed to enjoy the process, bouncing a little on his toes.

"Your turn, Gerry," I called out.

Gerry wrung his hands together nervously. "It's not going to hurt, is it?"

"Not even a little," said Aunt Mara.

"And no cats will be where I'm going, right?" His eyes darted toward Hades. Hades lifted his front paw and went about cleaning his claws while keeping his eyes locked on Gerry. Gerry shuddered.

"I can't make that promise," Aunt Mara said. "But you'll probably find you won't mind them as much there. And Hades is staying here, if that's any consolation."

Gerry took a few cautious steps to Jaystar and shakily held out his hands. In a few seconds, he was gone.

"Who's next?" I asked Aunt Mara. I suspected neither Bruce nor Smoker-Guy would be super willing.

"Charles! You're up!" Aunt Mara gestured for Smoker-Guy to come forward.

"Nuh-uh! I'm going right back to Pete's. There's a barstool with my name on it."

"Don't even give me that." Aunt Mara raised an eyebrow at him. "Hades wouldn't have been able to bring you here if there wasn't a part of you ready to move on. So get off your butt and get over here!"

Smoker-Guy's face fell. The cigarette hung loosely from the corner of his mouth. He shuffled over to our little group, his eyes on the ground. I guess Aunt Mara had a reputation even in the afterlife.

And then there was one.

Bruce. Aka Man-Bruce. Aka Brucie.

We all stared at him for a moment, at the bottom of the stair. It was strange seeing him without his phone in hand.

"Your turn, Bruce," Aunt Mara said.

To my surprise he pulled himself to his feet, then he lifted his head to look at us. "She's not a bad person," he mumbled. "What's going to happen to her?"

"Lucy did kill someone, Bruce. She'll have to answer for that. In the meantime, you get to see your family, and when it's Lucy's time, you'll see her too."

His eyes glistened. "I'll really get to see them?" he asked, and I was taken back to the photo in the newspaper of him as a child.

"You will," Aunt Mara said.

He stepped closer and held out his hands to Jaystar. "If you see her again, tell her I love her."

And then there were none.

Chapter 26

I t had been almost a week since I'd arrived in Widdershins, and I already felt I was getting a taste of what normal in Widdershins was like. It was certainly not what normal looked like anywhere else. For starters, my aunt was a witch, my best friend was a Reaper, my … Eli … because I still wasn't really sure what Eli was to me, was some sort of witchy law enforcement guy, and I could apparently teleport. Not that I'd done that since the basement fiasco with guns and ghosts. And then there was Hades. Maybe the least normal of any of us.

It was Saturday afternoon and Jaystar, Aunt Mara, and I were in the basement, aka Aunt Mara's apothecary. Or that's what it was for the moment. Papers had been signed, but it was still going to be another week before Aunt Mara could properly move into the red-bricked shop, across the road and down a ways from Miss Maisy's Tea Shoppe. That was going to be her public-facing apothecary. The one where she was simply a store owner with a fascination for herbs and crystals, not an actual witch.

Jaystar sat on the couch, his left ankle resting on his knee, a mug of Cosmic Clearing tea in hand, and his bag on the seat beside him. Most surprising was the fact that he shared the couch with Hades, who had perched himself at the other end, in a sort of truce. Jaystar's cat allergy seemed to have cleared up too. I suspected it was Hades's way of thanking him for helping out with our ghost infestation.

Aunt Mara had recovered from her run-in with Christo. The cut on her head had almost disappeared, and her energy was as I had remembered it in first meeting her. Today she was wearing three-quarter jeans, with a lapis lazuli-colored sequined tank top exposing more cleavage than I'd seen on a woman her age before. Her stilettos matched her shirt. I guess this was Aunt Mara's "weekend casual". In her arms she held our family's grimoire, our Book of Shadows. She placed it on the coffee table so both Jaystar and I could see it, and then seated herself in the chair opposite mine.

"I think it's time I introduce you to the Bos," she said.

"Boss?" Jaystar asked.

"B. O. S. Bos. Book of Shadows," I told him, before taking a sip of True to You tea. "Although, I think we've kind of been introduced." I cringed at the memory of flooring Lucy with it. It had been smart thinking on Eli's part that he hid it under the couch and planted a book on herbology in my hand instead. The sheriff had taken it away as evidence.

"I suppose you have," Aunt Mara said, raising an eyebrow at me. "But since we're all here and need to start your training, I thought a proper introduction should be had."

I wasn't quite sure how one was introduced to a book, so I took another sip of my tea.

"Jaystar. It's time." Aunt Mara held her hand out to him, and he did a double-take before a look of understanding settled on his face. He placed his cup on the side table beside him and rummaged in his bag.

He pulled out the vial of ink I'd seen the first day I met him. Its blue-black contents seemed to shimmer. My heart sped up. I'd seen Aunt Mara give it to him in one of my visions. Right before I sensed something else entirely from Jaystar. A gentle heat rose in my cheeks, and I studied my tea for a moment.

"Alice, are you paying attention?"

I nodded and focused on the vial she was twisting between her fingertips.

"A Bos is a keeper of a witch's ancestral magic. It's added to generation upon generation. In the wrong hands ... let's just say the consequences could be catastrophic."

"Christo was searching for this. Did he know what it was?" I asked.

"No. He simply thought I had a recipe book of secret herbal concoctions that would make him rich. It's why he broke into the basement. You had said Bruce's herbal package had been tampered with. I suspect that was Christo sleuthing. It was probably what led him to believe Bruce was making secret deals with me. Silly man." She shook her head. "The thing is, he's not the only one who would like to get his hands on this. There are others. Witches, in fact. And with you here, I suspected they might be enticed to come out of the broom-closet and seek it out."

"Why?" I asked.

"Because you, my dear, come from a very powerful and important lineage of witches. There are some who might be a little threatened by your arrival in Widdershins."

I shuddered. Holy cheese. This wasn't sounding like the relaxing Saturday chat I'd been expecting.

"Before you arrived, I thought it safest I give the book to Jaystar."

"To me?" Jaystar spluttered and had to cough to clear his throat. "But you never gave me the book, and why would it be safest with me?"

Instead of answering, Aunt Mara twisted off the top of the vial, held it up so we could both see, and went about pouring the liquid onto the sigils engraved on the cover. I cringed as she did so, thinking how the ink would stain the ancient leather. It didn't. Instead, it disappeared completely.

"Open it," she said to me.

I put down my tea and gently took hold of the cover. The cover alone was heavy, and I wondered again how it was I'd been able to swing the book with force.

I let the cover fall open on to the tabletop and inhaled sharply. There, on the first page, was the Lovell family tree. It extended for generations. Right down near the bottom was Aunt Mara. My mother. Me.

"I don't understand," I said. I flipped over a page to a table of contents, listing spells and recipes and chapters on creatures I'd assumed were mythical or I'd never heard of. The contents continued for several more pages before the entries began. I shook my head. The book was bursting with words and pictures, and yet I had seen its empty canvas less than a week before.

"I thought it safest to temporarily remove its entries so if it fell into the wrong hands, its contents would still be safe. And there's an interesting thing about Reapers. They're neither Magical nor Non-Magical. Neither fully of the world of the living, nor fully of the world of the dead. It makes them hard to track."

"But I wasn't a Reaper when you gave it to me," Jaystar said.

"Not true, my boy. You've always been a Reaper; it was just dormant. And it might have stayed that way if Bruce hadn't died and Lucy hadn't committed murder. But being a Reaper was in your blood."

"And you knew?" he asked incredulously.

She raised an eyebrow as if the very question was ridiculous.

"Well, it's a good thing you are a Reaper, or Alice would be in a lot of trouble right now for telling you she's a witch!"

"I didn't actually tell him," I protested. "He guessed, and Eli kind of confirmed it."

"It's true," Jaystar said.

Aunt Mara sipped her tea and said nothing.

"Knock, knock!" A man's voice boomed down the stairwell.

"Down here," Aunt Mara called up to him.

Hades opened an eye and studied the stairwell, stretching to attention when Eli appeared in the room.

My breath hitched, and I quickly took another sip of tea to try to hide it. Eli was serious and bossy and all sorts of infuriating. But he also made my heart race. And made me feel safe. And I couldn't deny there was something between us. Something I wasn't yet comfortable thinking about.

"Eli!" Aunt Mara cooed. "Come sit down and join us."

Eli looked around. Limited by choice, he took a seat beside Jaystar. Both men grunted a hello and glanced away awkwardly as they shuffled so they were still as far as possible from each other. Hades climbed onto Eli's knee and instantly made himself at home, purring as Eli stroked his back.

"Wonderland," he said, nodding by way of greeting me.

"Eli."

"You've been showing them your Book of Shadows." Eli gestured to the book on the table.

Suddenly protective of it, I closed it.

"Alice has a choice to make," Aunt Mara said. "And I thought this might help."

Eli eyed me. I shrugged. I wasn't sure what Aunt Mara was getting at.

Aunt Mara sighed. "Your mother's dying wish was that you spend a year here at Hollyhock Cottage, learning about your heritage. But I think it's only fair for you to make that choice for yourself. You've had a rocky beginning, and as I've alluded to, there may be some challenges ahead."

I felt Eli's and Jaystar's eyes on me. Oh lordy. I couldn't look at either of them. I'd already made up my mind.

It had certainly been a rocky week. I'd been kicked out of two coffee shops, although I wasn't sure Christo's Café was going to be a problem anymore, or if there was even going to be a Christo's Café for much longer. I'd learned not only that witches exist, but that I apparently was one too. I'd been accused of murder, nearly arrested, held up at gunpoint, and shared a house with a basement of ghosts. A house that happened to belong to a small black cat happily receiving belly rubs from Mr. Tall-Dark-and-Serious. I watched as a bead of dribble slipped out the corner of Hades's mouth. Ew!

But I'd also found family. Living, breathing, kind-of-scary family. And I'd made friends. I considered Jaystar, and he gave me a crooked grin. I smiled back.

And then there was Eli. He knew my mother. And he was protective of me. From snippets of conversations with Aunt Mara, it sounded like Eli had put himself on the line for me more times than I was aware. I wasn't sure what was going on with him and the High Council, but I couldn't shake the uneasy feeling that the High Council's interest in me was only just beginning.

I rifled for the brochure I'd stuffed in my back pocket, and put it beside the Bos.

"What's that?" Eli asked.

"I'm enrolling in night classes at the college. Herbology. I figured with Aunt Mara's new apothecary, she's not going to have time to teach me everything, and I want to be able to help out."

"You're staying?!" Jaystar bounced in his chair, a wide smile on his face.

"Wonderland?" Eli's eyes locked on mine.

"I'm staying," I breathed.

Hades regarded me, his amber eyes wide discs. He rolled himself back onto all fours, crouched down, and leaped across to my knee. Then he circled around twice and curled up into a ball.

See, Alice, think positive thoughts, and positive things will happen. Or weird, strange, unfathomable things. I gently ran my hand over his silky black fur. How angelic he looked when he slept.

"Right. Well, I guess it's been decided. No time for dilly-dallying. Jaystar and Eli you can help." Aunt Mara pushed the Bos to the side of the table, clearing some space, and leaned forward on her knees. "First, I think we need to start with teaching you to keep your thoughts hidden better. And then, Alice, *then* we'll see about getting you a snack."

She'd read my mind.

Free eBook!

Thank you for purchasing *Hades's Haunt*. I hope you enjoyed it! Book 2 of the Widdershins Magical Mystery Series, *Hades's Hex*, is launching in time for Halloween 2026. Preorder your copy here: https://books2read.com/hadesshex You can expect more magic, more murder, more mayhem, and of course, more Hades.

If you would like to stay updated about *Hades's Hex* or any of my other books, be sure to join my mailing list at https://BookHip.com/PBVBN or visit my website at https://jobuer.com.

By joining my mailing list you'll be the first to learn of new releases and special offers, and get a behind-the-scenes glimpse of my life as an author. I'll also send you a copy of my Gothic short story collection, *Between the Shadows*, for **free!**

Enjoy this book?

You can make a big difference to keep this writer writing!

Reviews are an author's secret weapon.

Honest reviews of my books help bring them to the attention of other readers and allows me to promote them to a bigger audience. In turn, this opens many more doors for me to keep writing and sharing Hades's stories with you.

If you've enjoyed this book, I would be super grateful if you could share the love and leave a review on Goodreads, BookBub, or on the storefront you've purchased this from.

And remember to tell your friends too!

Thank you so much!

Jo xx

About the Author

Jo Buer is a Kiwi-Canadian gothic suspense and paranormal mystery author. She writes stories with gothic heart and ghostly mystery, with a dash of romance, and often a cat or two.
Jo lives in Aotearoa New Zealand with her wonderful husband and four free-spirited felines: Atlas, Gaia, Zeus, and Hades.

You can connect with her at:
https://jobuer.com
https://www.facebook.com/jobuerauthor
https://www.instagram.com/jobuerauthor

Subscribe to her newsletter at:
https://BookHip.comPBVBNSV

Also by Jo Buer

Paranormal Cozy Mystery

Hades's Hex (Book 2 of the *Widdershins Magical Mystery Series*)
Coming Halloween 2026!

***

Gothic Suspense

Unspoken Truths (Te Tapu Gothic Book 1)
Broken Lies (Te Tapu Gothic Book 2)

Rest Easy Resort

Between (A Gothic Novella)

Hunger Pangs (A Gothic Novelette)

Voices (A Collection of Short Stories)

Between the Shadows (A Collection of Short Stories)

Acknowledgements

Writing and publishing any book is always a team effort. I am immensely grateful to everyone who has supported and inspired me throughout the creation of *Hades's Haunt*. Thank you, my wonderful cheerleaders!

First and foremost, I would like to express my deepest appreciation to my incredible family and friends. I am so grateful for your support, readership, and understanding. Without you, writing any book would be a near impossible task.

To my lovely students, thank you for keeping me young, teaching me the value of curiosity, and the power of storytelling, and for offering me your non-sweary swear words. I hope you enjoy seeing them within these pages.

My dear readers, I am so thrilled to have you on this journey with me. Many of you found me through my gothic fiction and have followed me as I've taken a small detour in genre. There will be more gothic fiction, I promise. Just as there will be more paranormal cozies. Your support of me, as an author, and for my books, is a privilege I don't take lightly. Thank you.

A special mention goes to my amazing editor, Hannah, whose keen eye for detail and invaluable suggestions have elevated this book to new heights. Your expertise, dedication, patience and flexibility have been invaluable, and I am truly grateful for your time, effort, and friendship.

Also, my two wonderful friends, Sally and Jennifer, who took on the informal role of proofreading this book. Your input and encouragement mean the world to me. I have learned so much from both of you. Your commitment to ensuring *Hades's Haunt* is the best it can be is deeply appreciated.

And on that note, any spelling, punctuation, or grammar gremlins that have *still* found their way into this manuscript, despite the best efforts of others, are mine alone.

I big thankyou to my ARC readers who took the time to read and review the early versions of this book. Your enthusiasm and support is invaluable.

Last but certainly not least, a special mention goes to my feline companions who inspire many of the mannerisms, expressions, and antics of the character of Hades. I have so much love for the real life Hades and his siblings, Atlas, Gaia, and Zeus, as well as those who have passed. You certainly make the best writing companions!

To all those who have played a role, big or small, in making this book a reality, thank you from the bottom of my heart. This book would not have been possible without each and every one of you.

Jo xx